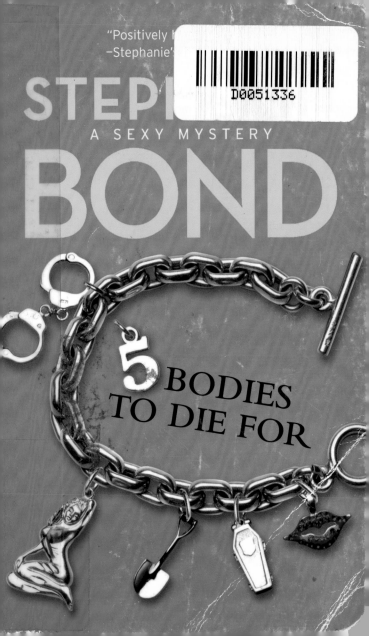

STEPH

A SEXY MYSTERY

BOND

5 BODIES
TO DIE FOR

Look for three sexy
new mysteries from

STEPHANIE
BOND

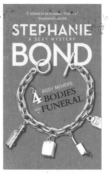

April 2009

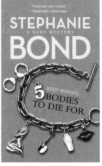

May 2009

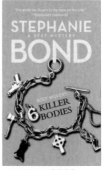

June 2009

ISBN-13:978-0-7783-2705-9
ISBN-10: 0-7783-2705-1

Praise for STEPHANIE BOND

Of *Body Movers*
"This is a series the reader will want to jump on
in the very beginning."
—Writers Unlimited

"Bond has successfully switched to the crime genre,
bringing along her trademark humor and panache."
—Booklist

Of *Body Movers: 2 Bodies for the Price of 1*
"Body Movers is one of the most delightful series I
have read in quite some time.
Stephanie Bond shows her audience what a
wickedly funny mystery should be all about."
—Suspense Romance Writers

"This series is simply splendid. Vivid, quirky, flawed,
wonderful people fill its pages and you care about
what happens to them. Like the prior volume, it is
replete with humor as well as action. I can hardly
wait to see all these characters again."
—Huntress Reviews

Of *Body Movers: 3 Men and a Body*
4 1/2 stars! "Bond continues her popular
Body Movers series with a fast-paced and wickedly
humorous story that skewers fame and celebrity
obsession with deadly accuracy."
—Romantic Times BOOKreviews

"Where the [Body Movers] series
goes next continues to be an intriguing mystery.
Readers who love a combination of
suspense and sexy romance will find their thrills
in Bond's latest offering."
—BookPage

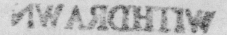
Also by Stephanie Bond

4 BODIES AND A FUNERAL
BODY MOVERS: 3 MEN AND A BODY
BODY MOVERS: 2 BODIES FOR THE PRICE OF 1
BODY MOVERS

STEPHANIE BOND

5 BODIES TO DIE FOR

MIRA®

ISBN-13: 978-0-7783-2705-9
ISBN-10:   0-7783-2705-1

5 BODIES TO DIE FOR

Acknowledgments

The middle book in a trilogy is a bit like the middle child—it tries to please everyone, tries to fill in all the gaps to keep everyone happy and moving along. (Can you tell I'm a middle child?) Writing this second book in the BODY MOVERS trilogy of books 4, 5 and 6 was a big challenge, and I couldn't have gotten through it without my editor Brenda Chin, who eagerly asks, "What happens next?" with all the confidence that I somehow *know* and will pull it off. Thank you, Brenda, for high expectations and constant encouragement.

Thanks, too, to Margaret O'Neill Marbury and Valerie Gray for your ongoing support of the BODY MOVERS series within MIRA, and to all the sales, marketing and production people behind the scenes who work to get the BODY MOVERS books into the hands of readers. A big, big thank-you to Michael Rehder at MIRA for designing the amazing charm-bracelet covers—I love them!

Thanks to my agent Kimberly Whalen of Trident Media Group for keeping the ball rolling. As always, thanks to my critique partner, Rita Herron, for our weekly meetings to discuss pages and possibilities over glasses of wine.

To my husband, Chris, who still moves me after eighteen-plus years.

And to my readers—thank you for allowing me to entertain you.

1

Carlotta Wren shoved her head in the freezer, closing her eyes and allowing the frosty blast to cool the flush on her face and neck as she tried to absorb everything that had happened over the past few days.

A serial killer was on the loose in Atlanta. Dubbed The Charmed Killer by the press for his signature of leaving a charm in the mouth of his victims, the unknown assailant was racking up bodies at an astonishing rate—four women dead in a week, culminating in the murder of an assistant district attorney. According to Detective Jack Terry, the Georgia Bureau of Investigation was joining the high-profile case.

And the Wren family was firmly in the middle of the fray.

She and her brother, Wesley, had been the body movers on the first two cases, and had been called in on the third, although Carlotta had had to step aside when she'd realized she had once crossed paths with the victim. Wesley had met the fourth victim, the deceased A.D.A., while settling his most recent legal trouble. And their father, Randolph "The Bird" Wren, a fugitive now for more than ten years for a white-collar crime, had been named a possible suspect. First, because one of the charms left behind had been a bird, and second, because one of the victims had worked in the same office building where he had once worked. Carlotta was sure she hadn't helped matters by handing over the charm bracelet her father had given her when she was a teenager to the police, but she was hoping it would help to clear Randolph.

Meanwhile, Jack had warned her she might have to take a polygraph to clear herself, due to her proximity to the bodies.

Minus ten points.

A moan from the living room roused Carlotta from her churning thoughts. She reached for an ice tray to fill an ice bag, but the trays were empty, of freaking course. When her gaze landed on a bag of frozen peas, she grabbed it, closed the freezer door and walked back to the living room.

Peter Ashford lay on the couch recovering from the stun-baton zap she'd inadvertently administered when she'd mistaken Peter for an intruder. After discovering that someone had been living in their guest bedroom unbeknownst to her and her brother, she'd been skittish.

Carlotta leaned over to brush aside Peter's blond hair with her fingers and place the bag of frozen peas on his forehead. "This is the best I can do. Feeling better?"

He was still pale, but his deep blue eyes seemed more alert. He nodded and reached for her hand. "It was stupid of me to come in the house unannounced. But the door was unlocked and I thought I'd surprise you."

She smiled. "You did."

"That'll teach me."

"And that'll teach me for leaving the door unlocked." She sighed. "I have to learn to be more careful."

"I'm so glad you've agreed to move in with me."

She bit her lip. It had been a decision she'd made once she fully understood that she wasn't safe in the town house, not with uninvited houseguests coming and going, and a mysterious black SUV stalking the curb.

Oh, and there was the matter of her Monte Carlo exploding in the mall parking lot two days ago when she was supposed to have been in it.

"I'm not moving in," she murmured. "I'm just staying with you until things settle down." But she could tell from the light in Peter's eyes that he hoped having Carlotta in his house would help her to fall in love with him, and with the lifestyle she might've had if Peter hadn't ended their engagement when her father had been indicted all those years ago. She was open to the idea of growing closer to Peter, but for now, all she wanted to do was feel safe.

She left his side to pick up her phone and dial Wesley— again. Again, he didn't answer, and again, she left him a message to call her right away. He was probably out working his new job as a bike courier and couldn't hear his phone. When Wesley learned that fugitive Michael Lane had stolen the money that Wesley had won in a card game and had stowed in his sock drawer for repairs around the house, he'd be furious.

Peter tried to sit up, then winced and laid back.

"Take it easy," she admonished.

"What if that psycho comes back?"

"There's a cop in the driveway. Jack sent him over to keep an eye on things until he gets here."

"Did you see this Lane guy?"

"No," she said, gesturing toward the hallway. "I went into my parents' room and found the scrubs Michael had been wearing when he jumped over the side of the bridge." She swallowed hard, reliving the fear. "It looks like Michael was living here all the time we thought he was...dead."

Michael Lane was a former coworker of Carlotta's at Neiman Marcus. He'd headed up an identity-theft ring that had resulted in two women losing their lives...and when Carlotta had figured out what he'd been up to, he'd tried to kill her, too. He'd been cooling his heels in the psych ward at Northside Hospital until deemed fit to stand trial, but Michael had escaped and after a televised foot chase, he'd chosen to jump over the side of a bridge into the Chattahoochee River instead of surrendering to police.

But it appeared the presumed-dead fugitive had gotten the last laugh.

Peter made an angry noise in his throat. "I can't believe that madman was here while you slept. He could've murdered you in your bed."

"But he didn't," she said, trying to sound soothing.

It was true that she thought she'd dreamed someone was watching her at night, but decided it was best not to mention to Peter that Detective Jack Terry had inadvertently protected her one of those nights—by sharing her bed. Besides, she and Jack had both agreed that it would be their last...lapse. Jack wasn't looking for a relationship, and she needed someone with more stability.

Like Peter.

"Has the feeling returned to your fingers?" she asked him.

He made a weak fist. "Getting there."

When she'd called Jack after realizing she'd zapped Peter by mistake, he'd said Peter would be fine in a few minutes. But what if he had a heart ailment or other condition? "Maybe I should take you to the emergency room after all."

"No, really. I'm already feeling much better." Then he gave her a wry smile. "Please don't make me tell total strangers that my girlfriend used a Taser on me."

She laughed ruefully and decided not to correct him on the "girlfriend" part. "I'm so sorry."

"I'll let you make it up to me."

A knock sounded at the front door. When Carlotta went to check, she was relieved to see Detective Jack Terry standing on the stoop, large and competent. Not stopping to analyze the rush of emotion that his presence triggered, she opened the door, her mood dimming at the sight of Jack's new partner, Detective Maria Marquez, standing behind him.

"Hey," Jack said, his rocky face solemn. "Are you okay?"

"Yeah, come on in." She stepped aside and nodded to Maria as the woman walked by. Scant hours ago, she'd seen both of them at the memorial service for A.D.A. Cheryl Meriwether. When she'd first called Jack after she'd found Michael's clothes, he'd told her he was busy, but would be there soon. In the background, she thought she'd heard Maria and other noises that made her wonder if Jack had already found a new project for his tool.

The woman was stunning, to be sure, with honey-colored hair, almond-shaped eyes and curves all up and down the highway. Worse, the woman was smart—a profiler who had recently relocated from Chicago. She was single and, based on a phone call that Carlotta had overheard while Maria had once babysat her, the woman had left an unhappy situation. She was ripe for the picking, and Jack had good hands.

The two of them made a spectacular-looking couple, Carlotta conceded as she closed the door behind them.

From the couch, Peter awkwardly pushed himself into a sitting position. The bag of frozen peas slid off his head and landed on the floor with a smack. Jack leaned over to pick them up and handed them back to Peter with a little smile.

"I heard that Carlotta lit you up with her stun baton."

Peter looked up at him, but the movement made him grimace. "She has good reflexes."

Jack looked back to her and smiled. "Yes, she does."

Carlotta gave him a warning glance.

"We need to take a look in your parents' room," he said, suddenly all business.

"Go for it," Carlotta said, leading them down the hall. Jack and Maria stopped at the closed door to pull on gloves and slip paper booties over their shoes.

Jack turned the knob and pushed open the door. "What made you come in here? Did you hear a noise?"

"No." She hung back in the doorway while they proceeded into the room that was pretty much the way her parents had left it, aside from being searched by the police after the couple had disappeared. Carlotta's gaze went to the box of dried-up cigars on her father's nightstand. One of the charms left in the mouth of a victim was a miniature cigar, and in light of the other suspicions leveled against her father, she had simply wanted to check out his stash…and maybe get rid of it, so the police didn't have any other circumstantial evidence against Randolph.

Jack followed her line of sight to the cigar box and nodded in mute understanding. In a shared glance, he telegraphed that Marquez didn't have to know…for now.

"When I walked in," Carlotta continued, "the room felt different—cleaner, for one thing. I could smell antiseptic. Then I noticed the scrubs and recognized them as the ones Michael had been wearing when he jumped off the bridge."

Maria looked incredulous. "How could someone have been living in here and you not know it?"

Carlotta bristled. Maria had accused her of being a little clueless in other areas of her life before—like when it came to knowing things about her best friend, Hannah Kizer, for example. The woman must be convinced that Carlotta was oblivious to everything going on around her, and at the moment it was hard to argue the point. "I dust in here occasionally, but normally the room is closed off. There's really no reason for me or Wesley to come in here."

Jack walked over to inspect the door leading out to the deck. "This is how Lane got in and out?"

"Probably. We keep that door dead-bolted, and it was unlocked when I came in."

"Are there signs that he was in other parts of the house?"

Carlotta squirmed. "Uh, yeah. He did…chores."

Maria arched a beautiful eyebrow. "You mean, like washing dishes?"

"And…laundry. And running the vacuum and…I think he might have mopped the kitchen floor."

Maria laughed. "He was doing housework, and you didn't notice?"

Carlotta gritted her teeth. "That's right. Are you annoyed, Detective, that this doesn't fit the profile you worked up for Michael Lane? You did say he'd kill me if he got the chance. Obviously, you were wrong."

"Lucky for you," Maria said pointedly.

"What's with the masks?" Jack cut in, nodding to the two colorful masks lying on the floor—a dog and a cat.

Carlotta stooped to retrieve them. "Peter brought them. He was wearing the dog mask when he came up behind me. That's why I used the stun baton—I didn't realize it was him."

Jack frowned. "Why the hell was he wearing a dog mask?"

"It's a scene in a movie," Maria said, snapping her fingers.

"Breakfast at Tiffany's," Carlotta murmured, fingering the masks. The scene where Paul and Holly steal masks from a toy shop during their day-long love splurge. Her favorite scene, and Peter had remembered.

Jack looked utterly lost. "Does this have anything to do with our crime scene?"

Carlotta shook her head and backed away. "I think I'll let you two do your job. I'll be in my room if you need anything."

She turned and walked back down the hall to her bedroom, thinking of what she needed to pack. Her skin crawled anew at the thought of Michael strolling through their house, ransacking drawers, eating snacks and watching TV. Had he stood over her while she slept and considered finishing her off?

She walked into the girlish room that hadn't changed much since they'd moved in after her parents had lost their big home in the exclusive area of Buckhead, after her father had been fired from his job at an investments firm where he'd been accused of bilking clients. She hung the masks on the corner of her dresser mirror, then went over to the white four-poster bed to pull out a suitcase from underneath it, then set the bag on top of the coverlet. She'd be glad to get away from this room, away from this town house for a while. Staying with Peter would be like going on vacation…as long as she could keep things between them from moving along too quickly.

Carlotta removed clothes and shoes from her closet, packing the suitcase as tightly as she could, wondering how long she would be away and how this one decision might change her life forever.

At a rap on the door, she turned to see Jack stick his head inside. "Can I come in?"

"Sure." She turned back to her task of removing underwear from her dresser drawer.

"Going somewhere?" Jack asked.

She folded a pair of red lace panties and set them on top of the pile of clothes. "Peter invited me to stay with him for a while, and I accepted."

Jack picked up the red panties between thumb and finger to study them. "You're moving in with Ashford?"

"No," she corrected, still folding underwear. "I'm staying with Peter until things settle down around here."

"Until I catch The Charmed Killer?"

She nodded and instinctively wrapped her hand over the charm bracelet she wore. The charms were supposedly prophetic, but so far, they'd only proved to be disconcerting. After all, a killer was on the loose using the trinkets as his signature.

Jack pursed his mouth. "I think it's a good idea."

She gave a little laugh. "I thought you might since you said I should marry Peter."

"That's not why I think it's a good idea." He brought the panties to his face.

Carlotta snatched them away. "Then why?"

He shrugged, unfazed. "Because I'm sure that palace of his is a fortress. You'll be safe there. Which means I can investigate The Charmed Killer without worrying about your pretty ass being in harm's way. I'm sure Ashford will keep you busy with polo matches and dinners at the country club."

"Does this mean I won't be seeing you?"

"You'll miss me, huh?" Then he was suddenly serious. "Carlotta, I'm liaising with the GBI and your name keeps popping up in the investigation. We're going to have to get you cleared, although this new development with Lane is a big step forward."

"You think Michael is The Charmed Killer?"

"We'll have to double-check the time line, but right now, he's the best suspect we have."

"But Shawna Whitt was murdered before he escaped from the hospital."

"We don't know exactly when Lane escaped, and we still don't know if the Whitt woman was murdered. Since she was cremated, we may never know."

"But the charm in her mouth—"

"Could've been placed there postmortem. Maybe Lane broke into her place and scared her so badly she had a heart attack, then he placed the charm in her mouth. Or maybe he heard about the death and the charm after he escaped from the hospital and decided to adopt it as his signature. Who knows how a crazy man thinks?" Jack wet his lips. "All I know is that thinking about Lane being here in this house when you were asleep makes *me* a little insane."

"But he didn't kill me, Jack. He had the chance, and he didn't kill me."

"Maybe he tried. We still don't have a line on who planted that bomb under your car. You said yourself that the Monte Carlo was only here, at Coop's, and at the mall. Michael was here and he's certainly familiar with the mall parking lot."

She bit her lip. "Michael isn't the type to plant a car bomb. He isn't technical, or gadgety."

"You can buy ready-made explosives if you know where to go."

She sighed. "Michael is the one person we know wanted me dead, so maybe he did plant the bomb. But it just seems like a lot of trouble to go to when he had the opportunity to off me in my own bed."

"Can't argue there," Jack said, then averted his gaze. She could tell he had his doubts about Michael being their man. He pulled a small notebook from an inside jacket pocket. "When do you think Lane got in the house?"

"I'm thinking Friday, after you removed the motion detectors. And I believe he left sometime Sunday or yesterday."

"How do you know?"

She didn't want to tell him about the money that Wesley had won in a card game. It wasn't exactly the kind of thing her brother was supposed to be doing while on probation.

"Come on, you said on the phone something about Lane having ten thousand reasons to leave?"

She closed her eyes briefly. "Wesley had ten thousand dollars hidden in his room and realized this morning it was missing."

Jack frowned. "Go on."

"Wes last saw the money Sunday morning, so Michael must have taken it sometime Sunday or yesterday."

"So Lane might've been gone before you and I came back here Sunday?"

When Jack had spent the night. She nodded, knowing the information would ease his conscience—and his ego.

"Have you noticed anything else missing?"

She shook her head, then glanced around her bedroom, comparing what she saw to the images a person's subconscious picks up from of their surroundings every day. When her gaze landed on her bulletin board, she stopped and walked closer to study the random mementos she'd tacked onto the mesh surface—tickets stubs to shows, things she'd cut out of magazines, and photos, some of the items so old they were curled around the edges.

"What?" Jack asked, coming to stand behind her.

"Something is missing." She stared at the empty spot, trying to remember what had once been there, then the answer slid into her mind. "A photo."

"A photo of who?"

"Of me," she murmured. "Michael had taken it during a holiday party at work. He gave it to me."

"Must've wanted a souvenir. Anything else missing?"

She sighed. "Not that I can tell, but who knows."

Jack made a few notes, then closed the notebook. "Let me know if you think of anything else. Go to Ashford's and lay low. We're going to have a CSI team go over the entire town house in case Lane left something here that relates back to one of the murders. Take only what you need."

Panic blipped in her chest. If Michael had left something behind in their house, the Wrens would be even more closely intertwined with The Charmed Killer case. And she didn't like the idea of the police going through her personal things.

"And forget about the body-moving business for a while," Jack added.

"But Coop—"

"Could stand to take a break himself."

She blinked, surprised to hear Jack's concern for Dr. Cooper Craft, the former M.E. who had been relegated to moving bodies for the morgue and had hired Wesley to assist. It was how she'd been drawn into body moving herself, and how she'd been drawn to Coop, who had been acting strange lately. "So you *do* think something's wrong with Coop."

"Nothing an AA meeting can't fix. Don't get caught up in Coop's problems, darlin', you've got enough of your own. And keep that stun baton handy." He wiped his hand over his mouth, trying to smother a smile. "You got Ashford good, huh?"

"You don't have to take so much pleasure in his pain."

"You're moving in with the man. Let me have a little fun at his expense."

"I'm not moving in with Peter…I'm staying at his house."

Jack stepped closer and lifted her chin. "In his bed?"

Carlotta's chest tightened. "What do you care, Jack?"

He leaned his face close to hers. "Because getting you back home gives me that much more incentive to get The Charmed Killer off the streets." He grabbed the red panties in her hands, and walked away, holding them high before shoving them into his jacket pocket with a grin. "I'll hang on to these for motivation."

Carlotta shook her head as he disappeared through her door, confounded as always by the man's push-pull on her heart. She had no doubt that Jack would get the maniac off the streets. Her live-in arrangement with Peter notwithstanding, she only hoped it was sooner rather than later.

She glanced around her room with an eye toward what the police would find that might make her uncomfortable.

Her teenage diaries.

Carlotta moved toward the dresser. She'd found them when she'd unearthed the charm bracelet that her father had given her. She couldn't remember the exact contents of the diaries, but since they'd encompassed her burgeoning relationship with Peter and the time immediately after her parents' disappearance, she didn't want strangers analyzing her personal drama for their own entertainment.

She pulled out the diaries—one for each year of high school—and stowed them under clothes in her suitcase. When she started to close the dresser drawer, she suddenly noticed the corner of a file—her father's client file that Wesley had stolen from Randolph's attorney, Liz Fischer. She didn't want it to wind up in the wrong hands. So she slipped in the file, then closed the bag and zipped it shut. Moving in with Peter was the right decision, Carlotta told herself. She desperately needed a change of venue.

Carlotta picked up her cell phone to check for messages and frowned. Meanwhile, where was her brother and why wasn't he returning her calls?

2

Wesley was valiantly trying not to throw up. He'd passed on a drive-through lunch in anticipation of the job that he'd spent hours working up his nerve for, and it was a good thing, too.

The severed head at his feet looked like a prop for a haunted house. The edges of the neck skin were black with dried blood and curled, like a macabre ruffle. Red and white strings of sinew dangled out of the gaping hole that had once connected the head to a torso. The head's eyes were partially open, and the skin was dark in places, hinting of a beating the man had received before he'd taken his last breath. The sparse, dark hair was a matted mess, caked with dirt and blood.

Wesley stood holding pliers, giving himself a pep talk. Mouse had ordered him to remove the head's teeth, which would make it harder for the cops to identify the head if it was found. This wasn't what Wesley'd had in mind when he'd agreed to go undercover in The Carver's loan-shark organization in exchange for having charges of attempted body snatching downgraded to a misdemeanor and additional hours added to his community service. By offering his services to Mouse to help him collect on overdue accounts, he'd hoped to kill two birds with one stone—fulfill the D.A.'s demands while clearing his own debt to The Carver. When he'd balked at performing the grotesque act, Mouse had told him he had Wesley's jacket with the dead man's blood on it. Wesley believed him. When he'd tried to recover his confiscated jacket from Mouse's trunk, he'd found a severed finger inside.

"Just do it," Mouse yelled. He stood nearby eating a Big Mac and fries.

They were on an abandoned construction site in east Atlanta where the city leaders' overly optimistic projections of growth had led to lots of digging, followed by lots of reneging. The site was deserted, hemmed in by a few trees, but there were no people or houses within sight. Just baked dirt, tinged red with Georgia clay, as far as the eye could see.

"Have you done this before?" Wesley asked his companion.

"Oh, yeah. You get used to it."

Wesley gagged.

"You're thinking about it too much, little man. Fucking do it already."

Wesley took a deep breath and lowered the safety glasses over his eyes. Then he knelt on the ground, averted his gaze and felt for the man's mouth. The dead flesh was cold and pulpy and the head reeked, like a rancid piece of meat. Wesley groped until he found the mouth, then pried open the stiff lips. He glanced down and grew light-headed at the sight of his hands in the mouth of the disembodied head.

"Start with the front ones," Mouse advised, chewing on his burger. "They snap off like dried corn."

Wes swallowed hard and positioned the pliers with a shaking hand around one of the big square front teeth. The stretching and pulling had made the man's eyelids pop open, revealing his cloudy irises. Wesley squeezed the pliers, but when he pulled up, the head slid against the ground and spun out of his grasp, rolling like a melon.

Mouse belly laughed, obviously enjoying the show.

Wesley wrestled the head back in position, then put it between his knees to hold it still. Panicky and sickened, he repositioned the pliers and pulled as hard as he could. Something pinged against his safety glasses, and when he looked down, half of the tooth was gone. Bile backed up in his throat, but before he could change his mind, he broke off the other half of the tooth and dropped it in the Micky D's disposable cup that Mouse had conveniently provided.

"See, that wasn't so hard," Mouse urged him on.

One by one, Wes rid the head of its teeth. Some of them broke off, and some of them came out root and all. There was no blood, thank God, but plenty of flying gum tissue to muck up the safety glasses. Mr. Dead Man had spent a lot of money on his choppers, because he had caps, and two in the back were gold.

"I'll take those," Mouse said, extending a handkerchief for Wesley to drop them into.

"What will you do with them?"

"Sell them."

"Who the heck buys gold teeth?"

"Well, most of our sources have dried up because it's gotten too risky, but now those companies that buy gold through the mail make it real easy. They send me a postage-paid envelope, I drop in the gold teeth, and a couple of weeks later, I get a check, easy-peasy."

Wesley's eyes bulged. "They don't wonder where you got an envelope full of gold teeth?"

He shrugged. "They don't care. Ain't America grand?"

The molars and the wisdom teeth presented the greatest challenge, but by then, Wesley had gotten the hang of it and twisted them out like pulling stumps out of the ground. When he dropped the last tooth into the cup, he sat back on his heels and tore off the safety glasses. The head rolled a quarter turn, its mouth a snaggly hole. Wesley stumbled to his feet, walked to the nearest bush and threw up.

Mouse chuckled, then picked up the cup of teeth and headed back to the Town Car. "When you're finished, let's go."

Wes wiped his mouth with his sleeve. "What about the head?"

"Leave it. It's supposed to be a hundred degrees today—the bugs and the birds will take care of it."

"What about the skull?"

"Hell, if someone does find it, they'll probably take it home and put it on their bookshelf."

Wesley walked back to the car to put the tools and gloves in a bucket in the trunk. He stopped for a moment and let the reality of what he'd done wash over him, then he slammed down the lid with revulsion.

"Hey, take it easy," Mouse called. "Get in."

Wes crawled into the front seat, hot and sweaty, the stink of rotting flesh in his nostrils.

"Moist towelette?" Mouse asked, extending one of those little foil packets that barbecue joints pass out to customers.

He took it and tore it open, then unfolded the disposable towel and held it against his face, breathing in the antiseptic smell. God, that was the worst thing he'd ever done. He had a feeling he'd be having nightmares about it for a while. He needed a hit of Oxy, bad. He reached for his backpack just as his phone rang from inside. Wes pulled it out and frowned. The screen said he had eight messages and the incoming call was from Carlotta—something was wrong.

"I need to get this," he said to Mouse, then flipped up the phone. "Yeah?"

"Wes, where are you? I've left you a half-dozen messages."

"Um, I've been working. Is something wrong, sis?"

He listened with incredulity as she told him how she'd discovered that Michael Lane had been living in their parents' bedroom. He shook his head, his mind racing at the implication—the psycho had been roaming around their house at all hours, doing chores? "That's crazy. For how long?"

"We think since Friday."

"Jesus Christ, why aren't we dead?"

"Good question. Michael obviously had ample opportunity to do whatever he wanted."

He hated hearing the fear in his sister's voice. "They don't know where Lane is?"

"Not yet. But at least Jack knows he's on the run again, so they have an APB out on him."

"I'm going to install a security system in the town house," he said. Guilt tightened his chest. He should've done it before now, considering all the trouble the pair had been in lately. He wasn't doing a very good job of taking care of his sister after years of her taking care of him.

"I think that's a good idea. But meanwhile, Peter invited me to stay at his house until the dust settles."

He frowned. "You're moving in with Peter?"

"I'm staying at his house," she corrected. "And Jack is having a CSI team go over the town house, so you should come, too. Peter has plenty of room."

He remembered the man's huge home from when he and Coop had gone there to remove the body of Peter's wife after she'd drowned in the pool. "Thanks, but I'll probably crash with Chance."

"Okay," she said, although he could feel her disapproval vibrating over the line. Carlotta didn't like his buddy Chance Hollander—she thought Chance was a bad influence on him. Little did she know that he'd just performed oral surgery on a severed head while Chance was probably watching cartoons.

"Wes, there's something else. It looks like Michael stole your money before he left."

His stomach fell. "No…no….*no*. Are you sure?"

"I didn't touch it, so if it's gone, that only leaves Michael."

He leaned his head back and groaned.

"I'm sorry, I know you had plans for that money. But in the scheme of things, we're lucky to be alive."

"Yeah, I know. But still."

"So, how's the courier job going?" she asked cheerfully.

He glanced down at the cup of teeth in the console and his intestines cramped. "Fine and dandy."

"Good. I'll have my cell phone with me, and here's the number at Peter's."

"Okay," he said, taking down the information. "Later."

He disconnected the call and sighed.

"Trouble at home?" Mouse asked.

"You know it." Now he *really* needed a hit of Oxy.

Reaching into his backpack, he palmed a pill into his mouth and chewed.

"What's that?"

"What's what?"

"Whatever you just put in your mouth, smart-ass."

Wesley frowned. "What do you care?"

"Didn't take you for a druggie," Mouse said, looking almost disappointed.

"Don't sweat it, man. It's just something to take the edge off." He wrapped his fingers around the section of his arm where The Carver had lived up to his nickname by etching the first three letters of his name into Wesley's forearm after Wesley had humiliated The Carver in a stunt at a strip club. "My arm still hurts, dude."

"Maybe so, but drugs'll mess you up."

Wesley lifted an eyebrow. "That's rich coming from you."

"I'm just saying, little man, watch yourself."

The cool pleasure of the Oxy coursed through his system, making the day's events a rosy haze. Still, high or not, he realized that he needed cash, and Mouse wasn't the kind of guy to pass out bonuses. "Are we through for the day?"

"Yeah. I have to go to my niece's dance recital. Where can I drop you?"

"Not at the house—the police are there." Wes lifted his hand. "Don't ask, man, it's a long story." On impulse, he pulled out his phone and brought up Coop's cell number. After a few rings, Coop answered.

"Hey, Wes, what's up?"

He wet his lips, suddenly nervous to talk to the man he'd let down by conspiring to steal a body they'd been transporting. "I was wondering if you had any work for me tonight?"

The silence on the other end indicated that Coop wasn't going to be easily persuaded to trust Wesley again. "I don't know. We need to talk."

"Okay, where are you?"

"At the morgue, working in the lab."

"Can I come by?"

Coop sighed into the phone, then made a frustrated noise. "Uh, sure."

"Great. See ya." He closed the phone and glanced at Mouse. "Can you drop me at the morgue?"

Mouse nodded. "Sure."

"Turn at the next street."

Mouse laughed and put on his signal. "I know the way, little man. I know the way."

Wesley swallowed, picturing Mouse driving by the morgue and pitching out bodies like apple cores. He leaned his head back on the headrest. What had he gotten himself into?

3

"When you pull up to the gate," Peter said, "just enter my code—four three nine nine." He demonstrated. "And the gates will open."

They did, swinging back like great black wings, welcoming Carlotta into the privileged neighborhood of Martinique Estates. Peter's Porsche two-seater surged forward, like a giant cougar. The guard at the pristinely designed gatehouse waved as they drove by.

Cruising past palatial custom homes, Carlotta was struck with a sense of déjà vu. She and her family had once lived in a private subdivision like this one. They'd belonged to the neighborhood pool and volleyed on the neighborhood tennis courts. But these days, in addition to the multiple pools and other shared amenities, individual home owners, like Peter, were likely to have their own pool and their own private add-ons.

Each home was its own little estate.

When he pulled in to the downward-sloping driveway of his sprawling brick home, Carlotta had to catch her breath. She had seen it before, of course, but not in daylight, and not through the eyes of someone who would be living there. The house was impressive, with a paved circular driveway in front that featured a huge fountain, with wide steps leading to the two-story entryway. Palladium windows and gleaming white trim gave the eye a pleasing break from the intimidating mass of brick. The landscaping was lush and flawlessly manicured.

To the right of the house was the pool. Carlotta was glad it was daylight. The memory of seeing Peter's wife, Angela, lying under night-lights next to the pool where she'd drowned was branded onto Carlotta's brain. But in the brightness of day, with the sun high and the trees full, it was tempting to believe that the tragedy hadn't happened in this perfect neighborhood.

Peter touched a button on his visor and one of the doors to a four-car garage opened, revealing his other vehicle, an SUV. She assumed he'd sold Angela's Jaguar.

"My insurance company is sending a rental car tomorrow," she murmured, remembering her own transportation situation. As much as she'd hated the blue Monte Carlo, she hadn't wanted to see it blown to smithereens, not when she owed more on it than it was worth.

"Nonsense," Peter said. "You can drive the convertible, or the SUV, whichever you prefer."

"Peter, I couldn't."

"Why not? Otherwise one of them will just be sitting in the garage while you drive a rental. That doesn't make sense."

She hesitated. "It just doesn't seem right. People will talk."

"People are going to talk anyway." He gestured to another house before pulling in to the garage. "My next-door neighbor is in the Junior League, so I figure Tracey Lowenstein will know about our situation in less than twenty-four hours."

Tracey Tully Lowenstein, renowned socialite and daughter to Walt Tully, Carlotta's godfather and her father's former partner at what used to be Mashburn, Tully & Wren Investments. When Carlotta's father had been indicted for fraud, the name Wren had been removed from the firm's letterhead, and from the Buckhead social register. Tracey seemed single-handedly determined that Carlotta would not be readmitted to the upper echelon.

"And I don't care," Peter added, putting the car into Park and turning off the engine.

"I have to buy a car soon, or get the Miata fixed." Although one would probably cost as much as the other. And with her wrecked credit still on the mend, she probably wouldn't qualify for a new car loan—or for financing to get the Miata repaired.

"You don't have to rush into anything," he said. "While you're here, use the extra car."

Carlotta pressed her lips together. His argument seemed logical, but Peter always seemed logical. It was how he had talked her into accepting a cell phone on his plan, because the incremental cost to him was negligible, while she couldn't get a new one until her credit mess was straightened out.

He reached over to cover her hand with his. "Let me spoil you, Carly."

His blue eyes were so sincere. Shortly before Angela's death, she had run into Peter at a cocktail party she'd crashed and thought she would die from wanting him. He had turned out to be everything they had planned he would be—successful and wealthy. Married and living in a world that had shunned her, he had seemed so far out of her reach. But he'd kissed her that night, had told her that his marriage to Angela wasn't good, and that he wanted Carlotta back in his life. When Angela had died a violent death and Peter had been blamed, it seemed that once again, all was lost…especially when Peter had confessed to his wife's murder. But in the end, it was revealed that Angela had been living the double life of a Buckhead housewife and a high-class call girl. Peter had confessed to protect the reputation of a woman he felt he'd driven to reckless behavior with his indifference.

The experience had endeared him to Carlotta, and even though he came out of it a free man, she had felt that it was too soon, that they were both too raw to resume their relationship. And then there was Jack…and Coop…

"Drive the Porsche," he said, gesturing to the interior of the luxurious car. "Have fun."

"What if I do something to it?"

"That's what insurance is for." Then he winked. "Besides, if I can't get you to fall in love with me again, maybe you'll fall in love with my car."

She laughed and stroked the armrest. "It is beautiful." Then she smiled. "Okay, but only until I get the Miata fixed."

"Fair enough. Let's go inside. I'll get your suitcase."

Carlotta stepped out of the car and glanced around the garage that was nearly as big as the town house she and Wesley shared.

"I'm starved," Peter said, energetically pulling her bulky bag out of the small car trunk. "I think that zap you gave me stirred my appetite. I was thinking of grilling out by the pool. How does that sound?"

Her mouth parted in surprise, then she chided herself. Peter couldn't very well live in this house and forever avoid the place where Angela had drowned. "That sounds fine. Do you grill?"

He looked sheepish as he moved toward the door leading to the house. "I'm learning, if you don't mind being a test subject."

She laughed. "I don't mind. Wesley does all the cooking in our house." She hesitated before following him inside, feeling self-conscious. She stepped into what appeared to be a mudroom that contained a door to a powder room and a wide closet.

"The laundry room is behind those doors," he said, pointing. "My housekeeper, Flaur, will take care of your clothes."

"Oh, that's not necessary," she said quickly. Except for the clothes that Michael Lane had inexplicably washed, dried and folded while she and Wesley were away from the house, she was accustomed to taking care of her own laundry.

In the mudroom, several of Peter's jackets hung on a Peg-Board and a couple of pairs of knockabout shoes sat on the floor. They walked through another door to enter a spacious great room, which brought back more memories of that night. Straight ahead was a jaw-dropping kitchen, to her right, a den and sunroom with an eating area, flanked by sliding glass doors that led out to the pool area.

The long wood table in the sunroom was where she'd sat with Peter, consoling him after Angela's body had been found. The garish "designer" silk flower arrangement that had sat on the table, the one Peter said he and Angela had argued over because of the expense, was gone, replaced by a demure lidded vase. The wall of cherrywood bookshelves in the den above the fireplace were studded with bric-a-brac, but seemed more streamlined than before. Peter had obviously removed some of Angela's possessions from his home, yet her influence remained in splashes of feminine color and the occasional designer collectible. And in a single framed black-and-white picture of Angela taken in happier times.

Wood-lined ceilings soared overhead, with more wood at their feet, polished to a shine. The first floor also featured a formal living room, a formal dining room, an office, a butler's pantry and a home theater.

"Wesley would love this," she said, gesturing to the plasma TV and surround-sound speakers.

"He's welcome to come over anytime and use it," Peter offered. "My house could use some living."

"It's such a lovely home, Peter," she said, running her hand over the curved moldings of a chair rail. Every element of every room was finely designed and crafted. "Did you and Angela build it?"

"Yes. Angie selected all the finishing details and the decor."

The implication hung in the air between them—if they'd married instead, Carlotta would've been the one sorting through Italian-tile samples and choosing custom-cabinet hardware. She knew that Peter was wealthy in his own right, and would inherit another fortune when his parents passed, but seeing firsthand how he lived—how she might've lived—left her feeling a little light-headed.

"Angela had good taste," she said finally.

He nodded, then retrieved her suitcase and gestured toward the stairs—one of two staircases, she'd learned during the tour. "I'll show you your room and you can unpack while I get dinner started."

She followed him, holding on to the handrail as she climbed the wide staircase. Ahead of her, Peter was animated as he pointed out different rooms and some of the pieces of art that he particularly liked. He seemed almost giddy to have her there, but Carlotta felt a heaviness all around her, as if there was a presence in the house…Angela's aura.

Then she gave herself a mental shake at her absurdity. Angela was gone, and Peter was ready to move on.

Still…it felt eerie to be given full run of the woman's house, especially in light of Angela's outright dislike of her. Carlotta couldn't blame her, though. During the investigation of the woman's death, it was revealed that Peter carried a picture of Carlotta in his wallet. Angela must have known, and it had to have eaten at her.

"This is my room," he said, stopping to allow Carlotta to peek inside. The room was enormous, with an elaborately trayed ceiling and skylight. At the end of the room was a sitting area, with a fireplace and flat-screen TV, with a veranda beyond sets of French doors.

Near the bed, she saw a dressing room through a doorway that she assumed serviced his-and-her walk-in closets. Through another doorway she glimpsed the bathroom and a waterfall shower.

The bedroom furniture was dark and heavy and of the highest quality—the king-size bed alone had probably cost as much as his Porsche, she surmised, picturing Peter's long frame stretched out on its length. The linens and curtains were earth toned and sumptuous, the inlaid designs in the wood floor a masterpiece. She wondered if he kept the Cartier engagement ring he was "holding" for her somewhere in this room.

"It's…wonderful," she murmured, but shrank a little inside, mortified at what he must think of her housing situation. When she moved back to the town house, things had to change.

"I'm glad you like it," Peter said. "The room I had in mind for you is across the hall."

She followed him to a set of double doors that opened into a suite that was as light as his was dark. The furniture was maple, the linens fresh and airy, the area rugs plush. It was feminine in every sense, including the enormous closet and the spalike bathroom. Angela's influence was apparent in every corner of this space. "It's wonderful," Carlotta murmured.

"There are three other guest rooms if this one doesn't suit you, including one in the basement."

Her eyes widened. "You have a basement?"

He grinned. "Where else would I put the game room and wine cellar?"

"Where else indeed?" Carlotta did a full turn in the center of the room, noticing that she had a veranda of her own, facing the front of the house, where the veranda off Peter's room faced the rear. "It's positively lovely, Peter. I feel like a princess."

"Good," he said, then picked up a lock of her hair. "You deserve to feel like a princess. Take your time settling in. When you come down, I'll show you the alarm system so you'll feel safe when you're here alone."

"Okay." When he closed the door behind him, she fell backward on the luxurious bed, enjoying the bounce of the mattress. She gazed up at a skylight that was lined with prisms, turning the sun's waning light into a thousand shimmering rainbows. Her life up until now seemed a thousand miles away.

"Oh," Carlotta sighed, "I could so get used to this."

4

Wesley waited until the Town Car pulled away, then walked up to the front door of the Fulton County Morgue, a building so nondescript that most people driving by didn't notice it. He'd never been through the front door before—as a body mover for Coop, he'd always entered through a side or rear delivery door with their solemn cargo. He walked up to a reception desk and flashed his body-hauler ID, then asked for Coop.

"Dr. Craft is in the lab," the woman at the desk told him. "Sign in and go on back. It's next to the crypt."

"Got it," he said, then signed his name and sauntered back, whistling under his breath. The Oxy seemed to be wearing off more quickly than before—a headache sparkled in his temples and his eyes felt itchy. But he didn't want to dose before seeing Coop, not when he was trying to prove to the man that he could be trusted again.

He shivered as he walked down the wide, harshly lit hallways—the expression "as cold as a morgue" was no exaggeration. The place was forty fucking degrees. Good for dead people, not so good for people with a pulse.

He found the lab and pushed open the door to the sound of raised voices. On the other side of the room, two men squared off. Tall and shaggy Dr. Cooper Craft, former chief medical examiner, wore a lab coat over jeans and black Chuck Taylor tennis shoes. Short and owlish Dr. Bruce Abrams, *current* chief medical examiner, wore slacks and a sport coat. The slighter, older man was bristling, his birdlike neck stretched forward.

"Cooper, I've come to terms with you being here in the lab. But I can't have you undermining my authority with the other M.E.s."

Coop shrugged, unfazed. "Then tell your people to stop coming into the lab to ask me questions."

"They're accustomed to seeking your approval," Abrams said. "It's up to you to remind them that you're not their boss anymore, that—" The man wiped his hand over his mouth.

"That I'm just a lab rat and a body mover," Coop supplied. "No problem, Bruce. I didn't mean to cause you extra trouble. I know you're swamped with this Charmed Killer business."

The other man nodded, then pulled out a handkerchief and mopped his forehead. "Between the police and the media, I'm feeling the pressure."

"Let me know if can help," Coop said.

The man jammed the handkerchief back into his pocket. "Just stay out of my way."

Abrams turned and stalked toward the door, flicking his gaze over Wesley before walking past him, out of the room.

Coop lifted his hand to Wes. "Come on in. Sorry about that."

Wes walked in. "If Abrams doesn't want you here, how did you get the job in the lab?"

Coop made a rueful noise. "The State Coroner's Office asked me to come in and tackle the backlog of unsolved cases. It was meant to lighten Abrams's load, but he doesn't see it that way."

Coop moved toward a microscope, as if he'd already dismissed the matter. "Hand me that tray of slides on the table, will you?"

Wes hustled and carried the slides carefully, concentrating in order to control the shaking of his hands.

"Thanks," Coop said, taking them from him.

He watched as Coop removed a slide, put it under the microscope and adjusted the focus. "Whatcha looking at?"

"DNA samples," Coop said without raising his head.

"Cool. I thought they had computers to do that stuff."

Coop gave a little laugh. "Call me old-fashioned. Besides, the morgue doesn't have the budget of a network television show."

"Can I take a look?"

Coop shrugged and stepped back. "Sure." Wesley removed his glasses, then leaned over to press his eye against the eyepiece and turn the smaller fine-focus knob.

"I see you know your way around a microscope," Coop said.

"I was pretty good in biology. What kind of DNA sample am I looking at?"

"Basic blood sample."

"What's it for?"

"I'm trying to identify a body."

"And this is the only way?"

"It is when there's no head."

Wesley jerked up, his mouth suddenly devoid of moisture. "No head?"

Coop walked across the room to a slab where a sheet-draped body lay. He pulled back the sheet and Wesley was able to cover his dismay over the sight of the decapitated, decomposing body by recoiling from the stench.

"Here," Coop said, handing him an open jar of Vicks VapoRub. "Wipe this under your nose."

Wesley did, and while the ointment overpowered the stench of decaying flesh, it also went straight to the sensitized nerve endings in his face. His eyes watered and his nose ran like a faucet.

"This guy was found in Piedmont Park, no head and a missing finger," Coop said, pointing to the missing digit. "I'm hoping his DNA will match something in the system. The computer *can* do that."

"What about fingerprints?" Wesley croaked.

"Burned off, probably with acid. Somebody didn't want this guy identified."

Bile backed up in Wesley's throat.

"You okay?" Coop said, then covered the body. "Didn't mean to shake you up. I thought you were immune to this by now."

"I'm okay," Wesley said. "Just out of practice, I guess." He wiped at his eyes and nose. "I was wondering if I could come back to work with you."

Coop pulled off his gloves. "I don't know if that's a good idea."

"Come on, Coop. I've learned my lesson. I won't screw up again."

"I already have another guy working with me. Abrams's nephew."

"Is he as good as I am?"

Coop frowned. "No."

Wes smiled. "There you go. I'm good at this—you said so yourself."

Coop shook his head, but Wesley could tell he was wavering.

"Will you give me another chance? I could really use the cash to pay on my court fee."

"Carlotta told me you got a job as a bike courier."

His cover for working with Mouse and The Carver. "Uh, yeah. But it's only part-time. I need something in the evenings, and I know that's when you're busiest."

Coop pressed his mouth together, then sighed. "Okay, I'll give you another chance."

Wes grinned in relief. "Great. You won't regret it."

"I doubt that," Coop said, then began to store trays of slides. "Beat it, I gotta get out of here."

"Any chance I could get you to drop me at the police station?"

"You in trouble again?"

"Nah, I just need to talk to Jack about something. No big deal."

"Okay, let me finish up here."

"What can I do to help?" Wes hurried to follow Coop's directions to get the lab back in order. It was the best he'd felt all day. Knowing he was going to work with Coop again gave him something to look forward to.

Now that he and Meg Vincent were on the outs.

Not that they'd ever been on the ins…or anything. His coworker just liked messing with his head.

He used a paper towel to remove the Vicks ointment, then followed Coop to his van, hoping he didn't look as shaky as he felt. He needed another hit, but he wasn't going to risk it around Coop.

The interior of Coop's van was cluttered, which was unusual. Paper coffee cups and crumpled napkins littered the console, as well as several parking receipts from Piedmont Hospital. That was strange. When Coop made pickups from the hospital morgue, he pulled the van around to the rear loading entrance. There were no parking receipts involved.

"So how's the community service going?" Coop asked when they got underway.

"At ASS?" Atlanta Systems Services. "Fine, I guess. I was off today because they're doing some construction in the building." Maybe Meg would miss him, the little tease.

"And your probation meetings?"

"Fine." Except for the fact that, unbeknownst to his probation officer, her boyfriend was a thug who had it in for him.

Coop shifted in his seat. "How's Carlotta?"

Wes grinned. "What took you so long? She's okay. Did you hear that lunatic Michael Lane, the one who tried to throw her over the balcony at the Fox Theater, has been living in our parents' room and we didn't even know it?"

"What?"

"Yeah, crazy stuff. They thought he was dead when he jumped off the bridge into the Hooch, but he must've survived. Dude sneaked into our place and he's been living there ever since."

Coop inadvertently applied the brake. "Did he hurt Carlotta?"

"No. That's the kicker—he just did a few chores around the house, stole some money and took off. She found his clothes this afternoon and figured it all out."

"It must've been after the memorial service for the A.D.A. I saw her there and she didn't mention it."

"Yeah, it was."

"Do they think Lane is The Charmed Killer?"

"I don't know—maybe. She said that our entire house is a freaking crime scene."

"Where is she?"

Wesley pressed his lips together. He knew Coop was crazy about his sister. And they might be together now if Wesley hadn't stowed away on their trip to Florida a few weeks ago and sabotaged their romantic weekend. But prior to that, Peter had gotten Wesley out of a serious jam and he'd promised the man he'd do what he could to keep Coop and Jack away from Carlotta.

"Wes?"

He exhaled. "Carlotta is at Peter's."

Coop's eyes widened. "She moved in with him?"

"More like staying with him, she said. You remember how big the dude's place is."

"Not big enough," Coop muttered as they pulled up to the midtown police precinct.

"I'm staying with my buddy Chance, so call my cell when you need me," Wes said, opening the van door to swing down. "Thanks for the ride."

Coop gave him a little salute, but Wes could tell he was preoccupied, thinking about Carlotta staying at Peter's house. No doubt about it, Coop had it bad for her.

Wes watched the van pull away, unable to shake the feeling that something was wrong with Coop. Carlotta was afraid that he was drinking again, and maybe she was right. Or maybe it was the pressure of being back inside the morgue that he had once run. Regardless, Coop seemed a little off his game, and it worried Wes to see him that way.

As Wes turned, he spotted something out of the corner of his eye—the black SUV with tinted windows that had been haunting the curb of the town house on and off for weeks. The occupants had never made themselves known, but with the spectrum of trouble he and Carlotta had been in over the past few months, it could be anyone from a testy loan shark to a vengeful murder suspect to a pissed-off mall customer. The SUV pulled away and although Wes craned to see the plate, the vehicle was too far away and moving too fast to make it out.

But since no one was shooting at him, really, how bad could it be?

He strolled into the police station, flirted with Carlotta's friend Brooklyn who thought he was cute, then got her to call Jack. She buzzed him through a secure door, and when he walked inside, he spotted Jack getting a Coke out of a vending machine.

Jack waved. "Want one?"

"Nah, thanks. You look like hell, dude."

"Don't call me dude." Jack fed in coins, then retrieved his can and cracked it open. "What's up?"

Wes held up the red phone that Mouse had given him. "You told me you could have a GPS chip installed in case I got in a jam." Mouse's "chore" for him this morning made him nervous about what might be on the horizon. He wanted the security of a panic button.

"Let me get somebody on it," Jack said, taking the phone. "It'll take about thirty minutes. Wait here, I need to talk to you."

Jack disappeared, then returned a couple of minutes later. "Have you talked to Carlotta?"

"Yeah, I know about Michael Lane. That's some jacked-up shit."

"Yeah." Jack's expression revealed how angry he was that Carlotta had been in danger. Wes couldn't tell if Jack really liked his sister, or just liked his role of self-appointed protector. "Can you add anything to the story? Do you remember anything strange?"

"Just that little things were getting done around the house. I thought Carlotta was nesting or something."

Jack frowned. "She said you had some cash in the house that was stolen."

"Yeah, about ten grand. If you catch the dude, I want it back."

"Don't hold your breath. And do I need to remind you that you're on probation? Gambling is not on the menu."

"It was just a friendly card game," Wes said.

"Uh-huh. Listen, about this work you're doing for The Carver…"

Wesley swallowed past a dry throat, suddenly regretting not taking that Coke. "Yeah?"

"Well, this Charmed Killer case is taking all my time right now, so don't rush anything. Just network and keep your eyes and ears open, especially when it comes to Hollis Carver's son, Dillon."

"Okay, but so far, the only person I'm networking with is Mouse."

"So chat him up. See what he knows."

Wesley shifted from foot to foot, not at all sure he wanted to get to know Mouse better. "Did you know that Carlotta moved in with Peter?" he blurted to change the subject.

Jack scowled. "She's *staying* with him until this maniac is off the streets."

Wesley arched an eyebrow. "Is that what she told you?"

A muscle worked in the big man's jaw. "I'll go see if your phone is ready."

5

After several blissful moments of daydreaming, Carlotta pushed herself off the feathery guest bed and unpacked. The few clothes that she'd brought looked pitiful hanging in the expansive closet that also featured a steam-iron press, but it was a treat having so much space. She walked around the suite, exploring every inch.

The room was meticulously clean, but showed signs of having been lived in. Carlotta stepped on something imbedded in the carpet and unearthed a small broken silver pin shaped like a cat, no doubt left behind by a houseguest or perhaps a housekeeper.

She set the pin on the counter in the lavish bathroom and ran her hand along the pale granite flecked with gold. Luxury bath products lined the vanity shelves. Spa-quality towels and a white robe lay folded on the edge of the jet garden tub. She wondered idly if Angela had ever come in here for privacy, sinking up to her neck in bubbles when she had the chance.

And then a realization sunk in—this had been Angela's room. She and Peter had apparently spent at least some of their marriage sleeping in separate beds. Carlotta felt a pang for the dead woman, sorry that Angela's life—and death—hadn't turned out as she'd planned. Carlotta and Angela hadn't been best friends in high school or afterward when their social paths had diverged, but Carlotta had never wished the woman ill, not even after Angela had married Peter. To be here and uncovering all her secrets… it felt intrusive, almost an insult to the woman's memory.

The troubling thoughts pushed her out of the room. As she closed the door, she glanced across the hall. While she was appreciative that Peter hadn't tried to persuade her to share his room, the proximity alone worried her. On top of the nagging sense of betrayal she felt staying in his dead wife's room, she knew that close quarters had a way of escalating intimacy.

But wasn't part of her decision to be here with Peter to give them the chance to explore their chemistry?

With her heart and head clicking, Carlotta descended the stairs, once again awestruck over the sheer size of the house. If Michael Lane could live in the town house without her and Wesley knowing about it, a family of five could live hidden in this place without anyone being the wiser.

Through a set of open sliding glass doors leading out onto the pool area, she heard the telltale noises of grill-wrangling. When she stepped outside, she spotted Peter at the far end of the patio, in the outdoor-kitchen area. Mingled scents of chlorine and spices filled the humid air.

He waved her over and, after slipping off her shoes, she made her way across the stone lanai surrounding the breathtaking pool. Crystalline blue water slapped gently against the sides. The memory of Angela lying near the pool's edge dressed in a black trench coat and boots, her eyes open and staring, rose in Carlotta's mind. She gave herself a mental shake and walked toward Peter.

She'd forgotten the lavishness of the outside living area—a recent addition, Peter had hinted, that Angela had wanted more than he had. Besides the pool, there was an in-ground hot tub and a waterfall. The landscaping was magnificent, with huge potted trees and urns making it feel like a European villa. And behind the alfresco kitchen that featured commercial-grade appliances and a firebrick oven sat a small building separate from the house—a guest-house-slash-pool house. Allegedly, it's where Angela had entertained her paying customers.

Carlotta marveled that Peter hadn't sold the entire property after the whole ordeal, but she rationalized that he must have his own reasons for staying put.

"I forgave her," he said, as if he could read her mind. He glanced up from the grill where he turned thick steaks and brightly colored vegetables with a pair of tongs. "That's why I didn't sell the house…or burn it to the ground."

Two glasses of red wine sat on the bar. Carlotta slowly climbed onto a stool and reached for one. "I wasn't going to ask."

"Everyone else has—my friends, coworkers, my parents, even Angela's parents. No one can imagine why I'd want to live here after everything that happened."

"This is your home," she murmured. "Besides, I'm sure you have good memories here, too."

He nodded, reaching for the other glass of wine. "A few. But the truth is, Angie and I led separate lives, even when we were both here. I don't feel bound up in memories because we didn't make many." He made a rueful noise. "That probably sounds cold."

"No, I understand what you're saying."

He took a drink from his glass. "Still, even though our marriage wasn't good for her or for me, I feel obligated to do right by her. And part of that is keeping the house she loved. Plus, I couldn't stand the thought of ghouls coming round to tour the place, just to see where she'd been murdered. They would've, you know. Even her so-called friends were vultures. After she died, they brought food and gifts of condolence, but sooner or later, they were all demanding the gory details. It was sickening."

Carlotta's heart squeezed for what he had endured at the hands of people who pretended to be his friends. "I know what that feels like to some degree. I'm so sorry."

He nodded, then smiled. "That's all behind us now. We can't change the past…only the future." He lifted his glass of wine. "To the future."

She clinked her glass to his and drank deeply, glancing at him over the rim. With his shirtsleeves rolled up, his hair tousled and his face flushed with heat, he looked incredibly handsome. Awareness curled in her stomach—Peter had been her first lover. At one time, they'd known each other's bodies intimately, couldn't get enough of each other. She could feel his body pulling on hers now, calling her home.

Sleeping across the hall from him might be harder than she'd anticipated.

"Did you get unpacked?" he asked, then took a drink from his glass.

She nodded. "Yes, the closet is wonderful, the room is wonderful and the house is…wonderful. Thank you for having me as your guest, Peter."

His eyes glowed with a banked fire. "You can stay as long as you want."

The way he looked at her fueled her own curiosity. She expected him to flirt with her—over dinner and as the evening wore on and the wine went down. But he was the perfect gentleman, keeping the conversation light, even steering clear of talking about their recent agreement to start looking into her father's assertions that someone within his old firm had framed him.

Instead, they laughed and teased and discussed movies and nonsensical things, as if he sensed that she was happy to avoid talking about The Charmed Killer and the panic unleashed on the city. To avoid thinking Michael Lane was the sicko they were looking for. The only time Peter hinted at the danger she was in was later in the evening, when he showed her how to operate the alarm system.

"I have an early breakfast meeting," he said. "But when I leave, I'll reactivate the alarm. When you get up, you'll need to turn off the motion detector before going down-stairs, by pushing this button."

He demonstrated and she nodded. Simple enough.

"The alarm will still be on for the doors and windows on the first floor, so if you want to go outside, push this button. At that point, the entire system is off. But I don't recommend you do that."

She nodded. "I understand." The house might be wired for bear, but if the alarm was off and someone made it past the guardhouse, a person would be a sitting duck. The neighbors were too far away to be of much help.

"When you leave the house, there's a panel next to the door leading to the garage. Push the button to reactivate the motion detector and close the door behind you. There's no alarm on the garage door, so you have all the time you need to get into the Porsche and out of the garage."

She nodded, mentally reviewing things in her head. "This thing isn't going to go off if I get up in the middle of the night, is it?"

He smiled. "Not if you stay upstairs. The motion detectors are just for the first floor."

She bit her lip. "And if I set off the alarm by mistake?"

"Within a few seconds, the monitoring service will call to see if everything is okay. They'll reset the alarm if you need them to."

"Okay." Carlotta smiled. "If you don't mind, I think I might go ahead and turn in. I need to check in with Wes, and let Hannah know where I am."

"I'm tired myself," Peter said, then winked. "It's not every day I get shot with a Taser."

As they climbed the stairs together, her heart rate accelerated and her hand felt slippery on the railing. Suddenly the palatial house seemed small, the air claustrophobic. When they reached the landing, Peter turned to her and lowered a very nice kiss on her mouth. She kissed him back, surprised at her all-over reaction. He raised his head and studied her face. The air sizzled. She wondered if Peter was going to ask her to spend the night with him, and what she would say if he did.

Then he smiled. "Good night, sleep tight." He disappeared into his room and closed the door.

Carlotta stood there for a few seconds, then retreated to her own room, blaming her response on the wine. And wondering why Peter hadn't tried to take advantage of her.

Inside the guest suite, she picked up her cell phone and her purse and headed for the veranda. Outside in the muggy night air, she glanced over the scattered lights of the neighborhood and lit up a cigarette. She inhaled it greedily while dialing Wesley's cell number.

"Hey, sis," he answered. "How do you like being back in the 'hood?"

She smiled. "I can't lie—Peter's house is nice."

"What's that sound? Are you smoking?"

She turned her head to exhale. "What? No, I'm not smoking."

"The Surgeon General says smoking is bad for your health."

Carlotta frowned. "You're smoking right now, aren't you?"

He exhaled into the mouthpiece. "Yeah. But it's an organic cigarette, so it's cool."

She gave a little laugh. "Peter has plenty of room if you change your mind and want to stay here, too."

"Thanks, but I'm settled in Chance's extra bedroom for now. He lets me smoke inside. I'll bet you're out on a fancy porch or something, sneaking around, aren't you?"

She looked at the exquisitely furnished veranda and flicked her ashes away from an upholstered chaise. "Or something. Have you been back to the town house?"

"No. Jack said he'd let me know when the CSI team was finished so I can install a security system."

She frowned. "When did you talk to Jack?"

"Uh, earlier. I just wanted to see what was going on, that's all."

"Did he have any news?"

"Not that he shared with me."

"Okay. So I guess I'll see you when I see you?"

"Yeah. I'll check in."

"You'd better." She disconnected the call, then sucked

on the cigarette until her cheeks hurt. God, it tasted so good.

She punched in Hannah's number, but no surprise, her friend didn't answer. Carlotta left her a message with her whereabouts and the reasons why, then ended the call, shaking her head.

Normally, she wouldn't think twice about Hannah not answering her phone. Her culinary friend, who dabbled in catering—and body moving when Coop permitted—had a lot of men, er, *irons* in the fire. But recently, Jack's profiling partner, Maria, had accused Carlotta of not knowing anything about her good friend. Carlotta had bristled at the allegation, but admittedly, it had made her curious about what was going on when Hannah couldn't be located or made vague excuses to escape.

She tapped some ash off the end of her cigarette, causing the charms on her bracelet to clink. She fingered them, shaking her head over the idea perpetuated that the charms on the bracelets sold by Olympian Eva McCoy for charity were not only unique to the wearer, but were also predictive. Her particular bracelet's charms were a puzzle piece, an "aloha" charm, three hearts bound together, two champagne glasses toasting and a woman whose arms were crossed over her chest—which looked a little too much like a corpse for Carlotta's comfort.

If she looked hard enough, she could find connections to her life. She *was* trying to figure out the puzzle of her father's guilt or innocence, for example. And shortly after donning the bracelet, she'd met Mitchell Moody, the son of June Moody, the woman who ran Moody's Cigar Bar. Mitch was currently on military leave from Hawaii.

It was a flimsy connection, but a connection nonetheless.

As far as the three hearts linked together, one might say that it could refer to the three men in her life: Jack, Coop and Peter. The champagne glasses…well, she would certainly celebrate once The Charmed Killer was apprehended…with someone.

And the weird corpse-looking charm, she didn't want to think about.

Carlotta took a final deep drag on the cigarette, then exhaled leisurely while she glanced over the roofs of the quiet neighborhood. Where she and Wesley lived in Lindbergh, she'd grown accustomed to the boom of car radios and the scream of sirens. Here, the only thing disturbing the peace were suburban crickets.

She squinted at a flash of something—light? metal?—from the house closest to Peter's, which was slightly up the hill and partially hidden by trees. There was a movement outside a window. As she continued to stare, she could make out more details and realized that someone was standing on a terrace in partial light.

Staring at her with binoculars.

Unnerved, she walked back inside and secured the door, dismissing the incident as typical neighborly snooping. In light of Angela's scandalous behavior, she suspected more than one set of binoculars had been trained on the Ashford house over the past few months.

She suddenly felt very exposed.

After washing her face and donning silky tap pants and a matching camisole, she snuggled down in the mountain of pillows and set the alarm on her phone so she wouldn't oversleep. She needed to allow extra time to get ready for work, not to mention drive an unfamiliar car along an unfamiliar commute. While she was scrolling through the features, her phone rang, startling her so badly she nearly dropped it.

She hadn't realized how skittish she'd become.

But when she looked at the caller-ID screen, she smiled. *Jack.*

She connected the call. "Are you calling to tuck me in?"

His sexy laugh rumbled over the line. "Yup. What are you wearing?"

"Sweatpants and big fuzzy socks."

"Good, that should keep Ashford in his place."

She sighed. "What do you want, Jack?"

He made a rueful noise. "I mentioned that the GBI is coming on board The Charmed Killer case."

"Yeah."

"They want to interview you as soon as possible."

Her heart raced—when would this ghastly situation end? "I can come down in the morning before I go to work. Eight o'clock?"

"Okay."

"Jack, will you be there?"

"Couldn't keep me away."

"Good night."

"You, too."

6

Carlotta woke to a piercing noise. As she reached for her cell phone to turn off the blaring alarm, her mind raced to orient herself. Light poured in from a veranda—Peter's veranda. In a rush it all came back to her—coming home with him and being ensconced in the lap of luxury, sleeping like the dead imbedded in a mattress fit for royalty, the ugliness of The Charmed Killer far, far away. She stabbed at her phone, but the frantic alarm didn't stop.

And then she realized the wail wasn't the alarm on her phone. It was the house security alarm.

Her heart vaulted to her throat. As she leaped out of bed, she wondered if Peter had inadvertently tripped it as he'd left for work. But the clock showed it was seven-thirty—much later than he said he'd be leaving. She rushed to the closed bedroom door and scanned the small security panel on the wall above the light switch. A red light glowed next to the words Motion Detector. Someone had set off the device on the first floor—meaning they were *inside the house.*

Carlotta's throat convulsed in fear. If Peter was running late and had accidentally set off the alarm, he would've disarmed it by now. She turned the dead-bolt lock on the door and backtracked to her cell phone, only to find the battery dead.

The crashing noise of glass breaking sounded from the first floor, confirming her fear that someone was in the house. From the nightstand, a landline cordless phone rang, startling her so badly she cried out, then she clamped a hand over her mouth, realizing she'd just advertised her whereabouts to the intruder. She scrambled to answer the phone. "Hello?"

"This is the security monitoring service," a man said. "We were alerted that your home alarm has been tripped. What is your password?"

Carlotta frowned. "Password? I don't know. I don't live here."

"Excuse me?"

"I mean, I'm a guest in the house. I think there's an intruder—I heard something downstairs."

"I'll send the police," he said, his voice full of solemn concern, "but I need to put you on hold and contact the owner at an alternate number. What's your name?"

"Carlotta Wren. When you call the local police, give them my name and tell them to contact Detective Jack Terry of the APD. This might have something to do with a case he's working on." It *was* possible that Michael Lane could be stalking her again. And there was a serial killer on the loose.

Assuming they weren't the same person.

"Will do, ma'am. Stay on the line."

"Okay, please hurry." She looked around the room for an escape route. The veranda was on the second floor, so unless she was willing to jump to the concrete driveway below, it wasn't an option. There was the back stairway down the hallway, but that meant leaving the relative safety of the bedroom.

She looked for a chair to wedge under the doorknob, but the only ones in the room were two upholstered models and a stool for the vanity, all too short. She set down the phone and tried to slide the dresser in front of the door, but the furniture wouldn't budge.

Then she heard a sound outside the door on the landing, a scuffing against the wood floor. Panic seized her. In the distance she heard the wail of sirens, but they were still far away. The peal of the alarm ended abruptly, leaving a whine of stunned silence in the air.

A thump sounded against the door.

"Go away!" Carlotta screamed. "The police are here!" But she knew it would still take precious minutes for them to arrive, possibly break into the house, and find her.

Plenty of time for her to be strangled and have a charm stuffed down her throat.

Carlotta retreated until her back slammed into a wall. She considered fleeing to the closet or the bathroom, but that would only take her farther from the last-ditch escape route of the veranda if she had to jump or shimmy down a tree in her skimpy pj's.

"I have a gun," she yelled, then picked up a lamp and wielded it like a baseball bat.

A scratching noise sounded against the door, sending terror rippling through her.

Then Carlotta frowned. Scratching? She took a step forward, then stopped. It was probably a ploy to draw her closer. Then an ax would crash through the door and the face of a maniac would appear.

She stood stock-still, her heart thrashing in her chest as

a muted sound came from the other side of the door. Carlotta crept forward and pressed her ear against the wood.

Meow.

Carlotta's shoulders fell in abject relief. If the maniac "intruder" was deranged, it was on catnip. Peter's cat must've escaped from wherever he kept it and set off the motion detector.

She set down the lamp and unlocked the dead bolt. When she carefully opened the door, a yellow streak of fur shot through her legs and under the bed. Carlotta stuck her head out in the hall for a quick scan, but the rest of the house vibrated with stillness. The whine of the police siren grew closer. Turning back to the bedroom, Carlotta walked over to pick up the phone. "False alarm," she said to the guy on the other end. "And the police are here. Thanks for your help."

She disconnected the call, then dropped to her knees to lift the bed skirt and look for the cat. From a far corner, two green eyes glowed back. The alarm had probably scared it to death.

"Me, too," she murmured to the cat in a soothing voice. "Come on, I won't hurt you."

It released a shaky little *meow.* Carlotta sprawled on her stomach and inched her way under the bed. "Come on, kitty. It's okay."

The cat stretched out its neck and sniffed her fingers.

"That's it, you're safe with me," Carlotta urged, sliding closer.

Suddenly the cat bared its teeth and swiped at her. The claws found their mark on her hand and Carlotta howled in pain. She jerked up her head and banged it against the bed railings, which made her howl again. She suddenly realized the danger of being in a confined space with an hysterical cat. Worse, when she tried to shimmy back out, she found herself lodged between the floor and the bed.

Damn, being off work so long with a broken arm had added a little padding to her backside. She tried to move, then grunted. And to her front side, as well.

The sound of voices came from downstairs. "Police! Is anyone here?"

"I'm up here!" she called, but her voice was muffled. She frantically tried to make her way back out from under the bed and managed to retreat a few inches by the time footsteps approached.

"Are you okay?" a male voice called, sounding hollow.

"Yes," she said cheerfully, wondering what kind of picture she presented. "You can go now, it was a false alarm."

Carlotta gasped when hands closed around her ankles. She slid out in a whoosh, then flopped over on her back and looked up.

Into Jack's sardonic face.

"Hi," she ventured with a little wave.

"Hi." He gestured to her lime-green tap pants and matching camisole. "I thought you were sleeping in sweatpants and big fuzzy socks."

"I lied."

He reached down and helped her to her feet. "You okay?"

"Except for the floor burns." She winced and touched the lump on her head. "And I konked myself pretty good on the bed railing."

He retrieved her robe from a chair and handed it to her. "Were you hiding from the intruder?"

"Not exactly."

He pinched the bridge of his nose, as if he was struggling for patience. "Is there another reason you were under the bed?"

A *meow* sounded and the cat appeared, rubbing against Jack's pant leg.

"Meet the intruder," Carlotta said, nodding to the blond Persian. "She must've set off the motion detector."

"There's a broken wineglass on the kitchen floor."

"She must've knocked it over. I didn't even know Peter had a cat."

"Figures, though," Jack muttered.

"It probably belonged to Angela," she chided, then crouched down and offered the fluffy feline her hand to sniff. The cat hissed and swiped, drawing blood this time. "Ouch!" Carlotta yelped, pulling back.

"She must prefer males," Jack offered. Then he stepped back into the hallway and called, "False alarm, guys. Thanks for your help."

He came back in the room and crossed his arms, looking her up and down. "You gave me quite a scare."

"Sorry. I guess I overreacted."

"Don't worry about it. This is the reason I'm okay with you being here—Ashford's house is even pussy-proof. Now I can relax."

She gave him a withering look. The cordless phone rang and she hurried to pick it up. "Hello?"

"Carlotta," Peter said, his voice high and agitated. "Are you okay?"

"I'm fine, Peter. It was a false alarm."

"The security monitoring system called me at work. I'm on my way home."

"I'm sorry for the commotion," she said, "but you don't have to come home. Jack's here."

"Jack?"

"He came with the police who responded to the alarm."

"Oh. Did you accidentally set it off?"

"No, your cat did."

"My cat?"

"Yes." Carlotta rubbed her finger over the angry raised scratches on her hand. "And she's a little mean."

"Carly, I don't have a cat."

She frowned and her gaze went to the feline twisting happily between Jack's legs. "Are you sure? She's fluffy and blond—a Persian, I think, with green eyes."

He laughed. "I'm positive I don't have a cat. It must belong to a neighbor and slipped into the house when one of us wasn't looking."

"That's strange," she murmured.

"I'm just glad you're okay," he said. "Are you sure I don't need to come home?"

"No, everything's fine. And I have to leave soon. The GBI wants to talk to me about The Charmed Killer case, so I thought I'd get that over with before going to work."

"Well, I have to admit that I'm glad the GBI is taking over the investigation. Jack and his people don't seem to be making much headway."

She lifted her gaze to Jack and he frowned, as if he sensed Peter was talking about him. "I should get going," she said. "Thanks for checking on me, Peter."

"I left you the Porsche," Peter said, sounding…husbandly.

"That's very generous. I'll see you later?"

"Can't wait. Have a good day."

"You, too," she murmured, conscious that Jack was listening. She punched a button to end the phone call, then shrugged. "Peter says it's not his cat. It must belong to a neighbor and got into the house somehow."

Jack made a noise in his throat. "I'll check the doors and windows and search the house just to be sure no one else came in."

She nodded, thinking of Michael.

"Want me to put the cat outside?"

"I suppose so. Her owner is probably looking for her. Or maybe she'll find her way back home."

Jack scooped up the cat, who purred and rubbed its head on his lapel. "I'll look around and wait for you downstairs. Do you need a ride to the station for the interview we discussed?"

She pressed her lips together. "Uh, no. I have transportation."

"Did you get the Miata fixed?"

"No."

"A new car?"

"Uh, no. Peter loaned me one of his."

Jack's eyebrows went up.

She squirmed. "It's practical, at least while I'm staying here."

"I have to hand it to Ashford. He's giving you a taste of the good life."

Carlotta lifted her chin. "What's wrong with that?"

"Not a thing," Jack said lightly. "Maybe I underestimated him."

"Peter is accustomed to getting what he wants, and he doesn't have to throw muscle around to get it."

"Muscle? What muscle?" Jack casually flexed his own bulging biceps.

"Real mature, Jack. I'm going to take a shower."

He grinned. "Want some company?"

"No," she said, pushing him out into the hallway and closing the door behind him. Yet, as she showered in the luxurious bathroom, she thought back to when she and Jack had shared a showerhead only a few days before—right after her car had exploded. The incident had shaken them both and they agreed that due to mounting complications, it would be the last time they would give in to temptation.

Yet they seemed addicted to each other.

She showered and dressed hurriedly, pulling her still-damp long dark hair into a ponytail. When she descended to the first floor, she found Jack standing next to the sliding glass door. His back was to her, and he was on his cell phone.

"Yes, sir, I do understand what's on the line, sir…yes, sir, I know it's a shit storm…yes, sir, I know this is our jurisdiction and I don't like the state badges here any more than you do…yes, sir, I won't let you down." He disconnected the call and rubbed his neck in fatigue.

Carlotta walked up to him and took over the impromptu massage, kneading the muscles in the top of his shoulders through his shirt.

"Mmm, that's nice," he said.

"Did you sleep last night?"

"Some."

"Jack, you're no good to anyone if you fall asleep behind the wheel and kill yourself."

"I'm fine," he said, straightening and turning around. He glanced over her outfit—gray miniskirt, a bone-colored jacket and lime-green blouse—his gaze lingering on her legs that ended in five-inch Chloe pumps. "Is your strategy to distract the state guys with that lame excuse for a skirt?"

She smiled. "Think it'll work?"

He groaned. "Only if they're not blind."

Carlotta laughed. "Any more leads on the case?"

"As if I could discuss them with you."

"But no more bodies?"

"No, thank God... At least none that we know of."

"Have you found Michael Lane?"

"No. He hasn't contacted you, has he?"

"You know I would've told you."

"Right." He glanced at his watch. "Ready to go? I'll follow you to the station."

"I'm ready, I need to set the security alarm. What did you do with the cat?"

"I put her outside and she ran away, so maybe she'll find her way back home."

Carlotta nursed a stab of remorse. "I hope so. Where is the broken glass?"

He gestured toward a utility closet. "I swept it up."

She arched an eyebrow. "Pretty domestic of you, Jack."

"Just trying to keep you safe. I'd hate to see you hobbled, just in case you have to outrun our killer." He arched an eyebrow. "Or Ashford."

"Peter is being a perfect gentleman."

"Are you sure he isn't gay?" Jack asked. "If you were in my house, you wouldn't be sleeping across the hall."

Carlotta angled her head. "Do you have a house, Jack?"

"We're going to be late," he said, easily changing the subject. "Believe it or not, my job consists of more than watching your sweet ass, as entertaining as that might be."

"Where's your partner?" Carlotta asked. "Getting her beauty sleep?"

"Marquez is with the Gibbies, going over the profile for The Charmed Killer."

Carlotta harrumphed. "I thought she had decided it was someone with the last name Wren."

"She never suspected you."

"Right. She only suspected that I was planting those charms on the bodies after the fact."

"She's just doing her job." Jack gave her a pointed look. "We all are."

"Meaning you haven't ruled out my father as the maniac who's going around murdering women?"

"Personally, I think Michael Lane is a more likely suspect."

She frowned. "I got the impression that you didn't think it was Michael."

He averted his gaze. "We're still working out the time line."

"I suppose that's better for Randolph," she mused.

He tapped his watch. "Let's get this over with."

"Right."

Carlotta turned off the lights, then grabbed her purse and carefully reset the alarm before stepping into the garage. Jack followed and pulled the door closed behind him, sweeping his gaze over the structure that was finished with details nicer than most home interiors. Carlotta depressed the button for the garage-door opener. As the door rose, it ushered in morning light that bounced off the mirror finish of the sleek little two-seater sports car.

Jack caught her eye and grinned. "I could take the Porsche if you'd feel safer driving the sedan."

"Nice try. Just don't rear-end me."

"Gee, you didn't mind the other day," he said, waggling his eyebrows.

Carlotta glared at him, then opened the door and swung into the Porsche, admittedly nervous. As she adjusted the seat to accommodate her shorter legs, her pulse tripped higher. What if she did do something to Peter's car?

She put her hands on the steering wheel and forced herself to relax. As long as she was careful and drove slowly, what could go wrong? She was allowing the luxury of the car—of Peter's life—to intimidate her. Which was ironic, considering that if she'd married him, she'd probably have a fleet of luxury vehicles to choose from on any given day. Feeling more confident, she pressed the button to lower the convertible top, determined to enjoy the car to its fullest.

She turned over the engine and held her breath as she slowly backed out of the garage into the circular driveway. Beautifully shaped pavers surrounded a tall concrete fountain that dropped sheets of crystal-clear water into a tulip-shaped basin. She glanced in the rearview mirror at Jack sitting in his sedan, waiting to pull out behind her. He gave her a wry little wave. She exhaled and shifted into Drive. So far so good. The engine purred around her like a vibrator set on low speed. The distinctive hood sloped down and away from her. She felt sexy and powerful, wrapped in leather, a light breeze lifting her ponytail. She lowered her sunglasses and sighed. She was meant for this life. Carlotta pressed the gas pedal and the car surged forward as if it had been let out of its cage. She knew how it felt.

Suddenly a screeching noise sounded and a blob of

scratching, snarling fur landed in her lap. Terrified, she yanked the wheel and tried to hit the brake, but wound up hitting the gas instead. The car lurched forward.

Into something hard enough to stop it cold.

The cat, meanwhile, acted as if it was possessed and climbed her shoulder, emitting humanlike screams. Carlotta flailed at it with her hands, but it sunk its claws into her scalp. She shrieked as pain shot through her head.

Then suddenly, the attack ceased. She glanced up to see that Jack had removed the deranged cat.

"Scat! Get out of here!" he shouted. "Carlotta, are you okay?"

She pushed her hair out of her eyes and was struck with horror—she had plowed the left side of the Porsche into the fountain. She nodded, then burst into tears. "Peter's going to kill me."

Jack sighed. "He's not going to kill you. It's just a scratch down the side. Come on, let's get you out of there."

He reached in to help her slide to the passenger side, then she heard him curse and felt herself being ripped out of the seat. A horrific crash sounded, followed by the splintering of glass.

When Jack set her on her feet, she turned around. The top of the concrete fountain had fallen through the windshield of the Porsche and was now resting in the driver's seat among torn metal and leather, exactly where she'd been sitting. Water from the broken fountain gushed into the open convertible.

Jack made a rueful noise. "Okay, *now* Peter's going to kill you."

7

Carlotta waved as Peter drove away in his SUV.

"Ashford took it better than I would have," Jack admitted as he held open the door for her at the midtown APD precinct.

"It's just a car," Carlotta muttered, feeling like a naughty child.

"Right. It's a good thing you're wearing that belt you call a skirt."

"Peter's a reasonable man. He knows it was an accident. Besides, like he said—his insurance will pay for the car."

"True. Now he can get next year's model," Jack said drily.

"See? All is well."

"Meanwhile, what are you going to do for transportation?"

She sighed. "Peter said he could get me a rental, but for now I think I'd feel less destructive riding the train."

"Since we still don't know who planted that bomb under your Monte Carlo, I have to agree. But last time I checked, MARTA doesn't run past Ashford's subdivision."

"I'll figure out something," she murmured.

He stopped to check Carlotta in at the front desk. She

said hello to her friend Brooklyn and followed Jack through a secured door into the bull-pen area that housed workstations, cubicles and offices. The area hummed with voices, printers and the ringing of telephones.

Her grip on her purse was slippery and her pulse ratcheted higher. "I'm nervous about the interview."

Jack scoffed. "You already wrecked a Porsche this morning, what else can you do? The way I see it, the day has nowhere to go but up."

"Very funny. You'll be in there with me, won't you, Jack?"

His mouth flattened into a line. "I'll be watching. Just remember that you're here of your own volition. You can stop the interview if you feel uncomfortable."

"You're late," chided a female voice.

Carlotta turned to see Detective Maria Marquez approaching. The woman managed to look fresh yet threatening in a pale blue pantsuit and shoulder holster. Her demeanor toward Jack was territorial, but Carlotta wondered if Jack even noticed.

"There was a mishap," Jack said, pouring a cup of coffee.

Maria eyed Carlotta knowingly. "Right. Well, the state guys are getting restless."

"How did your session go?" Jack asked, taking a drink from the steaming cup.

Maria shrugged. "They asked questions, I answered." Her glance cut to Carlotta, then back. "We can talk about it later."

Carlotta pursed her mouth. The woman was purposely excluding her, while letting her know that she and Jack had plenty of private time.

"Did they offer up the state lab to process our evidence?" Jack asked.

"When we get some."

Jack swallowed coffee and nodded. "Fair enough."

"They're waiting for Carlotta in interview room two," Maria offered, then walked away.

Jack topped off his coffee and looked at Carlotta. "Ready?"

"I guess so."

He led her down a hallway to a closed door. "I'll be right on the other side of the glass. Just be truthful. Everyone's after the same thing here—to get you cleared."

"And my father," she added. But at the sight of the muscle jumping in Jack's jaw, she frowned. "And my father, right, Jack?"

"Carlotta, this is about you. Let your father take care of himself. From what I've seen, he's pretty good at it."

He rapped his knuckles on the door, then opened it. Two suited men sat adjacent to each other at a rectangular table that was piled high with files. She assumed that one of them was Randolph's, one was Wesley's and one was hers. Her pulse kicked up a notch. The men stood and adjusted their waistbands as Carlotta and Jack walked in.

"Agents Wick and Green," Jack said, nodding to the slim black man and the stocky white guy, respectively, "this is Carlotta Wren."

The men said hello and she responded in kind.

"Ms. Wren has agreed to voluntarily answer whatever questions you have about The Charmed Killer case. She's eager to help, aren't you, Carlotta?"

She nodded, suddenly realizing that both men's eyes were locked on her legs. Jack cleared his throat, and the men were suddenly all business.

"Have a seat, Ms. Wren."

"Can we get you something to drink?"

"No, thank you," she said, lowering herself into the empty chair.

Both agents looked at Jack expectantly.

"I'll be outside," he said unnecessarily. After making eye contact with Carlotta, he backed out of the room.

Once the door was closed, Agent Wick gave Carlotta a friendly smile and eased out of his jacket. "I'm originally from Buffalo and I haven't acclimated to the Southern heat yet."

"I told him he'll get used to it," Agent Green said to her, as if he and she were on the same team and Wick was the outsider. Translation: Green—good cop, Wick—bad cop. They both sat down and made a great show of getting settled, adjusting ties, sipping coffee and scooting chairs closer to the table.

Carlotta smiled. "I don't mean to be rude, gentlemen, but I have to be at work soon, so…what can I do for you?"

Wick pursed his mouth. "Okay, let's do this." He took a folder that Green passed to him and opened it. "What do you do for a living, Ms. Wren?"

She glanced at the glass behind Wick and imagined Jack's comforting presence behind it. "I'm a sales associate at Neiman Marcus at the Lenox Square Mall."

Green jotted down her answer. Apparently, he was the note-taker.

"That's where Michael Lane worked," Wick said.

Carlotta nodded. "Yes, that's where I met Michael."

"You were friends?"

"Yes. Good friends, actually."

"What changed that?"

She shifted in her chair. "The night I realized he was

behind an identity-theft ring and was responsible for the deaths of two women."

"You confronted him?"

"That's right. We were in the Fox Theater at the time, and he tried to kill me."

Wick took another sip of coffee. "How?"

"By pushing me over a balcony."

"You obviously survived," Green interrupted.

"Yeah, I was lucky. Someone broke my fall." She glanced at the glass again.

"Have you seen Michael Lane since that time?" Wick resumed.

"Only on television, after he escaped, when he was being chased by the police."

"I understand that when he jumped over the bridge, you were the one who informed the police that Michael couldn't swim."

"That's right, Michael once told me himself."

"So you assumed he'd died in the fall?"

"Yes."

"But he didn't."

She sighed—this was going to be tedious. "Apparently not. I found evidence that Michael Lane broke into the home I share with my brother and was living in our guest room, unbeknownst to us."

"That's quite a story," Wick said wryly.

Carlotta didn't respond.

"Your brother," Green broke in, glancing over the file in front of him. "That would be Wesley Wren?"

"That's correct."

"And both of you have records?" Wick asked, taking the file. "Your brother for computer crimes and you for assault?"

Carlotta squirmed. "I once used a tire iron on a man my brother owed money to, but that was in self-defense."

"And your brother's computer hacking? Was that also in self-defense?"

"No," she conceded. "But Wes is on probation and doing community service. He's paying for his crime."

"Your father is Randolph Wren, is that right?" Wick asked.

She tried not to react. "Yes."

"And he's a fugitive."

"Isn't that what your file says?"

Wick smiled. "Yes, it does. Do you know where your father is?"

"No."

"When was the last time you saw him?"

A few weeks ago at a Florida rest area. "Just before Christmas, my senior year of high school."

"He and your mother abandoned you and your brother?"

"Hey, ease up, partner," Green said, then gave Carlotta a sympathetic look.

They were playing her. "Yes, my parents abandoned me and my brother."

"Must've been tough," Green offered.

"Wesley and I both are fine," she said evenly.

Wick made a rueful noise in his throat. "Your files say otherwise. It says here that last year you were questioned in the murder of a man named Gary Hagan."

"And does it also say I was cleared?" she asked. "He was found dead at a party I attended—everyone was questioned."

"It says here that you crashed that party."

She shrugged. "Party crashing isn't a capital offense.

Besides…I don't do that anymore." Unless she had a very good reason.

Wick scanned the file, using his finger as a pointer. "You were also a suspect in the murder of, let's see… Angela Ashford?"

"And cleared again," she said. "Angela was the wife of a good friend of mine."

"Hmm. Then you reportedly jumped off an overpass and committed suicide?"

"That was actually Barbara Rook, a woman who stole my identity. And she didn't jump—she was murdered. The D.A. asked me to go along and plan my own funeral to draw out the murderer, who turned out to be Michael Lane, by the way."

"It's our understanding that you were asked to plan your own funeral to draw out your parents, not the murderer."

She hardened her jaw. "Well…it didn't work." Only Wesley and Coop knew that Randolph had shown up in disguise. She hadn't even known it until she found the note he'd slipped into her pocket.

"But wasn't your father a suspect in the Barbara Rook case?" Wick asked.

"My father seems to be a convenient suspect when there's no one else to pin things on."

Wick sat back in his chair and crossed his arms. "Looks to me as if trouble runs in the family. I understand you were also on the scenes when three of the victims of The Charmed Killer were discovered."

"I was there, but after the fact. I was helping to remove the bodies from the scene."

Wick leaned forward. "You're a salesclerk at Neiman's, but you moonlight as a body mover?"

Her hairline felt moist. "Yes?"

Wick squinted. "I'm sorry, is that a question?"

Carlotta swallowed hard. "I mean yes…I sort of got into body moving accidentally."

"Let me guess—you just happened onto a crime scene one night and started folding and stacking body bags?"

She frowned. "No. My brother began working with Cooper Craft, who contracts with the morgue to haul bodies. I went along a few times to help."

"Pardon me for saying so, but that seems like a pretty strange job for someone like you."

"I don't mind. Someone has to do it."

Wick consulted another file. "So what can you tell us about the crime scene of the first presumed victim, Shawna Whitt?"

Carlotta thought back to the woman's neat house, the hush of her bedroom, and how the young woman had been lying in her bed so peacefully. "When Coop and I arrived, the police had finished processing the scene. It appeared as if she'd died of natural causes. Coop was the one who noticed that she had a charm in her mouth."

"Coop?"

"Dr. Craft. He used to be the medical examiner."

"Yes. He's coming in later today to talk with us. What happened next?"

"Jack asked Coop—"

"Jack?"

She swallowed. "Detective Terry. He was on the scene when we arrived."

"Why was Detective Terry on the scene of a woman who had presumably died of natural causes?"

"You'll have to ask him."

"I'm asking you. Did he say?"

She searched her memory. "I believe he said he was in the area when the call came in, dropping off his partner."

"Detective Marquez?"

"I assume so. She is his partner."

"Do Detectives Terry and Marquez have a relationship?"

She frowned. "What? I wouldn't know." She glanced to the glass behind Wick and could almost feel Jack's disapproval burning through it.

Wick made a noise in his throat. "Let's continue. You were also on the scene of the second victim, Alicia Sills, to remove the body?"

"That's correct. I was with my brother when Dr. Craft called him. We went on the call, along with a friend who sometimes helps out. The victim was lying on the kitchen floor. It looked as if she'd fallen off a step stool and suffered head trauma."

"The report says that you found the charm in the victim's mouth."

"Not exactly. The charm fell out of her mouth when we attempted to move the body."

Wick studied her, then angled his head. "Ms. Wren, did you place those charms in the mouths of the victims?"

"No," she said evenly. "I did not."

He nodded to the charm bracelet she wore. "You seem to be fixated on charms."

The room suddenly seemed stifling. "I have a charm bracelet, like a lot of other women do, especially since Eva McCoy made them so popular. That's not a fixation."

"You purchased the bracelet you're wearing?"

"Actually, a coworker gave it to me."

"Michael Lane?"

"No. Patricia Alexander. She bought one for herself and one for me. The proceeds went to charity."

"The foundation Olympian Eva McCoy set up to commemorate the charm bracelet she wore when she won the women's marathon. It's been all over the news. I understand that you were present when Ms. McCoy's charm bracelet was stolen."

"That's right," she said, wincing inwardly at the memory of being facedown in a birthday cake the thief had rolled into the event as a diversion to steal the bracelet. "But the bracelet was later recovered."

"It says that you were involved in that, as well."

"Yes," she murmured.

"Good for you," Wick chirped, then looked down at his file. "Back to Alicia Sills. Did you know that she worked in the same building as your father's former investment firm? The one he embezzled from?"

"Allegedly embezzled from," she said through gritted teeth. "And it's a huge office building. Thousands of people have worked there in the past ten years."

"Did you ever hear your father mention her name?"

"Absolutely not."

"Did you ever see her with your father?"

She scoffed. "No. These are crazy questions."

Agent Wick glared at her. "We'll be the judge of that, Ms. Wren." He snapped the papers he held to punctuate the fact that he was still in charge of the room. "Now to the third victim, Pam Witcomb. Apparently you knew her?"

Carlotta frowned, confused. "Pam Witcomb?"

"Says here that she was a prostitute."

"Oh, you mean Pepper. I didn't really know her. I'd only met her once."

"Where?"

"On the corner of Third and West Peachtree. I was waiting for a ride and she…was also waiting for a ride. We had a conversation."

"About what?"

She pressed her lips together and rolled her shoulders. Her blouse was stuck to her back.

"Ms. Wren, what did you and our murder victim talk about?"

"Um…chocolate cake and blow jobs."

Green coughed and Wick's eyes widened. "Excuse me?"

"Hey, we were just passing time. My ride came a few minutes later, and that was it."

"Where were you going?"

"Dr. Craft picked me up for a body-moving job that turned out to be Shawna Whitt."

Wick frowned and sifted through the papers in front of him. "Is that in the file?"

Carlotta shrugged. "I don't know why it would be. One had nothing to do with the other."

He pulled on his chin and nodded. "Okay, on to the fourth victim then—A.D.A. Cheryl Meriwether."

"I didn't know her."

"But your brother did."

She frowned. "Have you talked to Wesley?"

"No. His name is on a list of defendants that Meriwether worked with over the last six months." Wick crossed his arms. "The Wrens are connected in some way to every victim."

She gave a strangled little laugh. "That's…a coincidence."

"Is it?" Wick asked, his voice light, but his eyes hard.

"Of course," she said, but heat flooded her face.

From a bag he pulled the charm bracelet that her father had given her when she'd turned fourteen. From the bracelet dangled fanciful charms that represented the things she'd loved in her teens: handbags and shoes, animals, flowers, cheerleading pom-poms and a tiny convertible for the Miata he'd bought for her first car, among other things. A tiny locked book reminded her of the high-school diaries she'd taken to Peter's so no one would read them.

"Your father was also fixated on charms," Wick ventured.

She shook her head. "That's ridiculous. The bracelet was simply an age-appropriate gift for a teenager."

"So you don't think that your father is trying to communicate with you through these killings?"

Her mouth watered to say that her father *had* been communicating with her, and no one had died because of it. But of course she couldn't without opening another can of worms. She felt Jack's gaze on her, and wondered if she should come clean about Randolph's impromptu appearances. She wavered. It really came down to whether she thought her father was capable of doing such heinous things.

"Ms. Wren," Wick said in a steely tone, *"do you think your father is trying to communicate with you through these killings?"*

Agent Green was rapt and Agent Wick's eyes glowed, as if he was on the verge of breaking the case. Carlotta fought to draw enough air into her lungs. "No, I don't."

"So for the record, you don't know the identity of The Charmed Killer?"

Carlotta gripped the table and leaned forward. "*No*. Don't you think if I did, I'd tell someone to end this killing spree?"

The agent's dark eyes narrowed. "Maybe you like being in the middle of something so sensational."

So Maria had shared the "profile" she'd come up with for Carlotta, as someone who liked to inject herself into investigations. Carlotta seethed. "I want this to be over as much as everyone else."

"So you'd be willing to take a polygraph?"

"Yes. I already told the detectives that I'd do whatever was necessary to clear myself of any involvement. That's why I'm here."

Wick studied her until her skin prickled. Even Green shifted in his seat.

"I need to get to work," she said, and stood abruptly. Her chair fell back and clattered against the floor.

"Okay," Wick said, pushing to his feet. Green followed, although he was still scribbling in his notebook.

She made a move to right the chair.

"We'll get that," Wick assured her.

Carlotta strode to the door, in a hurry to get out of the warm room.

"Ms. Wren?"

She turned back.

Wick put his hands on his hips and glared at her. "Don't leave town."

Carlotta gave a wry little laugh. "No worry there. I don't have transportation."

When she walked out into the hallway, another door opened and Jack and Maria appeared.

"Are you okay?" Jack asked. Maria looked less concerned.

"Fine," Carlotta said, marching ahead. "But I have to get to work."

"Do you need a ride?"

"No, I'll call a cab." After she smoked a cigarette.

He grabbed her arm, then leaned in close. "Chocolate cake and blow jobs?"

She smiled and murmured, "Wouldn't you like to know."

"What about that polygraph?" Maria asked loudly.

Carlotta turned around. "Set it up for first thing tomorrow." Then she looked at Jack. "Thanks for coming this morning when the alarm went off."

He gave her a flat smile. "Just doing my job. Be careful out there."

She turned and headed for the door, her mind spinning. It was obvious the GBI thought The Charmed Killer was someone connected to her. Forget the cigarette—she could use a stiff martini.

"Please let this day get better," she whispered.

She walked through the lobby, then out into a hallway and pushed open a door to the outside. It was already hot and humid, the summer air as thick and moist as cake. She was rummaging in her purse for a cigarette when she heard a man's voice, a little too close to her.

"Carlotta Wren?"

She froze and curled her fingers around the stun baton Jack had given her. She looked up to see a stout, unfamiliar dark-haired man standing in front of her. Her fight-or-flight instincts flared. He had thick, bushy eyebrows and big hands with grease under his fingernails. When he took a menacing step toward her, she whipped out the baton and zapped him in the shoulder. For two seconds, the air was rent with the buzz of a giant mosquito, then the perp dropped to the ground, his eyes rolled back in his head.

She turned and fled back into the precinct lobby, shouting at Brooklyn to get Jack. The woman picked up a phone and a few seconds later, he came barreling out with his weapon drawn. In between gasping breaths, she explained what happened as she retraced her steps outside. The big man was still lying there, his feet twitching.

"Stand back," Jack warned, then bent over the guy and began to pat him down.

Carlotta's heart pounded like a bongo, half in fright, half in anticipation. If this man was The Charmed Killer, it would be sweet to apprehend him while the GBI agents sat inside taking notes.

From inside her purse, her phone rang. She looked to see it was Peter calling. She answered, her hand at her throat. "Peter, can I call you back?"

"I couldn't wait," he said. "I had to see how you liked the gift."

She frowned. "What gift?"

"I had a guy deliver a Vespa scooter to the police-station parking lot. I thought I'd surprise you. Do you like it?"

"A Vespa?" she said, then looked up to see a pink scooter with a huge bow on it sitting a few feet away. "For me?"

Jack followed her gaze, then gave her a wry smile and held up a Vespa key ring and key that he apparently found on the incapacitated man.

Carlotta winced. Minus ten.

8

Wesley removed his watch and dropped it in a bowl along with all the change from his pockets. Because he had to walk through a metal detector every day to clock in to his community service job at Atlanta Systems Services, he'd stopped wearing a belt. The strict security measures seemed to have taken its toll on everyone who worked in the government building on Pryor Street. Along with saggy, beltless pants, soft-soled shoes and minuscule purses were now the norm.

After an unexpected day off the previous day due to construction that had shut down the building, everyone seemed restless this morning, and short-tempered. But Wes had chomped an Oxy when he'd rolled out of bed and swallowed another after locking up his bicycle in the parking lot, so he was feeling nice and relaxed. The first chewed capsule had flooded his system with the drug, and the subsequent swallowed one would keep the buzz going as the time-release coating broke down.

The drug made the light streaming into the atrium-style lobby luminous, the scent of the live potted trees and plants crisp, the humming of the woman behind him harmonious. The Oxy amplified his senses and made all things rosy, a welcome reprieve from the nightmares of toothless heads that had plagued his sleep. He couldn't stop thinking about the poor schmuck, wondering if the guy had a kid thinking it was his fault that his father hadn't come home…

In front of him, someone set off the metal detector, eliciting groans all around. Like everyone else, he craned for a look, his pulse quickening when he saw it was his coworker Meg Vincent who had stopped the line. A female security guard waved her aside to be wanded. Wesley watched with amusement as the slim blonde stood with arms raised and legs wide as the guard ran a handheld metal detector over her eclectic outfit of flowered pants, striped T-shirt and short jacket. When the baton went off near her breasts, he smiled and nodded—she was wearing an underwire bra today. Nice.

Meg caught him staring and rolled her eyes. The line started moving again, and he shuffled through in time to catch up with her just as the elevator doors were closing.

"We're full," she said.

He stuck his foot in the gap to make the doors bounce open. "It'll hold one more skinny dude," he said, then slipped in next to her.

Meg stared straight ahead, ignoring him.

"Maybe you should stop wearing a bra," he whispered.

Her mouth tightened.

He smiled, enjoying her discomfort. If anyone had the right to be irritated with anyone, it was him—with her. Meg had done nothing but torture him since he'd started working at ASS, looking hot and being smart as hell to boot. He'd been so mesmerized by her that he'd agreed to join her and two coworkers at a damn chick flick in

Piedmont Park. Aside from the fact that he'd had to leave early for a body-moving job, he'd thought things had gone pretty well.

Then she'd accused him of being an addict—which he'd flatly denied—and announced that he could only be her boyfriend if he'd "straighten up."

Like a damn school kid.

And the cherry on top of that shit sundae was when he'd run into Meg later with a *guy*…on a *date*. And the preppie guy had looked as if he moved in the same circle as her parents—Meg's dad was some hotshot geneticist. If he'd needed proof that Meg had been toying with him, he had it.

When the elevator door opened on subsequent floors, she moved aside woodenly to let people pass. After the fifth floor, they were alone. She turned her back to him and jabbed the Close Door button. "You're stoned."

"No, I'm not."

Meg arched an eyebrow. "Lie much?"

"I might wonder how you'd know so much about it."

Her expression changed in an instant—from cynical to something else. The elevator doors opened onto the seventh floor and she walked off, her back rigid.

"Hey." He went after her, feeling contrite. "Don't say anything to McCormick. I need this gig."

She turned around. "It's just a community service gig to you, but some of us are here because we want to be. I won't say anything to McCormick, but I'm not covering for you, either. You've been dragging your ass on this encryption project because you think it's beneath you. But I actually like doing a good job, even if the assignment isn't a career builder. I'd appreciate it if you'd get yourself sober and kick it up a notch."

So she'd noticed that he was trying to stretch out the database-encryption project, hoping that McCormick would switch Meg to another assignment before she realized he was trying to pull information about his father's case from the courthouse databases under the guise of encrypting the data.

Meg leaned in and lowered her voice. "I'm not going to let someone like you pull me down."

Right between the eyes—someone like him. "Yeah, I saw your type the other night."

She straightened and crossed her arms, inadvertently pushing up her cleavage. "What's my type, Wesley?"

"From the looks of the guy I saw you with? Gay."

She shook her head and turned to walk toward the fourplex workstation they shared with Ravi Chopra and Jeff Spooner, geeks of the highest order who also happened to be decent guys. Like Meg, they were employed by the city IT department through a work-study program for Georgia Tech students.

And like him, they were both, um, *enamored* with Meg.

"Morning, boys," she sang.

When they lit up like little pets, Wesley wanted to heave. The woman was a hypnotist.

But with her lecture ringing in his ears, he pried his attention away from her breasts and got down to business on the encryption project. He'd been holding off on pulling test data that would include his father's information because he was afraid Meg would see it and realize what he was up to. He'd also procrastinated because access to the databases was strictly monitored and his user ID would be forever attached to the data he pulled if someone checked. One more infraction would probably land him in jail. His attorney, Liz Fischer, was good, but she'd warned him—in the aftermath of a screw—that she was running out of tricks to pull out of her hat.

Just the thought of Liz made his balls tingle. But not as much as knowing that Meg was wearing an underwire bra. Maybe it was the plaid one that he sometimes got a glimpse of when she bent over…

Then a thought hit Wes like a slow-moving locomotive. His brain worked in a lower gear under the influence of Oxy, but when the ideas made it through the goo, they made him *so* happy: Maybe having Meg on the project was a blessing in disguise.

All morning he kept his head down and his smile to himself while he put together the procedure that would pull enough data on either side of his father's records to hopefully render it invisible. At fifteen minutes before noon, when he was supposed to leave, he waved to get Meg's attention.

She looked annoyed, then removed the earbuds of her iPod. "Yeah?"

"I have to go in a few minutes, but I have the job ready to pull the test data we need from the databases I'm working on. McCormick said he'd have to grant me one-time access to the data before I can run the job. But since you have access, I was thinking it would save him a lot of time and trouble if you ran the job when you get a chance."

She considered him for a few seconds, then shrugged. "I guess it's all the same. Send me the Job Control Language."

"Done," he said, then jerked his thumb. "I'm taking off."

"Knock yourself out," she said, then put her earbuds back in.

An alien feeling of frustration crowded his chest. Why he felt so compelled to impress this girl, he didn't know. It also made him a little nuts that she totally saw through him. The dismay sent little shards of pain to his temple as he made his way out of the building and to his bike. He really wanted another Oxy pill, but he had an appointment with his probation officer, and he thought it best to be as sober as possible.

During the ride across town, he thought he noticed a black SUV with tinted windows about a block behind him. He blinked to clear his vision and willed the pounding in his head to go away as he strained for a better look. He couldn't tell if it was the same vehicle that had been dogging him, so he whipped left to go down a side street.

When he glanced over his shoulder, he saw the black SUV slow, then go past. He exhaled in relief, but still…this was getting creepy.

He didn't see the vehicle again, but his nerves jumped as he locked up his bike and walked into the building that housed the offices of Fulton County Probation Control. He signed in with the sourpuss at the front window, then eased into a chair in the waiting room. His head was really throbbing now, and his left eye twitched.

Wednesdays were the worst because he had to plan his Oxy hits around his meeting with E. Jones. He consoled himself with the knowledge that after he left, he had plenty of Oxy waiting for him. He'd used some of his poker earnings to buy a bag before Michael Lane had stolen the bulk of his cash. And living with Chance, he had easy access to the pills. Chance had even promised him more if he could talk Carlotta's friend Hannah into going out with him. Wes was still working on that deal.

"Wren, you're up!" the woman at the window shouted, then cut her eyes to a door leading to a hallway of offices. He knew the way well.

Outside E.'s office, Wes glanced in all directions. During his last visit, he'd run into E.'s boyfriend, Leonard, a thug whose apparent cover was selling pharmaceuticals when, in fact, the man worked for The Carver and ran drugs for Chance.

Thankfully the bully was nowhere in sight. Wes rapped on the door and E. called for him to come in.

"Have a seat," she said, surprising him with a bright smile. E. was a babe—long red hair and nice full breasts. But while she'd always been cordial, she'd fallen short of being friendly.

Until today.

"Are you having a nice day?" she asked, her eyes shining.

"Uh, sure," he said, lowering himself into a chair opposite her.

"Beautiful weather we're having, isn't it?"

"Yeah," he agreed, wondering why she was so chipper. He started to dismiss it as normal female flakiness until his gaze landed on the sparkler on her left ring finger. "What's with the rock?"

"Hmm?" She lifted her head, then followed his gaze to her finger and smiled, her cheeks turning pink. "Oh...I got engaged."

Wesley felt a little sick. "To Leonard?"

"Of course to Leonard. Who did you think?"

He shifted in his chair. "I didn't realize the two of you were so serious."

She laughed, the sound like a tinkling bell. "That's what grown-ups do, Wesley."

He wiped his hand over his mouth. E. had no idea what she was getting into.

"Aren't you going to congratulate me?" she asked. "I thought you and Leonard were friends."

"Congratulations," he said. "When are you getting married?"

"We haven't set a date yet. Right now, I just want to enjoy being engaged."

He smiled and nodded, but he longed to tell her that she was making a colossal mistake. The only upside was her pervasive good mood. Instead of the normal grilling she gave him, asking about his job and if he was staying out of trouble, E. seemed downright giddy.

"Sounds good," she said, closing his file. "Anything else?"

He considered telling her about Michael Lane having been in their house, but she might get nosy about where he was staying, and she already suspected that Chance was a bad influence.

"Nope," he said, pushing to his feet. "See you next week."

At the door, he turned back. "Be careful, E. You know there's a man out there killing women."

At the mention of The Charmed Killer, she sobered, then gave him a little smile. "I will be. Thanks for your concern, Wes."

He left the office feeling grateful but a little off-kilter at the ease of the appointment. No interrogation, no drug test. It was a gift, but he felt bad taking it, knowing that E. was being conned by Leonard the Lughead.

He was *so* ready for an Oxy hit. Standing on the heat-radiating sidewalk in front of the building, he popped one of the pills in his mouth and rolled it around for a few seconds before crushing it between his molars. A choking bitterness flooded his tongue, but was followed by a tide of ecstasy that swept through his throat, chest and limbs. Compromising the tablet's time-release coating allowed all its sweet goodness to pour into his pleasure centers at once.

All was right with the world.

"Hey, dumb ass!"

He pivoted his head to see the long black Town Car sitting at the curb, windows down. Mouse leaned forward to shout through the passenger-side window. "Get in!"

Wesley almost smiled. He and Mouse had fallen into a routine. His community service commitment had him working at ASS every weekday morning. Afternoons he spent with Mouse collecting on The Carver's past-due accounts. On Wednesdays, Mouse knew to pick him up after his probation meeting.

It was like being fucking married.

"Let me get my bike," he said.

By the time he'd unlocked his bike Mouse had popped the trunk. Wes glanced around the trunk before dumping his bike inside, glad to find it empty of body parts. Then he swung inside, happy for the cool interior. The advantage of riding around with a fat man was that the air conditioner was always on. And the chow was always plentiful.

"I got you two chicken sandwiches," Mouse said through a mouthful of food, nodding to the Wendy's bag that sat on the floor in the precise place the severed head-in-a-bag had sat yesterday. "I know you like those."

"Thanks," Wes said, reaching for the food. "What'd you get?"

"Baconater," Mouse said, hefting his half-eaten burger.

"My wife would fucking kill me if she knew I was cheating on my diet."

Wes arched an eyebrow at the man's bulk. "You're on a diet?"

Mouse stuffed a fry in his mouth as he pulled away from the curb. "I don't need you busting my chops, too."

Wes unwrapped one of the sandwiches and bit into it. "What's on the agenda?"

"Same old shit. A handful of college snots who think they can get away with not paying the man."

Wesley had convinced Mouse that he could help him collect from nontraditional clients by getting into places Mouse couldn't, including dormitories, student centers, frat parties, sports clubs and other college hangouts that provided a layer of security between debtors and collectors.

In the backseat of the Town Car was a box that held a plethora of props—fast-food-delivery vests and hats, mocked-up lanyards that read Campus Security, even jock props like sports equipment. Baseball jerseys helped him to look convincing on the occasions when he needed to carry a baseball bat.

Thank God he'd only had to use it to bash in a couple of minifridges. That had been enough to convince his reluctant customers his swing made up for his aim.

Today, though, he was so mellow from the Oxy, he didn't feel like bashing anything. So after he'd talked his way into a dorm at Emory University, a computer lab at Georgia State and band practice at Georgia Tech (by wielding a piccolo), he'd used an Oxy pill to lubricate his marks. Once they were floating toward nirvana, they parted with their daddies' money pretty easily.

"You got the magic touch today," Mouse said, counting

bills. "Here's something extra—get a haircut." He handed two hundreds to Wesley, which Wes added to the three hundreds he'd filched from the payments before delivering them to Mouse.

Remembering what Jack had told him about chatting up Mouse, he settled back in the leather seat and tried to sound casual. "So, how long have you been working for The Carver?"

Mouse shrugged, sorting the bills by denomination. "About fifteen years, I guess."

"How did that happen?"

Mouse laughed. "Same way it happened for you. I owed the man money, and decided I was better off collecting for him."

"Guess that's worked out for you."

"Pays the mortgage."

"Are you involved with other parts of the business?"

Mouse looked up. "What other parts?"

Wesley tried to look nonchalant. "I dunno. I just figured The Carver was into other things. Good businessmen diversify."

"The boss has other business interests around the region," Mouse said stiffly, sounding like a publicist, "but you don't need to concern yourself with them."

"Just wondering if that guy I detoothed was a customer, or if maybe he had personal issues with The Carver."

Mouse folded the wad of cash and stuffed it into an inside jacket pocket. "Maybe he was someone who asked too many questions."

Sweat popped out on Wes's upper lip. He swallowed hard and glanced at the nearest street sign to get his bearings. "I think I'll go ahead and take off."

"Want me to drop you somewhere?"

"Nah, this is fine. Pop the trunk?"

"Yeah. Later, little man."

Wesley climbed out and retrieved his bike, then watched the Town Car drive away, probably home to a three-car garage in a suburban cul-de-sac. He wondered if the man's family had any idea what he did for a living.

With a start he realized he didn't even know Mouse's real name.

Wesley threw his leg over his bike, about to head back to Chance's place, but at the sound of his cell phone ringing from his backpack, he stopped and pulled it out. Liz Fischer's name flashed on the caller-ID screen, and blood rushed to his groin. The last time he'd slept with her she'd called him on the rug for blurting out Meg's name in the thick of things, so he wasn't sure he'd hear from her again. The other worry that nagged at him was the fact that he'd told Liz his father had approached Carlotta at a rest area in Florida. He'd justified the slip by telling himself that since Liz had been Randolph's attorney, she had a right to know he was alive and well.

But, as he'd learned from his father's papers, Liz wasn't just Randolph's attorney, she'd also been his lover. And now that Wesley'd had time to think about it, letting Liz in on the secret might not have been the wisest move. What if she was sore at his father for taking off and decided to go to the D.A.?

His hand shook slightly as he flipped up the phone. Damn, the Oxy seemed to be wearing off more and more quickly. "Hi," he said into the mouthpiece.

"Hi yourself," Liz said, her voice cracking.

Wesley frowned. "Are you sick?"

"I've been better," she said. "It's been a rough couple of weeks. I wanted to let you know I'm going out of town for a few days."

"Okay," he said, puzzled. "This doesn't have anything to do with my dad, does it?"

A rueful noise sounded over the line. "No. I just need to think through some things."

"Okay," he said, still at a loss as to how, or if, he should respond.

"I thought you should know in case something comes up that needs my attention. How's the undercover work going?"

"Fine. Jack is so wrapped up in The Charmed Killer case that he told me to lie low for a while."

"Yeah, everywhere I go, that's all people are talking about. The women in my office are scared to death."

"Where are you going?" he asked.

"Um…I haven't decided yet."

"When will you be back?"

"Maybe a week or so. Call my cell if there's an emergency. Maybe all this serial-killer business will be over by the time I come back."

Wesley frowned. "Is something else bothering you, Liz?"

A pregnant pause sounded over the line. "Nothing you can help me with. I'll check in when I get back."

Wesley closed the phone, frowning. Liz Fischer wasn't the kind of woman who was easily rattled, especially by anything work related. So whatever was shaking her cage, it had to be serious…and personal.

9

Carlotta lowered the Vespa kickstand in the mall parking lot and carefully climbed off the pink scooter—not easy to achieve in a short skirt. Then she walked over to where Jack sat in his sedan and grinned. "I think I have the hang of it. But thanks for following me."

He squeezed the bridge of his nose. "I don't think this is a good idea."

"Why not?"

He gestured to the scooter wildly. "You're exposed. It's not safe."

"It's perfectly safe. There are scooters all over this city. And the helmet? Hello?"

"I know, but you…"

She crossed her arms. "What?"

Jack shook his head. "I don't know what Ashford was thinking."

"He was thinking that I needed transportation, and he knew I wouldn't accept a car. It's a very thoughtful gift."

"Just remember that the learner's permit is only good for six months."

"I know." She loosened the chin strap on the matching

pink helmet. "Do you think the salesman is going to be okay?"

"He'll be pissing sparks for a while, but yeah, he'll be fine."

"He was really nice about the whole thing."

"Thank the magic skirt," Jack said wryly, his gaze drifting down before he looked back up. "I'm glad to know you're not afraid to use the stun baton, but you might need to be a tad more discriminating."

She frowned. "I wanted to use it on Agent Wick this morning."

"That, I wouldn't advise. I talked to your boss about Michael Lane being on the loose again. You'll have an undercover security officer in your area in case Lane decides to put in an appearance."

She nodded, her gut clenching.

"Keep your cell phone with you and call me if you see anything suspicious."

"Jack, tell me the truth. Do you think Michael is The Charmed Killer, or don't you?"

He looked uneasy. "It doesn't matter what I think—we can't take any chances. Pay attention to everything and everyone around you." He wet his lips. "And stick close to Ashford. I'll see you tomorrow when you come in to take the polygraph."

"Any tips for when I take it?"

"Yeah—try to tell the truth." He waved, then pulled away, watching her in his side mirror.

Carlotta waved after him, muttering, "Easier said than done."

She removed the helmet and stored it in a compartment beneath the scooter seat. Just looking at the Vespa gave her a rush of pleasure—and guilt. It was an extravagant gift and she shouldn't accept it, but it was a gorgeous little plaything, and frankly, it felt good to have something pretty to take her mind off serial killers, exploding cars and long-lost fathers for the time that it took to buzz up and down Peachtree Street.

She jogged in to Neiman's, late as usual these days, and removed her cell phone from her purse before dumping it in her locker in the employee break room. She jumped on the up escalator, but when she saw her boss, Lindy Russell, riding on the down escalator, she tried to hide her face.

"I see you," Lindy said as they passed. "You're late."

"I have a good excuse."

"You always do," her boss offered over her shoulder. "I expect you to sell your tail off today."

"Yes, ma'am," Carlotta murmured, then turned to face forward. Lindy had let her off the hook so many times, she'd lost count. She loved this job and had nearly gone crazy when she'd been off work while her broken arm healed. Retail was her life, and she was really good at it— her name had been at the top of the sales charts more than any other associate at this location.

Until lately.

Recently, events had converged to distract, digress and divert her from what she thought was her calling. Wesley's involvement with body moving and with Coop had overlapped into her life, and Coop had on more than one occasion confronted her, challenging her to do more with her life, and with her mind.

She fingered the puzzle piece on her charm bracelet. Coop had told her she was good at solving puzzles, at helping people.

Then she frowned. And Maria Marquez had told her she was good at insinuating herself into investigations.

Carlotta tripped on the top step of the escalator, but caught herself. A good reminder that she needed to get her head back where it belonged.

When she reached her designated department, she noticed a stocky guy in an ill-fitting sport coat loitering between racks of women's clothes. Christ, all he needed was a ball cap that read Undercover. He gave her a conspicuous nod, then proceeded to scan the faces of shoppers in the department with all the subtlety of an X-ray machine.

But his presence did make her feel safer. Carlotta immersed herself in her job, switching on and reading customers to better understand how she could help them find what they were looking for. Valerie Wren hadn't been much of a mother, but she'd taken the time to tutor Carlotta from a young age on good tailoring and how to mix and match unusual color combinations and fabric textures. Both talents served her well when catering to the Neiman's clientele who came to her wanting a fresh look. She had the added insight of knowing how her customers' minds worked, the places they frequented and the social competition they faced, because the Wrens had once moved in those same circles.

Today the store was hopping. Customers congregated in the aisles, wide-eyed and talking in low tones. They seemed antsy and eager to buy, probably for much the same reason that she was so willing to keep the pink scooter—because it made her feel better. Apparently, serial killing was good for the economy.

Despite the macabre motivation, Carlotta was grateful

for the commissions she racked up over the next few hours. She was finally getting her groove back, and the rush of adrenaline made her realize she'd been crazy to let herself get distracted with amateur sleuthing. This was her life, and it wasn't half-bad.

Later in her shift she looked up to see fellow associate Patricia Alexander coming her way. Carlotta swallowed a groan. The blonde was a cross between a nemesis and a pesky younger sister. But at the moment she looked worried, so Carlotta tamped down her irritation.

Patricia thrust a folded section of newspaper toward Carlotta. "Did you see this in the *AJC?*"

Carlotta took the paper. "What does it say?"

"That The Charmed Killer is targeting women who wear charm bracelets." Patricia's hand covered the bracelet that she'd bought for herself, similar to the one Carlotta wore.

Surprise bled through Carlotta as she skimmed the article written by Rainie Stephens, a reporter who'd helped her recover Olympian Eva McCoy's stolen charm bracelet. Rainie cited "sources inside the APD" as indicating that the presence of a charm bracelet might be a trigger for random attacks on women.

"That seems inflammatory," Carlotta murmured. "None of the victims were wearing charm bracelets."

Patricia squinted. "How do you know?"

Her coworkers didn't know she moonlighted as a body mover. "I…must have read it somewhere." Besides, wouldn't Jack have told her if there was a connection?

"There must have been some reason to print it," Patricia insisted.

Carlotta handed the newspaper back to her. "Not necessarily. But if it makes you feel better, don't wear your bracelet."

Patricia's face fell. "But I really believe these charm bracelets can predict the future."

"I thought the spirit of featuring different charms on each bracelet was to encourage the wearer to try new things, not to predict the future." She was saying the words aloud to convince herself as much as Patricia. Just because her bracelet had a charm with champagne glasses didn't necessarily mean that something...*celebratory* was around the corner. If she believed that, she'd have to believe in the corpse charm, too.

So why did she feel so compelled to wear it?

Patricia held up her wrist and pointed to a miniature lion. "Then explain how I met a guy named Leo—" she pointed to a baseball glove "—who is a baseball player."

"How do you explain the broom?" Carlotta asked, pointing to a third charm on the woman's bracelet.

Patricia smiled. "That's easy. He swept me off my feet."

Carlotta rolled her eyes and decided not to ask about the dog charm or the horny steer head. She might get more information than she cared to know. "I have a solution."

"What?"

"Wear long sleeves," Carlotta said, tapping Patricia's bare arm with a wry smile. "I'm taking my lunch break."

"Want some company?"

"Er...I'm actually running errands," Carlotta improvised.

"Buying change-of-address cards?" Patricia asked lightly. "Word is that you've moved in with Peter Ashford."

Carlotta couldn't hide her surprise. "Where did you hear that?"

Patricia shrugged. "Neighbors talk."

Carlotta set her jaw. The neighbor with the binoculars? "It's only temporary. There was an issue of safety
at my place."

Patricia's eyes widened. "Does this have something to
do with Michael Lane being on the run again?"

"Is that in the paper, too?" Carlotta asked.

"Yeah, it said he'd broken into someone's house—wait
a minute! It was *your* house, wasn't it?"

"I'm not supposed to talk about it," Carlotta said, glad
to have an excuse. She didn't want to explain to yet
someone else how it was possible that a psycho could be
living in their guest room, undetected.

"So that's why you moved in with Peter?"

"I didn't move in. I'm only staying with him until this
all blows over."

Patricia's eyes gleamed. "But I can guess what the
sleeping arrangements are."

"I'm taking my break," Carlotta said pointedly.

Patricia looked over Carlotta's shoulder and gasped.
"Don't look now, but there's a mean-looking man in
resort wear who keeps looking at you. What if he's The
Charmed Killer?"

"Relax—he's a rent-a-cop."

Patricia pulled back. "Carlotta, don't take this the
wrong way, but I'm starting to think that your being here
makes it unsafe for the rest of us." She sniffed and walked
away, leaving Carlotta feeling nonplussed.

The woman wasn't wrong.

From inside her pocket, her phone rang. She pulled it
out to see Peter's number, and, after glancing around to
make sure no customers were within earshot, she connected the call. "Hi, Peter."

"Hi, I'm just checking on you."

She felt a rush of affection. "Thanks, I'm fine. The scooter is great, and Jack arranged for extra security here at the store."

"That was good of him," Peter said, although his voice was tinged with something other than wholehearted approval.

"I'm sorry, Peter, but I'm not supposed to be on the phone while I'm on the floor."

"I won't keep you. I just wondered if you'd like to go with me to the club tonight for a black-tie charity auction."

Excitement barbed through her chest at the thought of attending an event at the country club where Peter belonged, where her parents had once belonged. "I'd love to."

"Great. I'll see you at home?"

Home. "Yes," she murmured, then disconnected the call. Wonder filled her chest at how easily Peter could offer her access to places she'd been denied all of her adult life. Admittedly, part of the motivation for going would be to face down some of the people who had cast them out.

Then she gasped—she didn't have anything to wear. All her cocktail dresses were at the town house, which was off-limits. She glanced with envy in the direction of formal wear, but made herself resist the urge to splurge. No matter how much she wanted a new dress, she couldn't afford it. Her employee credit card hadn't been reinstated, and the one card she had left after a shredding party incited by Wesley couldn't bear the strain.

Jack had told her if she needed something at the town house, she'd have to have an escort. She dialed his number and he answered after half a ring.

"Carlotta? You okay?"

"I'm fine," she said. "I just need to get back into the town house."

"Why?"

She squirmed. "I need to get some clothes."

"Yesterday you had a suitcase full of clothes."

"Not the right kind," she hedged.

He sighed. "You want to compromise a crime scene to get a specific outfit?"

"Peter is taking me to an event at the club, and I need something fancy."

"By fancy, you mean something slinky and tight?"

"Probably," she agreed.

"Well, in that case…I don't think so."

"Jack!"

"You should be careful about false advertising. You don't want to lead the poor guy on."

She rolled her eyes. "Will you meet me at the town house or not?"

"What time?"

"Six o'clock."

"Okay. Be careful on that Hello Kitty tricycle."

"And how does a big macho detective like you know about Hello Kitty?"

He disconnected the call and Carlotta laughed, shaking her head.

10

Carlotta spent her lunch break in the food court eating a salad, but it was hard to relax with the hulking undercover guy—Herb, she'd learned—hovering nearby. She wound up tossing half the salad and sipping a diet soda while searching the faces of passersby for Michael Lane.

Where was Michael, and what was he doing? Was he enjoying the panic he'd unleashed? Was he basking in the power?

On the walk back to Neiman's, Carlotta spotted a jewelry kiosk that offered cases of gold and silver trinkets, most of it costume quality and trending young. At the sight of a tray of charms, though, she stopped and leaned in.

"May I help you?" the female attendant asked, then pointed to Carlotta's charm bracelet. "Something to add to your bracelet?"

Carlotta glanced back at the undercover security guy, who looked bored to tears with his babysitting stint, and was paying zero attention to what she was doing. Chances were good Herb wouldn't report any charm-buying activity to Jack.

Then she frowned. And what if he did? There was

nothing wrong with being a concerned citizen doing a little ad hoc investigative work, especially if it led to finding the source of the charms left in the mouths of the victims. She was in a unique position to have seen some of the charms at the crime scenes, so why not take advantage of her insider information? Carlotta looked back to the attendant. "I'm looking for some specific charms. Do you have any chickens?"

"We have some birds, but no chickens right now. We tend to sell out of them."

Carlotta arched an eyebrow. "Why?"

"A lot of people are into the Chinese zodiac, the year of the chicken."

It was something to keep in mind, at least. "Do you have any cigars?"

"That I think I can help you with." The woman bent over the tray and poked through the miniature replicas of everything from animals to foods to letters of the alphabet. A few seconds later, she removed a tiny charm and placed it on a black cloth for Carlotta's inspection.

Carlotta's pulse sped up. The miniature cigar with a tiny etched band looked identical to the one she'd personally witnessed falling out of the second victim's mouth when she and Wesley had prepared to move the body from the crime scene.

"I'll take it," she said. "Do you have any cars?"

"Several," the woman said, sweeping her hand over a section of the tray.

Carlotta bit her lip. She hadn't seen the car charm that reportedly had been in the third victim's mouth, nor the gun charm found in the mouth of the fourth victim. "I'll take the cigar, all of the cars, and do you have any gun charms?"

The woman looked surprised, then nodded. "Three different ones."

"I'll take those, too, one of each," Carlotta said, then slid her bloated credit card across the counter, hoping it would withstand the purchase. She exhaled when the woman bagged the charms and handed them over, along with a receipt to sign.

Carlotta walked back to Neiman's and guiltily stored the charms in her locker. Maybe collecting the same charms the killer had left behind would help her to figure out if Michael Lane was behind the senseless killings.

As she walked back to her station, she mentally reviewed her interaction with Michael over the past few years, trying to recall any personality tics that she should've picked up on, any red flags that would've indicated he was the narcissistic serial killer that Detective Maria Marquez said he was. True, he'd murdered two women over the identity-theft ring he'd spearheaded, and tried to eliminate her when she'd uncovered his plot, but killing for self-preservation was wildly different than killing for the sake of killing. She found it difficult to wrap her mind around her former coworker being that damaged.

With Michael weighing heavy on her heart and her mind, she was skittish all afternoon and grateful for the presence of the security guard who was practically hanging on the fixtures by the time she ended her shift. He escorted her out to the parking lot, where she thanked him, then straddled her new scooter and turned it in the direction of the town house. The wind on her face as she headed south on Peachtree Street felt soothing, and her spirits lifted. She told herself it had nothing to do with the fact that she was meeting Jack.

But when she rolled into the driveway of the town house to find Detective Maria Marquez leaning against the sedan that Jack normally drove, Carlotta conceded a stab of disappointment. She parked the scooter and dismounted awkwardly, then removed her pink helmet, thinking that the carmelicious detective wouldn't be caught dead with helmet hair.

"Nice ride," Maria said, her voice curling with amusement.

"Thanks," Carlotta murmured.

Maria moved toward the front door. "Jack said you needed to get an outfit?"

She made it sound so frivolous. "That's right."

"Give me your keys and tell me what you need, and I'll get it."

Carlotta handed over her keys and followed Maria as she climbed the stoop and unlocked the door. "It would be faster if I picked out the clothes."

Maria gave her a disparaging look, but Carlotta refused to back down from the standoff. It was clear there was more going on here than just picking out a cocktail dress.

"Okay," the female detective finally said. "But stay behind me and don't touch anything."

Carlotta made a face at the woman's back.

"I saw that in the window," Maria said.

Carlotta winced. "Sorry, it's just that this *is* my house."

"But right now it's a crime scene," the woman said, snapping on thin latex gloves before breaking through the yellow tape stretched across the entrance.

Carlotta followed her into the house, which was dark and still. "My bedroom is down the hallway, first door on the right."

The detective turned on lights along the way, revealing black residue around the light switches, on appliances and flat surfaces where they'd lifted fingerprints.

"Is there a reason why Jack didn't come?" Carlotta asked casually, following Maria into the bedroom.

"He's with the state guys."

Carlotta nursed a pang of embarrassment as Maria perused her juvenile white furniture, lingering on the bed in which Carlotta and Jack had rolled around a few times. "Has there been a development in The Charmed Killer case?"

Maria turned and frowned. "As if I'd tell you."

Carlotta crossed her arms. "Why not?"

"To begin with, you're not a law enforcement officer."

"But I'm involved in this case."

"Yeah—as a possible suspect."

Carlotta laughed. "You can't be serious. I think you're letting your personal feelings get in the way here."

Maria scoffed. "I don't know you well enough to have personal feelings for you, Carlotta."

"I meant your personal feelings for Jack."

The woman stopped, then dipped her chin. "I don't have personal feelings for Jack. He's my partner."

But Carlotta knew that look. Still, there was no use flogging the detective. Instead, she turned toward her closet and gestured to the residue-covered doorknob. "Will you open it for me?"

The detective obliged, and Carlotta flipped through the clothes jammed on the racks inside.

"Nice Valentinos," Maria murmured, stroking a gloved hand over a pair of silvery crisscross high-heeled sandals.

"Thanks." Carlotta pulled out a red crepe spaghetti-strap short cocktail dress with a swing skirt, and a cream-colored sheath with silver-chain trim. "Which do you think I should choose for a charity auction at a country club?"

Maria angled her head. "The cream one if you want to fit in, the red one if you want to be remembered."

Carlotta frowned. "Hmm…I can't decide."

"Take both and decide later."

"With the Valentino sandals?"

"Oh, yeah, they'll go with either dress." Maria pointed. "With the Lauren Merkin bubble clutch."

"Good choice," Carlotta agreed, then pulled it from a shelf.

She put both dresses in a garment bag, then backed out and Maria closed the closet. They retraced their steps to the front door, then Carlotta cursed. "I forgot about being on the scooter. I can't get these to Peter's."

"Give me the dresses," Maria said. "I'll follow you."

"That's not necessary," Carlotta protested.

"No problem. That way I can tell Jack you got home okay."

Carlotta was nervous having Maria behind her on the short ride to Peter's, but she conceded that the woman was going above and beyond the call of duty to make sure that she was safe. All for Jack, of course.

At the entrance to Martinique Estates, Carlotta punched in Peter's code and waved to the guard as she and Maria drove in. When she pulled the scooter into the driveway to the immense house, she grimaced at the sight of the broken fountain. Out of the corner of her eye she saw a flash of yellow fur disappear into the thick foliage of the landscaping. It seemed that the pesky stray cat hadn't yet found its way home.

"Nice place," Maria said from the car.

Carlotta climbed off the scooter and walked over to take the garment bag the woman held out the window. "It is, isn't it?"

"I can see why Jack is jealous."

Carlotta's head came up. "Jealous? I don't think so."

Maria's mouth twitched downward. "There's something you should know. The state agents took Jack off The Charmed Killer case."

Carlotta gasped. "What? Why?"

"Territorial issues. They want to run their own investigation and they think Jack's too close to some aspects of it."

Realization dawned. "You mean too close to me, don't you?"

"Among other reasons," Maria said. "Carlotta…you need to be more careful about the men you let into your life." Then she drove away.

11

Peter squeezed Carlotta's hand as they walked into the twinkling ballroom of the Bedford Manor Country Club. "Are you okay?"

"I'm fine," she said, conjuring up a smile. In truth, she couldn't get Maria Marquez's words out of her head. Jack had been removed from The Charmed Killer case. He must be going crazy.

"You look more than fine in that red dress," Peter said, raking his appreciative gaze over her. "You look amazing."

"Thank you." At the last minute, she'd decided against the dress that would make her fit in, in favor of the one that would make her memorable, as Maria had put it. And based on some of the looks they were getting from milling guests, she had hit the right note. "You don't look so bad yourself."

Peter preened in his black Joseph Abboud tux that fit his lean frame and broad shoulders flawlessly. "I was hoping you'd notice."

"I noticed," she murmured, giving herself a mental shake to return to the present. Hadn't she dreamed of this moment, when she would take her rightful place among to the people who had cast her out, on the arm of one of their own?

She pushed Jack's dilemma and The Charmed Killer from her mind as she glanced around at the beautiful people gathered at draped tables, wineglasses clinking and diamonds winking. No one in this grand room was worried about the sordid things that went on outside their community—their lives were insulated with glamour and amusement and privilege. Crime was something that happened to other people. She suspected the only reason they hadn't turned their backs on Peter when Angela had been murdered so fantastically was because of his parents' far-reaching influence.

"Mom, Dad," Peter said as the prim couple approached. "Good to see you." He embraced his mother and shook hands with his father. "You remember Carlotta Wren."

"Of course," his mother said with a nod.

Carlotta extended her hand to each of them in turn. "Good to see you, Mrs. Ashford, Mr. Ashford." The couple seemed unnerved by her presence, glancing around as if to see if anyone else had noticed she'd broken rank.

"I was told there are two empty seats at our table if you'd like to join us," Peter said.

"Oh, we'd love to," his mother said, then wet her lips. "But we promised the Daileys that we'd sit with them." She looked to her husband for confirmation and he nodded vigorously.

Carlotta's face stung at the reproach.

"Another time, then," Peter said easily. After the couple moved on, he said, "Sorry about that."

"Don't apologize for them," she said, feeling sorrier for Peter than for herself. The couple treated him more like a business acquaintance than a son. She wondered if her relationship with her parents would've ended up the same way. Assuming, of course, that they hadn't abandoned her. "We'll have fun tonight anyway."

He smiled down at her, his eyes shining. "Yes, we will." Then he nodded at her clutch. "Keep an eye on your purse, though. We've had some reports of women's bags going missing lately. It's become a bit of a problem. Security has been beefed up, but you can't be too careful."

"Surely no one would steal at a charity auction," she murmured.

"One would think," he agreed.

They walked among the tables until they found their assigned seats. A couple was already at the round table, the poufy-haired young blonde coiffed within an inch of scientific probability, and her older companion, bleary-eyed, his hand curled around a drink.

"Carlotta Wren, meet my neighbors, Sissy and Tom Talmadge."

"Hello," Carlotta said as Peter held out her chair.

"Hi there," the woman said, leaning forward on her elbows. "You must be Peter's new houseguest."

"Sissy and Tom live in the blue house just up the hill," Peter offered.

With a start Carlotta realized that this was probably the person who'd been spying on her with binoculars. "That's right. Peter and I go way back."

"I see," the woman said, her voice singsongy. "How long will you be staying?"

Carlotta blinked at the woman's unconcealed nosiness.

"As long as she likes," Peter answered for her. "Something to drink, Carly?"

"Red wine," she murmured. "A big glass."

"I'll be right back." He gave her a bolstering wink, then walked away.

When she looked up, she noticed that Sissy was watching Peter's retreating back with an expression akin to longing. The woman glanced back to Carlotta and smirked. "Peter is quite a catch." She slid a meaningful glance to her blob of a husband who sat in a stony stupor.

Carlotta's mind raced to change the subject. "Do you, by chance, have a blond Persian cat?"

"No. Why?"

"We've seen a stray around Peter's house."

"It's not ours. I'm allergic."

"Hello all."

Carlotta looked up to see Tracey Tully Lowenstein, the daughter of Walt Tully, a former business partner of her father's, and Tracey's trophy husband, Dr. Frederick Lowenstein. Tracey was seated and scooting her chair up to the table before she noticed Carlotta. The woman's eyes went wide.

"Carlotta, I didn't recognize you."

"It must be that lovely dress," Frederick Lowenstein offered, raking his wolfish gaze over Carlotta in a way that made her squirm.

Tracey glared. "No, it's not the dress. You just seem out of place here. What brings you to the club?"

Carlotta hadn't expected to be welcomed with open arms, but the thinly veiled hostility was disconcerting. "I came with Peter."

Tracey wrinkled her nose. "Of course."

At that moment, Peter returned with drinks in hand. "Hi, Tracey, Freddy." He set a glass of wine in front of Carlotta, and slid his hand down her back in a proprietary fashion as he lowered himself into the seat next to her. "Nice to see you again."

The last time they'd "seen" the couple, Tracey and Freddy had crashed her and Peter's date at an outdoor showing of *Breakfast at Tiffany's,* horning in on their blanket and their privacy.

"Carlotta, I hope you're not going to run out on poor Peter like you did at the movie," Tracey offered tartly. "You're as bad as Freddy, disappearing at the drop of a hat."

"I'm on call, dear," her husband chided.

Carlotta shifted on her chair. She'd left the movie that night because Wesley had asked her to help him with a body removal nearby. She'd thought she'd be back before the closing credits rolled, but after they'd learned the deceased was another victim of The Charmed Killer, that hope had died.

Tracey lifted her bejeweled hand and snapped her fingers at a passing server. "You, there. I need a martini, stat."

The server's back went rigid, then she swung around. "You also need some manners, lady."

Carlotta gasped. "Hannah?"

Her friend Hannah Kizer, a culinary student who also worked for catering companies, stood there holding a tray of empty glasses. Her goth makeup was more subdued than usual, but one of her eyebrows that went up was newly pierced—twice.

"Carlotta, what are you doing here?" Then her gaze landed on Peter. "Oh—right." Then she gave Tracey a fake smile. "Martini, coming right up, Your Highness." She strode away, but Carlotta excused herself and went after her.

"Hannah!" She caught up with her friend at the bar and touched her arm. "Hannah, why are you ignoring me?"

Hannah poured ingredients into a shaker. "Because I'm supposed to. Servers aren't allowed to fraternize with guests."

"But it's *me,*" Carlotta said with a laugh. "You can't just pretend you don't know me."

"I'm doing what's best for you," Hannah said lightly.

"What's that supposed to mean?"

Hannah guffawed. "As if your pretentious friends are going to welcome me into their circle."

Carlotta sighed. "They aren't my friends."

Hannah glared at her. "So why are you with them?"

"Did you get the message I left on your phone? I'm staying with Peter for a while."

"Yeah, I got it." Hannah's posture relaxed a bit. "Was Michael Lane really living in your house?"

"Yeah—crazy, huh? I have to stay somewhere, at least until the police process the town house."

"Is Wes staying with Peter, too?"

"No, he's at his friend Chance's place. The one who wants you, remember?"

"Yeah," Hannah said with a dry laugh. "Fat chance."

"You didn't return my call. Do you have a new married lover?"

Hannah averted her gaze. "No. I've just been busy."

Carlotta nodded, but again Maria Marquez's accusation of not knowing her friend came back to her. "Okay, well… don't be a stranger. Peter has a pool."

Hannah's expression was suspicious. "This living with Richie Rich—it's really temporary?"

"Yes."

"Are you sleeping with him?"

"No. And please quit calling him that. I'll think of a cartoon when I look at him."

Hannah grinned. "Is he buying you nice stuff?"

"He bought me a Vespa…after I wrecked his Porsche."

"Ouch. The scooter sounds fun, though."

"I'll take you for a ride sometime. When can we get together?"

"I keep hoping you'll call me on a body-moving job."

She frowned. "I promised Peter I'd give it up for a while."

Hannah made a face.

"Jack thinks it's a good idea to lie low, too."

"Because they think that Michael Lane is The Charmed Killer?"

"He's the prime suspect, I think. The GBI is investigating now."

"Have you seen Coop lately?"

Carlotta shook her head. "I heard that he's doing more work with the morgue. And Jack seems to think he's drinking again, or is on the verge of it."

Hannah looked concerned—she had a wild crush on Coop. "Since he was the one who found the first charm, he probably feels responsible somehow."

A head server walked by and gave Hannah a disapproving glance. She picked up the drink mixer and shook it vigorously. "I'd better get back to work," she said, putting a skewered olive in the glass, then bathing it with crystalline liquid.

"I'll take Tracey's drink to her," Carlotta offered.

"You don't have to."

"I want to," Carlotta said, trying to let her friend know that she felt awkward about the role reversal.

"Wait a minute, it needs a stir." Hannah looked around, then put her finger in her mouth and pulled it out, then used it to stir the martini.

"Hannah!"

"What? The alcohol will kill the germs," Hannah insisted. "Most of them, anyway. Who knows where that finger's been?"

Carlotta bit back a smile, then took the drink and carried it back to the table, where two other couples had joined the fray. Carlotta vaguely recognized the women and assumed they were friends of Angela's that she might have seen at the memorial service.

"Here you are," she said to Tracey and set the martini in front of her.

Tracey looked surprised—and suspicious. "Thanks." She took a healthy drink, then introduced Carlotta to the new people—Bebe and Will Plank, Jada and Artie Westby—as if Carlotta was Tracey's pet. Carlotta greeted them and reclaimed her seat next to Peter self-consciously. When his hand settled on her lower back she noticed the women exchanging knowing looks.

Tracey gestured to the charm bracelet on Carlotta's wrist. "Interesting choice of accessory, Carlotta. But aren't you afraid that The Charmed Killer might take it as an invitation? Or maybe you don't read the newspaper." She gave her table cronies a conspiratorial grin.

Carlotta's hand tightened on the stem of her wineglass. "While it's true that my having to work cuts down on my leisure reading, I heard about the article."

"But you chose to ignore it? Maybe you know something that the rest of us don't."

Carlotta frowned. "What's that supposed to mean?"

"Daddy got a call from a GBI agent today," Tracey said. "He wanted to know if he'd heard from your father lately. He said that Randolph is a suspect in The Charmed Killer case."

Carlotta felt the blood drain from her face as condemning stares turned in her direction. Peter's hand massaged her back. "That's…ridiculous," she murmured.

"Is it? Peter, you must have gotten a call, too. Daddy said most people in senior management at the firm were contacted."

Carlotta swung her gaze to Peter's profile. Her father had called him at work out of the blue a few months ago. Randolph had said he needed Peter's help to prove he'd been framed for the charges he'd been accused of years ago. Had Peter told the GBI about the phone call?

Peter gave her an apologetic look that sent a knife through her heart. "I did receive a call," he said to Tracey evenly. "I told the agent if he thought Randolph Wren had anything to do with these murders, he was grasping at straws."

Carlotta glanced away to gather her wits and to her horror, saw that Rainie Stephens, the *AJC* reporter, was standing within earshot. And from the expression on the redhead's face, she'd heard Tracey's comments. The woman made a movement toward Carlotta, but was intercepted by someone else and drawn into a conversation.

Carlotta could only guess what tomorrow's headline would be: Randolph "The Bird" Wren Implicated as The Charmed Killer.

Minus ten points.

Frederick Lowenstein stood suddenly, looking down at his pager.

"What is it, dear?" Tracey asked.

"Looks like the Lindelhoff baby decided to come early."

"Oh, no," Tracey pouted, then glanced all around and sighed. "But that's what it's like to be an important doctor—he goes whenever he's needed."

Freddy dropped a kiss on Tracey's cheek, then waved as he backed away from the table. Carlotta couldn't help noticing that Tracey seemed to relish the attention. But at least it had diverted the conversation from her father being a serial killer.

She picked up her wineglass, then looked up at Peter. "Why didn't you tell me about the GBI contacting you?"

"I'm sorry," he said, his eyes warm. "I didn't want to upset you."

She sipped from her glass, knowing that Peter's intentions were good, but still…

Dozens of servers suddenly appeared with laden trays and began to pass out salads. Hannah served their table from a rolling cart, shooting lasers into the back of Tracey Lowenstein's head when she walked behind her and leaving Carlotta feeling uncomfortably superior as her friend used tongs to reach over her shoulder and place a warm roll on her bread plate. Carlotta had been excited to attend the fancy event, but the shine was quickly wearing off. Even Peter's hand at her back was starting to feel invasive.

The host for the evening, a local weather personality, took the microphone. To Carlotta's surprise, he introduced Rainie Stephens from the *AJC* as his cohost. The vivacious redhead was engaging as she welcomed the crowd, announced that the silent auction would be going on all evening and introduced a clip about the animal shelter that would benefit from the crowd's generosity. The lights were lowered as the short piece ran, showing abandoned pets so big-eyed and forlorn that it left Carlotta feeling guilty for wishing bad things on the stray blond Persian that had caused her so much grief.

When the lights came up, everyone applauded politely, then turned to their meals.

Peter leaned in close. "I noticed several vacation getaways up for auction. How would you feel if I bid on a couple of them?"

A bite of bread wedged in her throat. "For us?"

He smiled. "Of course for us."

She swallowed hard to push down the dry morsel. "I—"

"My purse!" Bebe Plank was patting an empty spot on the table in front of her. "Has anyone seen my purse? It's a zebra-print Prada clutch, and it was right here."

Everyone at the table stopped to look, but to no avail. After several minutes of searching, it seemed apparent that the purse had been lifted.

"I say we call the police and have the waitstaff strip-searched," Tracey exclaimed. "Some of them look like hoodlums, with their tattoos and piercings." She gave Carlotta a pointed glance. "I know who my money's on." Then Tracey turned to stare at Hannah, who was refilling water glasses a couple of tables away.

Carlotta opened her mouth to say her friend would never steal, but something stopped her. Hannah had always openly disdained the country-club crowd. Carlotta assumed her friend had endured a meager upbringing.

Detective Marquez's words washed over her. She didn't know where Hannah lived, who her other friends were or where Hannah spent her free time. In view of how little she really knew about her best friend, could she swear that Hannah wouldn't steal something from someone she might perceive as having too much?

After all, Carlotta had considered Michael Lane a friend, and look how that had turned out.

12

Wesley looked up from playing Poker Slam when Chance strolled into the living room. His friend wore baggy briefs and black socks.

"I thought you'd passed out in the bathroom," Wesley offered.

"I was jerking off thinking about your sister's friend Hannah."

Wesley held up his hand. "Dude, please."

"When are you going to set us up? I'm dying here."

"I'm still working on it, okay?"

Chance yanked on his johnson through his shorts. "Can you lose weight in your dick? I swear it looks smaller since I started walking on that damn treadmill."

"Seriously, man, stop."

"Will you look at it and give me your opinion?"

"Okay, I just went completely deaf."

"Come on, man, I'm worried."

Wesley lost the poker hand he'd been playing and set his jaw in frustration. "The only way your tool will shrink is if you're doing steroids. Are you?"

Chance scratched his beer gut. "No."

Wesley took in his friend's white flabby body. "Shocking. But that means you're fine."

"'Roids make your dick shrink?"

"Your balls, actually."

"Dude, how do you know all this shit? You should go on *Jeopardy* or something."

"And you should read a book once in a while."

Chance laughed. "Why, when I can just ask you stuff? Having you around here is like having a search engine on the couch."

"Thanks," he said drily.

"Wait a minute—if I shrink my balls, won't my dick *look* bigger?"

"You're wearing me out, man."

Chance pointed a meaty finger. "While we're talking about schlongs, smarty-pants, that Oxy will mess with yours. That's why I steer clear of the stuff."

Wesley frowned. "I'm cool."

"For now. You keep eating them like candy, you're going to be serving boneless pork to the ladies, you get my drift?"

"How about I worry about my pork, and you worry about yours?"

"I'm just saying, man. Ease up before it gets away from you."

Wesley gritted his teeth against a throbbing headache. He needed a hit right now and was playing a poker video game to keep his hands from shaking. "Why don't you go put on some clothes."

Chance shot him the bird, but walked toward his bedroom. "I'm working on getting you into another card game," he called over his shoulder.

Another game would be nice, Wes conceded. To try to win back some of the cash that lunatic Michael Lane had stolen from his room. He'd had plans for that money. It was supposed to have made things better for his sister—pay for some upgrades around the house and replace her car. All those things would have to wait until he got lucky again.

Wesley turned back to the video-poker game, but he had trouble focusing. He took off his glasses and rubbed his eyes, then tried again. But his reaction time was slow, and twice he mistook one card suit for another one. He cursed and tossed aside the controller, then stood and paced, his mind bouncing all over the place, from E.'s engagement to her thug boyfriend, to the identity of the decapitated man in the morgue, to the killer who was stalking the city.

When he got shaky, his mind turned to Meg Vincent for some reason, as if she was something he could anchor his thoughts to. Then he grunted and pulled at his zipper—at least his dick was still working.

From his backpack, his personal cell phone rang. He pulled it out, but the call was from an unknown source. Wes frowned, then answered, "Yeah."

"Is this Wesley Wren?" The voice was male, relatively young and thick with a country twang.

"Who's this?"

"Kendall Abrams."

"Who?"

"My uncle is the chief M.E. at the county morgue."

"Oh, right. You're working with Coop?"

"Yeah. We got a pickup, but Coop isn't answering his phone. My uncle says you and me can go, if that's awright with you."

Jesus, the guy sounded like a hayseed. "Sure." Wes gave him the address of the condo building. "What are you driving?"

"One of the morgue's vans. See you in a few."

Wesley disconnected the call, uneasy about the fact that Coop wasn't answering his phone. He tried to reach him, too, just in case, but Coop wasn't picking up. Was the pressure of working with Abrams at the lab getting to him? It was obvious to anyone that the men had history.

It also occurred to Wesley, though, that the prospect of moving bodies had a lot less appeal if he wasn't with Coop. Or Carlotta...or even Hannah. Without them, it was just a job. And not a very pleasant one.

Chance came back into the living room. To his shorts-and-socks ensemble he had added a towel around his neck. "Want to order Chinese?"

"I have to go."

"To pick up a dead person?"

"Yeah," Wesley said, fishing an Oxy tablet out of his pack and tossing it back.

"Well, at least you won't need your dick for that," Chance said.

Wesley snapped, irritated at the interruption to his chew-buzz. "Shut up, dude. I got this under control."

Chance made a clicking noise with his chubby cheek. "That's what they all say."

Wesley swung his backpack to his shoulder and stalked to the door, ignoring his friend. He could quit the Oxy anytime he wanted to. He just didn't want to tonight.

13

Carlotta sipped from her wineglass as she strolled beside the tables featuring items up for bid in the silent auction. There were ski packages to Vail, Broadway packages to Manhattan, spa vacations to the wine country, gambling junkets to Vegas, cooking lessons in Paris, and sailing adventures in the Caribbean. To her dismay, Peter had bid on almost every trip for two on offer. She looked up and spotted him a few yards away chatting amiably with some guy whose name she couldn't recall. After a while, the faces and names all ran together.

She scanned other items up for auction—jewelry, art, sporting events—but her mind was elsewhere. She kept one eye on the kitchen entrance where Hannah had disappeared a few minutes ago and hadn't returned. When Bebe Plank's purse hadn't turned up, the police had been summoned, but Carlotta knew how things worked in these environments enough to know that the police wouldn't have made themselves known to guests. Instead, the cops would be shepherded into a private room, and have suspects delivered to them.

Or in this case, *suspect,* as in singular.

From inside Carlotta's bag, her cell phone rang. She

reached in and felt around the stun baton to pull out the phone. Wesley's name scrolled onto the display.

She connected the call and covered her ear. "Wes?"

"Hey, sis, are you busy?"

She looked around the packed ballroom. "That depends. What's up?"

"I'm on a body run and I could use a little help."

"Are you alone?"

"Uh—almost. And the house is in Buckhead." He gave her the address.

"That's not too far from Peter's neighborhood," she mused. "What happened?"

"No specifics. But the chief M.E. is already on the scene, so I get the feeling that it's big. Are you in?"

Another victim of The Charmed Killer? She weighed the experience of picking up a dead body against spending the rest of the evening at the charity auction. Fake laughter burst out behind her, making her wince.

"Sis?"

"I'm in," she said. "Pick me up in front of the Bedford Manor Country Club."

"Okay. We'll be there in ten minutes in a morgue van."

She disconnected the call and glanced at Peter across the room, still talking to Mr. Generic. Peter had been so good to her. She was probably going to regret this.

Resolved, she drained her glass of wine, then headed toward the kitchen. A man wearing an employee name tag stepped in her path. "May I help you, ma'am?"

Carlotta held up her glass. "Just looking for a refill."

"Our bar is over there," he said, nodding. "Or any of the servers on the floor can help you."

She smiled. "Get out of my way."

He held out his arm. "Ma'am, I can't let you go back there."

"I've already zapped two guys with a stun baton this week," she said, patting her bag. "But I don't mind going for a personal best if you don't."

He dropped his arm. Carlotta pushed through the swinging doors that led to the kitchen area, her head pivoting, ears perked.

"I didn't do it!" came the sound of Hannah's voice behind an office door left ajar.

Carlotta headed toward the door and flung it open. Hannah stood in a makeshift office/storeroom, her expression defiant. Bebe Plank and Tracey Lowenstein stood there and from their haughty stance, Carlotta suspected they had initiated the interrogation. A male uniformed police officer stood nearby, eyeing the tall Hannah warily. A block-shouldered guy was apparently leading the questioning.

They all turned toward her when she walked in.

"Carlotta?" the blocky guy said, his voice loaded with surprise.

Recognition hit her. "Herb." Her rent-a-cop from the store. "Do you work here at the club?"

"I got two kids in college," he offered with a shrug. "Are you a member?"

"A guest. And I was sitting at the table when Ms. Plank's purse went missing. I can vouch for Ms. Kizer—she didn't take it."

"This woman is not a member of the club," Tracey said, gesturing to Carlotta. "She's obviously covering for her thuggy friend who was hovering over Bebe's purse just before it went missing. No one else could've taken it."

Carlotta's mouth tightened. "Hannah is a friend of

mine, and she'd never steal. Anyone could've taken it when the lights were down for the film."

"Even you," Tracey said.

Carlotta gritted her teeth, but didn't respond.

Herb turned to Carlotta. "You say you know this woman well?"

"Yes. For many years."

"Does your friend live around here?" he asked.

She looked at Hannah, panicked by the thought that she didn't really know where Hannah lived. "Uh…yes. In the area."

"With my parents," Hannah supplied. "On West Paces Ferry."

Carlotta tried to hide her surprise. West Paces Ferry was one of the most expensive zip codes in the county.

"I don't believe you," Tracey said, her voice scornful.

Hannah's eyes narrowed, then she removed a wallet from her back pocket, removed her driver's license and thrust it toward Herb.

"West Paces Ferry address," he confirmed.

"That doesn't mean anything," Tracey insisted.

"Why would I steal a damn purse?" Hannah asked.

"For the money," Tracey said. "You couldn't make much as a server."

"Not when everyone tips as badly as you do," Hannah offered.

"Hannah has another job," Carlotta cut in. "We work together."

"At Neiman Marcus?" Herb asked.

"Uh…no. We have a side…thing." Carlotta dazzled him with a smile. "In fact, we were just called out on a job. So I'm afraid we have to leave."

"What kind of job?" Tracey demanded.

Carlotta swallowed hard. Telling Tracey about her part-time gig would be the equivalent of announcing it in the Peach Buzz section of the *AJC*. "For…the morgue," she said warily, then rummaged in her wallet and came up with the lanyard ID that gained her entrance to crime scenes and other places where dead bodies lay in wait. "Hannah and I are body movers, and this is an emergency."

Tracey looked horrified. "You move dead people?"

Hannah fished out her morgue ID and they both handed the cards to Herb. He and the uniform looked them over, then handed them back with a nod.

Herb faced Tracey and Bebe. "Ladies, it's your word against Ms. Kizer's. No one saw her take the bag, and she doesn't have it on her."

"She could've put it on the cart she was using."

"The cart was searched, ma'am. I think we're done here."

"Let's go," Carlotta said to Hannah.

They left with the protests of Tracey and Bebe following them like a cloud.

"Thanks," Hannah muttered. "Are we really going out on a job?"

"Assuming you can get away."

"Are you kidding?" Hannah reached around to untie her apron. "I'm so out of here."

On the way back through the ballroom, Carlotta scanned the crowd for Peter. When he looked up and saw her coming, he smiled. But his smile dimmed when he saw Hannah with her.

"Having a good time?" he asked, his voice tentative.

"Yes," Carlotta said. "But Wesley needs our help with something, so I have to step out for a little while."

Peter's face darkened. "More body moving? I thought we agreed you wouldn't be doing this anymore."

"I'll be back before you miss me," she assured him with a pat. "Have fun and don't worry." She had to tug her hand free and tried to tamp down the guilt she felt as she turned away. But she couldn't deny the excitement coursing through her veins.

"Leaving so soon?"

Carlotta looked up to see Rainie Stephens standing there, her eyebrows raised, no doubt along with her journalistic curiosity.

Carlotta shrugged carefully. "I left something at home. I'll be back."

"Good," Rainie said. "Because I'd like to talk to you about The Charmed Killer case." A phone rang and Rainie reached for her purse.

Carlotta backed away—she could guess what the call was about. "Let's go," she whispered to Hannah.

They trotted to the front door of the building, and out into the thick summer night. After the cloying atmosphere of the rarefied air in the country club, the oppressive humidity felt like freedom.

"Is Coop coming?" Hannah asked as they jogged down a set of steps.

"No, but I got the sense that Wesley had someone with him, someone he didn't fully trust."

The extended van was waiting for them. Wes jumped out and gestured for them to hurry.

"I need you for backup," he murmured as he helped Carlotta climb in the rear seat. "I can't get a fix on this guy."

When Kendall Abrams introduced himself, Carlotta

understood Wesley's concern. The kid gave her the creeps. He looked to be about Wesley's age, with black eyebrows as thick as bottle brushes, his eyes dark and darting. His molasses-thick accent made him sound like a hick, but he seemed observant, his eyes always moving. He also did not seem pleased to have her and Hannah around.

"What're they doing here?" he asked Wesley. "My uncle said to just bring you."

"On-the-job training," Wes responded easily. "Coop needs all the help he can get."

"She's not exactly dressed for it," Kendall grumbled, jerking his head toward Carlotta.

"There are scrubs in the back," Wesley said. "Chill, okay?"

"Where's Coop?" Carlotta asked to defuse the tension.

"Nobody can reach him," Kendall supplied. "My uncle thinks he's on the sauce again."

Carlotta exchanged worried glances with Hannah and mentally vowed to check up on him. Since their return from the Florida road trip where they'd picked up the body of a celebutante, Coop had been withdrawn. At first she'd attributed it to their flirtation with a fling that hadn't happened, but she was starting to think that something deeper and darker was afoot.

They pulled in to a neighborhood that was only a couple of miles away, this one not quite so grand as Martinique Estates, but nice nonetheless, with spacious homes and neat landscaping on moderate-size lots. A two-story brick-fronted home was ablaze with lights, the driveway and curb lined with various civilian and official vehicles, including two police cars, a car from the M.E.'s office, and a GBI van.

Her heart was pumping as they drove up to the scene. Because of the congestion, Wesley was forced to park along a sparsely lit curb, where residents' cars were spaced at various intervals between mailboxes. They all climbed out and Carlotta told them to go ahead while she changed clothes.

"I'm right behind you," she assured them, moving quickly. She pulled out scrub tops and bottoms, along with booties to put over her Valentino silver-strap sandals, then stepped into the shadows to change. She pulled on the scrub pants and lifted her cocktail dress over her head.

She smelled the man a heartbeat before he clamped his hand over her mouth. She screamed anyway, but the air backed up in her throat, giving her an instant headache. Terror seized her and she fought against his iron grip. No way was she succumbing to The Charmed Killer without a fight.

"It's me," a familiar voice whispered.

Jack. She went limp for a few seconds before her anger surged and she turned on him. "What are you doing?" she whispered harshly, covering her red bra with crossed arms, as if it mattered. "You nearly scared me to death!"

"Sorry," he muttered. "No one can know I'm here."

Realization dawned. "So this *is* another victim of The Charmed Killer?"

"So it seems."

"I thought you were taken off the case."

"That was a mistake." His voice was thick with anger. As her eyes acclimated to the darkness, she could see his tie was undone, and his hair was sticking up, as if he'd been raking his hand through it.

"So that explains the subterfuge. But how are you going

to investigate a crime if you're not even supposed to be here?"

"When I saw you get out of the van," he said, his voice suddenly cajoling, "I thought you might be willing to help."

"You told me to stop body moving, and now you want my help?"

"As if you'd listen to me. Nice bra, by the way."

She frowned and pulled on the top half of the scrubs outfit. "Jack, are you crazy? What can I possibly do to help?"

"Be my eyes and ears. Ask questions—be your nosy self."

"Can't your partner be your eyes and ears?"

"Not without jeopardizing her job. The state guys are watching Marquez to make sure she doesn't feed me information."

The thought of being in a position to give Jack something Maria couldn't gave her a little rush. "Okay, I'll see what I can do."

"Thanks," he said, his shoulders relaxing a bit. "If I'm not here when you come back out, I'll call you later."

He disappeared into the darkness, presumably to his car that was parked on another street. Carlotta took a moment to marvel over how her relationship with Jack had changed since they'd first met. Was it possible to bond over murder and mayhem?

Feeling the weight of her mission, Carlotta hurried toward the house, her head spinning with revelations.

When had she become the girl who would leave a black-tie event at the country club for a chance to jump headlong into investigating a serial killer?

14

Carlotta flashed her morgue ID and a big, toothy smile to get past the crime scene tape. Wesley, Hannah and Kendall stood waiting for her on the porch.

"They won't let us in," Wesley said. "They're not finished yet."

Carlotta wandered over to glance through a window and saw Dr. Abrams conferring with GBI agents Wick and Green over the body of a woman lying on the floor of what looked like a den. Detective Marquez stood nearby, listening intently.

From her clothing, Carlotta judged the victim to be in her thirties. She was dressed modestly, and her clothing was intact. She lay on her back, arms at her sides. The woman didn't appear to have any abrasions or other signs of outward assault, but her face was cherry-red and swollen.

"Did you hear what happened?" Carlotta asked Wesley.

He shook his head. "No one will tell us anything."

Carlotta spotted one of the uniformed officers standing near the crime scene tape looking her way. She elbowed Wesley. "Give me a cigarette."

"I don't—"

"I don't care if you're smoking," she cut in. "Give me one."

He relented. Reaching into his pocket, he tapped one out of a packet. "Need a light?"

"Not from you," she said. Then, descending the porch steps, she walked up to the cop who was keeping watch behind the yellow tape. "Hi," she said, smiling.

Even in the semidarkness, she could tell he blushed. "Hi."

"They're not ready for us to move the body yet, so I thought I'd grab a smoke. Do you have a light?" She knew he did because she'd caught the whiff of cigarette smoke on him when he'd let her through.

He pulled out a lighter and she leaned close to light the cigarette, then straightened and exhaled. "Thanks."

"You're welcome," he mumbled.

"These always calm my nerves," she offered. "This whole thing with The Charmed Killer has got me spooked."

He nodded solemnly.

"I picked up his first victim, and two others," she said with a shudder. "And now here's another one."

"Yeah," he said. "Pretty sick."

She drew on the cigarette. "Who found her?"

"One of the neighborhood kids going door-to-door selling gift wrap. He looked in the window and saw her lying there. Fool thought she was asleep. Hours later he decided to mention it to his parents and they called 911. I was the first to respond."

She made a noise to indicate she was impressed. "Were there signs of forced entry?"

He hesitated.

"I'm only asking because I live by myself, and I need to know how to protect myself."

"No, no signs of forced entry," he said, then pulled at his waistband and rocked back on his heels. "If you ask me, it was either someone she knew, or someone she allowed to talk his way inside."

Their guy must not look very menacing if he was able to easily gain entrance in to women's houses.

"Did she live alone?" Carlotta asked.

"Looks that way."

Carlotta tapped ash off the end of the cigarette. "She wasn't…assaulted, was she?"

"I went in when the coroner arrived and he said he couldn't be sure until he ran tests. But it didn't look like she was raped."

She exhaled. "Well, at least there's that."

"The GBI's involved now," he said. "This case is getting serious attention."

"It should be. It's like this guy is taunting the police, leaving those charms." She lifted her arm to show him the charm bracelet she was wearing. "It makes me afraid to even wear mine. I don't suppose you saw what kind of charm he left this time."

He looked over his shoulder nervously.

"I saw all the other ones," she said. "There was a chicken, a cigar, a car and a gun. Bizarre."

"This was a tiny pair of handcuffs," he whispered. "I saw the M.E. take it out with tongs."

"Ooh, creepy," she said, tucking away the piece of information. "Well, maybe he was sloppy and left DNA behind this time."

"I doubt it. When I walked in, I smelled bleach and I heard the CSI guys say the place was wiped clean, as if the person knew what he was doing."

Michael Lane was a neat freak—in fact, he'd always wiped down his locker at work with disinfectant and carried around gel hand cleaner. She wondered if the other crime scenes had been sanitized.

"The woman's face is pretty red," she offered. "Did you hear the M.E. say what he thought had happened?"

"Said it looked like poison, but he'd have to run tests."

Poison—a new M.O. for the killer who had suffocated, beaten, stabbed or shot his previous victims. She made a mournful noise, imagining the woman's last moments alive. "How awful."

"Yeah. Still, as dead bodies go, I've seen much worse," he offered in a tone that said he'd been around the block, yessiree.

"Right," she said, then dropped her cigarette and stubbed it out with her toe. "Thanks for the light."

The officer cleared his throat. "Maybe we could get a drink sometime."

Her mind swam for a polite brush-off.

"Carlotta!" Wesley yelled from the house.

"I'd like that, Officer…?"

"Childress, ma'am."

"I'd like that, Officer Childress," she said with a smile. "I have to go." She walked back to the porch where Wesley and Hannah were descending the steps.

"They're ready for us," Wesley said. "Abrams wanted to talk to Kendall, show him a few things. I thought we'd go ahead and get the gurney."

"Can you and Hannah handle it?" Carlotta asked.

"Sure."

"Okay, I'll see you inside." She jogged up the steps and into the house. When she heard the voices of the GBI agents coming her way, she darted into the hallway, relieved when they walked on by and outside. They were deep in conversation, followed by Detective Marquez. Carlotta tiptoed past the front door and into the room where Abrams was bent over the body, pointing out things to his nephew, Kendall.

"Notice the extreme coloring of the facial skin."

"Looks like a really bad sunburn," Kendall offered.

Abrams's mouth tightened. "It's a sign of poisoning. Do you notice that smell?"

Kendall sniffed. "Yeah, she's dead."

"Not that," the older man said, his voice shaded with frustration. "The smell of burnt almonds."

Kendall sniffed again. "No, I got nothing. So she, what, choked on an almond?"

Carlotta almost felt sorry for Abrams—it was clear his nephew wasn't the sharpest tool in the shed.

"Uh, no. Remember I said she was poisoned? The scent of almonds indicates cyanide poisoning."

"Hmm," Kendall offered with a scratch to his head. "That's bad, huh?"

Abrams sighed. "Very bad."

"Dr. Abrams," Carlotta ventured, walking closer. "What's the victim's name?"

He looked up and frowned. "Oh, Carlotta, I didn't realize you were here, too. The victim's name is Marna Collins, age thirty-eight. She was a middle-school teacher."

"How long has she been dead?"

"Why do you want to know?" he asked suspiciously, closing his black bag and pushing to his feet.

She shrugged carefully. "I just wondered if rigor had set in, in preparation for moving the body."

"Partial rigor," he said in a clipped tone.

"What's rigor?" Kendall asked.

Abrams frowned harder. "Rigor mortis occurs when the deceased's muscles begin to freeze."

Kendall still looked confused.

"The limbs begin to get stiff after three hours," Carlotta supplied. "Full rigor sets in around the twelve-hour mark." Partial rigor indicated that Marna Collins had been dead maybe six to eight hours.

"I didn't realize you were so knowledgeable," Abrams said, his eyebrows high.

"I watch TV," she murmured.

"My nephew here is studying forensic pathology," Dr. Abrams said, clapping Kendall on the back.

"It's just my first year, and I'm not real good at it," Kendall said miserably.

"You will be," Abrams assured him, then headed toward the door. At the entrance, Abrams turned back. "Carlotta, have you talked to Cooper lately?"

"Not for several days," she admitted.

"I couldn't reach him today and frankly, I'm worried about his state of mind."

Carlotta bit her lip. "I heard he was working in the morgue lab."

"That's right. I think it was someone's idea of keeping him busy. Idle hands are the devil's playground, and all that."

"Someone?"

"Someone above me who thinks he can be saved," the man said, then walked out.

His comments left her even more worried. Abrams had worked with Coop for years, had even reported to Coop before his fall from grace. Abrams had been privy to Coop's meltdown after he'd drunkenly declared a car accident victim deceased when, in fact, she'd been alive. Abrams had a reference point for Coop that she didn't have, so as much as she didn't want to believe that Coop was slipping into destructive behavior, it was looking more and more as if he was.

"What do we do now?" Kendall asked her, gesturing to the body, his eyes wide.

"Why don't you go see if they need help with the gurney," she suggested.

He loped out of the room. Carlotta positioned her back to the windows, slipped her cell phone out of her pocket and surreptitiously snapped a few photos of the victim and the surrounding scene. There were no signs of overturned furniture in the room or any other disturbances.

Carlotta stared down at the still body of Marna Collins, and her heart wrenched. "Who did this to you?" she whispered. "How did he earn your trust?"

"What are you doing here?"

Carlotta jumped and slid the phone back into her pocket as she turned to see Maria Marquez standing there. "I got called in to move the body. So, The Charmed Killer strikes again."

"What makes you think this is the handiwork of The Charmed Killer?"

Uh-oh. Her mind raced. "Why else would the GBI be here?"

The detective's eyes narrowed. "If any details about this murder get out, I'll know where they came from."

Carlotta swallowed hard, glad when Wesley, Hannah and Kendall arrived with the gurney and body bag. The guys lifted the body while she and Hannah situated the body bag and zipped it closed around the victim, a stomach-clenching final act. They wheeled the body out to the van and loaded it in the back.

Carlotta quickly changed back into her dress in the shadows of the van. Since Jack didn't accost her, she assumed he'd left the area. The guys dropped her and Hannah back at the country club before taking the body to the morgue.

"I might make the end of the auction after all," Carlotta said as they walked back inside. "Are you sure you're okay to come back?"

"I'm good," Hannah said. "I don't want those bitches to think they ran me off."

Inside, they separated, with Hannah moving toward the kitchen and Carlotta toward the table where she and Peter were seated. The abrupt change in environment was jarring, moving from the bleak sadness of a crime scene to celebratory excess.

Rainie Stephens was on the stage announcing the winners of the prizes of the silent auction. Carlotta felt the woman's gaze on her, but shrugged it off. She lifted a glass of wine from a serving tray and headed back to her table.

"Carlotta! Yoo-hoo!"

She knew that voice—couldn't seem to escape it. She pasted on a smile then turned to greet Patricia Alexander who was clinging to the arm of a dark-haired guy in an ill-fitting tux who looked a little less happy to be there than she did. "Hi, Patricia."

"Carlotta, meet Leo Tennyson." The woman beamed, her eyes big as she stroked the man's arm. Her bracelet tinkled with the charms that collectively, at least in Patricia's mind, pointed to him as being The One. "Leo is a professional baseball player."

"I think you mentioned that," Carlotta said with a smile. "Hello, Leo."

"Hello," he said, his tone and body language bordering on surly.

"What team do you play for?" Carlotta asked out of politeness.

"The Gwinnett Braves," he said. "It's the farm team for the Atlanta Braves."

"That's very impressive."

"Isn't it?" Patricia broke in, rubbing against him. "We're late because Leo had practice. I guess you're here with Peter?"

"That's right."

"That should have all the tongues wagging."

"Er...I should get back to my table," Carlotta said, gesturing. "Nice to meet you, Leo. Goodbye, Patricia."

Carlotta threaded her way through the crowded ballroom, then slipped into the empty seat next to Peter. He looked over and grinned in surprise.

She squeezed his hand under the table. "Told you I'd be back."

He looked so happy that guilt swelled in her chest—and gratitude. She was fortunate to have someone in her life who cared for her as much as Peter did.

"And the winner of the trip for two for a deluxe

romance package to Las Vegas," Rainie announced, "is Peter Ashford!"

Carlotta conjured up a smile while the room erupted in applause. Deluxe romance package? To Vegas?

"Doesn't that sound like fun?" Peter asked, squeezing her against him.

"Yes," she murmured. Across the table, Tracey Lowenstein smirked at her and applauded halfheartedly.

Carlotta tried not to panic—hopefully the trip was still weeks or months away. Nothing had to be decided tonight. She clapped politely as winners of the remaining auction items were called out, and at Rainie Stephens's announcement of the impressive figure that had been raised for the local animal shelter through the night's ticket sales, auctions and individual donations. She waited for Peter to ask her about the body-moving job, but he didn't. She had missed dinner, but enjoyed a few forkfuls of cheesecake with her wine, and slowly the ugly events of the Collins crime scene dimmed until they seemed surreal. She glanced around at the beautiful people in the beautiful room. There was a certain comfort in being insulated from the unpleasantries of the world.

Afterward, she and Peter danced to big-band tunes with other couples on the dance floor. Since Dr. Lowenstein hadn't returned, Tracey sat glowering at her while Peter spun her around expertly. He was tall and graceful and she felt sheltered in his arms. She'd forgotten how well their bodies fit together. When she was away from Peter, she had trouble remembering details about his face, the way he smelled. But when they were together, she could almost fool herself into believing they'd never been apart.

On the drive home, Peter was funny and charming. She

found herself studying his profile and tingling with pleasure that he wanted her. The man didn't mind that her family name was sullied, that she lived in a substandard part of town, that she was up to her gapped front teeth in debt and that she had totaled his Porsche.

It had to be love.

When they entered his house, it was very late. The wine was still coursing nicely through her bloodstream, making her limbs loose and her smile permanent. Anticipation swirled in her stomach as they climbed the stairs to the second floor, hand in hand. Would he ask her to spend the night in his bed? Did she want to?

At the top of the stairs, he turned toward her and pulled her into his arms for a languid kiss. She opened her lips to him, inhaling the musky scent of his skin and his cologne, reveling in the texture of his tongue as he explored her mouth thoroughly. She ran her hands over his muscular arms, registering how his body had changed from a boy's to a man's in the time they had been apart. Her body molded to him, yielding to the unique ways he awakened her. Her breasts grew heavy, her thighs moist. They were two grown, single, consenting adults, she thought, leaning into him to increase the intensity of the kiss. There was nothing to keep them from enjoying each other's bodies tonight.

Peter lifted his head, abruptly ending the kiss. "Good night, Carly," he said. Then he walked to his bedroom door and disappeared inside.

Carlotta stood there for a few seconds, perplexed and zinging all over. She wondered briefly if this was what it felt like to be zapped with a stun baton.

She was still breathing hard when she closed her bedroom door behind her. Was Peter not leaping at the chance to bed her out of a sense of nobility…or was he simply playing hard to get?

She reached up and massaged an aching breast. Whatever he was doing, it was working.

After changing into pajamas, she moved aside her father's file and pulled out the high-school diaries she'd brought with her, each one of them padlocked. She used the tiny tasseled key that fit all of them to unlock the first one, imprinted with the year that she'd been a freshman. The silly, girlish entries made her smile as she relived her anxieties about high school and fitting in. There were names of girlfriends she vaguely remembered and girls whom she thought would be lifelong friends, but that hadn't happened.

There were cheerleading tryouts and sweetheart dances and tests to take. Shopping excursions with her friends, birthday parties, vacations with her family. She especially enjoyed reading about her parents and noticed that she'd written about them as if they were older friends rather than authority figures.

She skimmed the first-year diary, then moved on to her sophomore one and found the entry that she'd been looking for.

Dear Diary,
Today I met a boy named Peter Ashford. Isn't that the grandest name? Peter Ashford. He's so handsome I can barely write about it, my heart is beating so fast. He could have any girl in the school, and he wants me. I'm the luckiest girl in the world.

Carlotta closed the diary and hugged it to her chest. Peter was arguably the most eligible bachelor in Buckhead.

He could still have almost any woman he wanted, and he wanted her. She *was* incredibly lucky.

From the nightstand her phone rang. She glanced at it and sighed.

Jack.

She wasn't ready to be pulled back into the real world, but she'd told him she'd help him. Carlotta set aside the diary, then connected the call. "Hi, Jack."

"Did I interrupt anything?"

"I wouldn't have answered if you had."

"So Ashford hasn't made his move yet, huh?"

"That's so none of your business."

"I know, but I have to ask. Okay, what do you have for me on the murder?"

She told him everything Officer Childress had relayed, from the description of the charm left, to the fact that the scene had been sanitized, plus what she'd found out about the victim and time of death from Abrams.

"Damn, you're good," he said at one point. "All I'm missing are pictures from the scene."

"I took some on my phone—do you want them?"

"Christ, did anyone catch you?"

"Marquez almost did. She threatened me against leaking anything. I think she suspects something."

"As long as she can't prove it. Bring your phone tomorrow when you come down to take the polygraph. I'll off-load the photos and get it back to you before you leave."

"Okay. Listen, Jack, I'm concerned about Coop—he seems to be M.I.A. Will you check on him?"

"Will do. Frankly, though, I'm more worried about you."

She hesitated, then said, "I'm fine."

"I could come over to tuck you in. In that big house, Ashford will never know."

She laughed into the phone. "Thanks anyway, Jack."

He made a rumbling noise.

"What are you doing?"

"Rubbing your red panties on my face."

"I'm hanging up now."

Carlotta disconnected the call and groaned, thinking about the men in her life. One guy was willing to bed her, but offered no commitment. One guy wanted a commitment, but was hesitant about the bedding part. And one guy had seemingly withdrawn from the competition altogether.

Minus ten. Minus ten. Minus ten.

15

Carlotta walked into Peter's kitchen humming a happy tune, but stopped short when she saw Angela Ashford sitting on the granite counter, dressed in a black trench coat and tall black boots.

"Good morning," Angela said sweetly. "I made coffee."

"Thanks," Carlotta murmured warily, then walked to the pot.

"So, Carlotta, how does it feel?"

She looked back to the beautiful, green-eyed blonde while she poured. "What do you mean?"

Angela lifted her hands. "To be living in my house, with my husband."

"It's only temporary."

"Right. That's what you keep telling yourself so you'll feel better about stealing my life."

"I didn't steal your life."

Angela's smile vanished. "Yes, you did, *shopgirl*."

"You don't have to get nasty about it," Carlotta said, sipping from her cup.

"But *I* was the one who picked up the pieces after you and Peter broke up. *I* was the one who ate alone while he went to dinners to build his client list. *I* was the one who endured his indifference and his coldness." Angela began grooming herself with her tongue.

"I'm sorry the two of you weren't happy together," Carlotta offered.

The blonde lifted her head and growled. "We could've been, if not for you. When I found that picture of you in his wallet, I thought I would die."

Carlotta winced. "I hate to point out the obvious, but you *are* dead." She nodded to her mug. "Great coffee, by the way."

"Thanks. I put cyanide in it. You should be feeling lousy any second now."

Carlotta's eyes went wide, and her lungs began to squeeze. "You didn't have to kill me."

"If I can't have Peter," Angela said with a feline smile, "neither can you. *Meow.*"

Carlotta's throat convulsed. She couldn't breathe. She gasped for air, but the cyanide was bleeding through her system, paralyzing her organs…

Angela purred with happiness. *"Meow…meow…meow."*

Carlotta sat up in bed with a start, clutching at her neck. Her chest rose and fell sharply, her heart thumped against her breastbone. Predawn light filtered through the doors leading to the veranda. A familiar scratching noise sounded. Carlotta looked down to see the stray Persian pawing frantically at the door. It was raining outside, and the creature was wet and shivering. She must have climbed a tree to get up there and was afraid to go back down.

Meow…meow…meow.

Carlotta shook the remnants of the disturbing dream from her mind and climbed out of bed. "I'm coming," she muttered.

When she stood, a headache shot to her temples, reminding her of the wine she'd drunk the night before at the auction event. All the details of the crime scene came back to her in a torrent, and she realized wryly that her subconscious had managed to blend The Charmed Killer's latest cause of death with her obviously unresolved guilt over betraying Angela.

She limped over to the door and opened it. The cat yowled as if scolding her for leaving it out in the rain, then darted inside and bounded up onto the bed, trailing mud and water onto the pale sheets.

"Not the Egyptian-cotton sheets! Shoo!"

But the bedraggled cat simply bared its teeth and hissed at her.

She shrank back, then frowned. "You ungrateful little…"

The big, sad eyes of all the animals from the shelter in last night's film came back to her and she tamped down her irritation.

"Never mind," she said with a sigh. "I was *planning* to leave my nice comfortable bed at the butt crack of dawn and give it over to a grubby stray."

The cat growled back from where she crouched in the covers.

Carlotta went into the bathroom and turned on the shower. She wasn't looking forward to taking that polygraph exam this morning. Maybe some development overnight had broken the case, or maybe Michael had turned himself in, and it would be a moot point.

She flipped a switch to release aromatherapy oils into the air, chose blues on the stereo system built into the wall, then stepped under the dual-massage showerhead.

Of course that meant she'd have to go back to the cramped town house with the broken television and shabby furnishings. Not that she wanted the killing spree to continue simply so she could have an excuse to live in Peter's house. She leaned her head forward and moaned at the sensation of a hundred fingers massaging her skin, while imported French conditioner fortified her hair. That would be selfish and unconscionable…

She gave the faucet handle a yank until icy water blasted her, rousing her from her luxurious stupor. She quickly rinsed her hair and stepped out of the shower shivering. After wrapping herself in a towel thick enough to sleep on, she stepped onto the floor that was nice and warm because of the heating coils beneath the tiles.

Which explained why the stray cat was now curled up on the floor near the door.

"I see you found a warmer spot after running me out of my bed," Carlotta muttered.

The cat meowed a retort, as if they were having a conversation. Carlotta frowned, recalling how Angela and the cat had seemed to be one and the same in her dream. She'd probably had the dream because she'd subconsciously heard the cat meowing and pawing at the door before she was fully awake. And because when Angela was alive, she had struck Carlotta as being catlike, with her lioness mane of blond hair, her green eyes and her twitchy, aquiline nose.

Carlotta stared at the cat and the cat stared back with such loathing intensity that Carlotta blinked first. If she didn't know better…

Then she truncated the idea and scoffed. But she *did* know better.

The cat blinked lazily and resumed her bored, blank expression.

Carlotta downed a couple of aspirin to help clear her head, then turned her attention to getting ready. If she got the polygraph exam over early enough, maybe she'd have time to ride over to Coop's place to check on him. She wanted to see for herself that he was okay. Being tucked away in Peter's house was a double-edged sword—it made her feel more safe, but also left her feeling insulated from the outside world.

Carlotta pinned up her hair in preparation to dry in sections, then plugged in the blow-dryer. Her thick dark hair was a trait of her mother's for which she was normally grateful, but it was a pain to dry thoroughly. She'd once asked her mother if they had Native American heritage because of their shared coloring and bone structure, but her mother had insisted they had European ancestors. Carlotta wished she'd pushed her mother for more answers at the time because she knew next to nothing about her deceased grandparents. Maybe they were Italian, she mused as she held a hank of black hair straight up with a wide-tooth comb to speed its drying.

She progressed from section to section and had nearly finished when a movement at her waist startled her. She looked down to see that the matted cat had jumped up onto the counter and despite the noise of the hair dryer, was nudging Carlotta's arm and pawing in the air.

"Scat," she said, fanning the hair dryer over the cat.

But instead of running away, the animal rolled its shoulders and leaned closer.

Carlotta pursed her mouth. If the creature was chilled to the bone, the warm air probably did feel good. "You could use a comb out," she murmured to the bedraggled feline, then rummaged for a metal comb in the drawer where she'd stored her toiletries.

She set the blow dryer on the lowest setting, but still expected the cat to run away when she started to comb and fluff her matted fur. But not only did the animal stand still, she closed her eyes in pure delight, her whiskers trembling orgasmically.

"You're accustomed to being groomed," Carlotta said wryly. "Which means you're someone's pet. Too bad your owner didn't declaw you."

By the time she'd combed out its luxurious blond fur, the cat was three times its original size. When Carlotta turned off the hair dryer, the poufed cat walked up and down the counter, rubbing against the mirror.

"Pretty pleased with yourself, aren't you?" Carlotta said.

The morning rain had yielded to the summer sun, so with the scooter in mind, Carlotta dressed in slacks, a silk shell and a cropped jacket. When she left her bedroom, she glanced at Peter's bedroom door and her face burned. She would've slept with him last night, but he'd been the one with the level head. Hopefully things between them wouldn't be awkward this morning.

From the kitchen below she smelled coffee and heard him moving around. He was talking on his cell phone. The fluffed cat bounded down the stairs in front of her, almost tripping her. When she walked into the kitchen, the cat was twining herself between Peter's legs, meowing for attention and licking his shoes. Peter was jacketless and had his back to her, but seemed engrossed in his phone conversation. "I'll ask Carlotta about it, Will, and I'll get back to you. Bye."

He closed the phone and sighed.

"Ask me about what?" she said lightly.

He started and turned with a smile. "Good morning."

"Good morning. Ask me about what?"

"You're up early. I made coffee."

She experienced a shot of déjà vu from her dream, and moved toward the pot. "Ask me about what?" she said again.

Peter crouched down to idly pat the cat's head. "I see the cat has returned."

"She woke me up this morning, meowing at the veranda door. When I let her in, she jumped up on my sheets and got them muddy."

"The housekeeper will take care of the linens."

Carlotta angled her head. "Peter, you're stalling."

He winced. "That was Will Plank on the phone. He said that another purse went missing last night."

She looked up from pouring her coffee. "And what are you supposed to ask me?"

His mouth flattened into a line. "About your friend Hannah."

Irritation spiked in her chest, but Carlotta tamped it down. "The police questioned Hannah last night and they were quite satisfied that she didn't have anything to do with Bebe's purse being stolen."

"Okay. Are *you* satisfied she didn't have anything to do with Bebe's purse being stolen?"

"Yes, I am." But she couldn't look him in the eye because before she'd interrupted the interrogation last night in the manager's office, she'd had some misgivings about Hannah herself. Now she realized her doubts had more to do with acknowledging that she hadn't reached out to get to know her friend than anything Hannah had done.

He set down his coffee and came over to loop his arms around her waist. "Then that's good enough for me."

She softened toward him, although she was still feeling awkward about the way the previous nights had ended. But she accepted his kiss, and didn't retreat when it deepened and he pulled her against him. A yowling noise sounded and they parted as the cat practically climbed up his leg.

"What the—" Peter carefully extricated the cat from his trousers.

"Watch out for the claws," Carlotta warned, but the cat simply licked his hands as if it couldn't get enough of him.

"Er…it must be hungry," he said, setting the cat back on the floor.

"She."

"Pardon me?"

"It's a she," Carlotta said, studying the cat. "Are you sure this wasn't Angela's cat? She seems…I don't know— *familiar* with this house."

"Angie didn't have a cat, although she loved them. She always said she was going to get one, but never got around to it."

"I found a broken silver cat pin in my bedroom."

He stopped, then nodded. "It was probably Angela's. You can toss it." He walked over to the cupboard. "Let's see what we can find to feed her. I wonder how we can find her owner."

"If you don't mind me using your computer, I could put together some flyers."

"Feel free to use the computer in the den anytime you want," he said, then pulled out a tin. "I think I have just the thing."

Carlotta made a face. "Sardines?"

"Angela ate them like popcorn. I could never stomach the things and was thinking the other day that I should toss them." He smiled as he peeled back the opening and dumped the contents onto a saucer. "Guess it's a good thing I kept them."

He set the saucer on the floor and the cat pounced on the tiny headless fish, devouring them in seconds, then licking the plate hard enough to move it across the floor. Peter laughed when the feline came over to lick and nudge his hand, meowing and begging for more.

"That's enough for now," he chided, standing. Then he looked at Carlotta. "I don't normally eat breakfast, but I have time to watch you eat."

She smiled, but shook her head. "I have to run. I have another appointment at the police department this morning."

His mouth twitched downward. "Again?" He walked backward as he tried to elude the cat that was purring and rubbing herself on his legs.

"I was asked to take a polygraph exam to clear myself."

He looked alarmed. "Do you need a lawyer?"

"No," she said with a laugh. "It's just a formality, because I was on the scene when the first victim was found. The GBI wants to eliminate the possibility that the charms were inserted in the mouths of victims after the fact."

"All the more reason for you to stop the body moving," Peter said lightly. He reached for the newspaper on the counter and turned the headline so she could read it:

The Charmed Killer Takes Fifth Victim.

She skimmed the story, written by Rainie Stephens,

who cited her "source inside the morgue" as saying that the charm pulled out of the victim's mouth was a woman's shoe. Carlotta bit her lip—that differed from the description of the handcuffs charm that the chatty police officer had given her. The same sources reported that the cause of death had been strangulation rather than poisoning, although granted, the M.E. might have altered his opinion after a preliminary examination at the morgue.

The article ended by saying that the police had added Randolph Wren to their list of "persons of interest" in The Charmed Killer case. The article went on to describe her father as a longtime fugitive from the law who still had ties to Atlanta and indirect ties to at least one of the victims.

Carlotta's heart thudded against her breastbone. Would Randolph see the item in the paper? Was the district attorney trying to lure him out of hiding to defend himself against charges of murder?

She looked up at Peter. "Did you read this? The insinuations about my father?"

He nodded. "Why didn't you tell me last night that this murder happened only a couple of miles away from here?"

"I didn't want to spoil the evening and…you didn't ask."

He looked contrite. "I know. I was angry. But I asked you to move in with me so you would be safe, Carly, and you're still taking chances. Why?"

She pressed her lips together. "I guess I feel involved in this case because I was there when Coop pulled the charm out of the mouth of the first victim, and because of Michael Lane."

"The man tried to kill you!" Peter said, flailing his

arms. "Then he stalked you under your own roof and again, could've killed you. Did it ever occur to you that this could be a little cat-and-mouse game for him?"

Carlotta frowned. "Are you saying that Michael might be killing these women to get back at me?"

Peter pulled his hand down his face. "Carly, who knows what this lunatic is thinking? But until he's caught, don't you think it would be safer if you removed yourself from the investigation?"

"You mean stop body moving?"

"Yes. Like you promised."

She balked. "I didn't promise...exactly."

Peter closed his eyes, then his shoulders sagged in defeat. "Maybe *I* should've given you a polygraph."

She raised up on her toes and kissed him on the mouth. "Have a great day. I'll see you tonight."

"I'm right behind you." But he stumbled over the cat that was underfoot.

Carlotta bit back a smile. The feline had apparently fallen in love with Peter. "What do we do about her?"

He sighed. "We can close her up in the mudroom for the day, she'll be safe there. I'll leave a box for her to go to the bathroom. Ready?"

When Peter turned his back, Carlotta grabbed the newspaper and stuffed it into her bag. She thought she might have to corral the cat, but it padded after Peter as if he were a big branch of catnip. Carlotta frowned and brought up the rear, feeling strangely like a third wheel.

The cat, however, was furious at not being allowed to follow them into the garage. Peter tried in vain to make her stay in the mudroom. Carlotta managed to push the cat back gently with her foot, but got her slacks picked and her leg scratched for her trouble. When Peter pulled the door closed, they could still hear the animal yowling.

"Sounds like old times," Peter said with a little smile. Then he sobered. "Was that crass?"

"No," Carlotta said sympathetically. "I know you and Angela had good times and bad times. It's all right if you want to talk about them, Peter."

He nodded and from the look in his eyes, she knew he was thinking of the way things had ended last night.

She put her purse in the storage compartment of the scooter that sat next to Peter's SUV. When she put on the helmet, he stepped in front of her to tighten the strap.

"How's the scooter?"

"I love it," she said. "It's the most fun I've had in a long time."

"I'm glad."

Peter's expression went solemn and she braced herself for what was coming next.

"Carly, you'll never know how hard it was for me to walk away from you last night."

Her lips parted. "Then why did you?"

"Because I want you to come to me of your own volition, not because you've had too much wine or because you feel like you owe me something for letting you stay here…or because I just want you so damn much. If it happens, I want it to be because you want me, too."

Her heart pounded. "Okay."

"Okay." He kissed her and when he pulled back, his eyes were glazed with passion. "I'll be thinking about you all day. Call me if you have problems at the police station. I can have a lawyer over there, pronto."

"Thanks, Peter. You always look out for me."

"When you let me."

Peter's words reverberated in Carlotta's head as she wound her way through traffic. He could sense she was holding back. It was noble of him to wait until she was ready, to wait until the time was right. That meant the ball was in her court.

Too bad she'd never been good at sports…

16

Carlotta walked into the police precinct and checked in with Brooklyn, who was standing behind the Plexiglas window.

"You're here bright and early," Brooklyn said.

"I'm scheduled to take a polygraph exam."

"Yeah, I see it here," the woman confirmed, scanning a computer screen. "But the examiner won't be here for another thirty minutes. Do you want a magazine?"

Carlotta pursed her mouth. "Is Jack in by chance?"

"Man's been sleeping here."

"Officers can sleep here?"

"Yeah, but he's here more than most. But something tells me he wouldn't mind if you woke him up, baby doll." She hit a button and a buzzing noise sounded. "Take a left at the soda machine and go to the black door at the end of the hallway."

Carlotta nodded and walked through the secure door from the lobby. The bull pen and offices on the other side were subdued compared to their normal levels of activity. She spotted Agents Wick and Green standing across the room, but they were angled away from her. She slipped out of sight and down the hallway. At a black door, she hesitated, then put her hand on the knob and turned.

The interior of the room was dark and quiet…except for a familiar low snore. She smiled and stepped inside. Rows of bunks were situated on either side. All the beds within her immediate sight were empty. A night-light illuminated her way to a bunk in the far corner. As her eyes acclimated to the darkness, she could make out Jack's large form. He lay on his back wearing slacks and an undershirt, his broad chest rising and falling. His rugged features were relaxed and handsome, but his eyes twitched, belying his otherwise peaceful posture. Still, she enjoyed the chance to study him unobserved—he was such a physical man that seeing him shut down was almost jarring.

He looked so tired she decided not to wake him and turned to go. Then his hand darted out to grab her and he pulled her down on top of him. Carlotta gasped, squirming. "Jack, what are you doing?"

"Right now I'm missing that magic skirt," he murmured thickly. "It's harder to get into your pants when you're wearing pants, but I'm game."

She pushed at him and wound up straddling him, with him holding her wrists. "I thought you were asleep," she said, exasperated.

"I sleep with one eye open."

"And a hard-on?" she asked wryly.

He grinned. "You noticed, huh? Well, since you're here—"

"You're incorrigible."

"I know." He sighed. "If you're not going to shag me, I guess I should get up."

"You have to let me go first."

He made a rueful noise. "And therein lies my dilemma."

Their gazes locked and she wished she knew what was going on behind those gold-tinted eyes of his. He released her wrists and she pushed to her feet. Jack swung his legs over the side of the bunk and stretched his arms overhead with a grunt.

"Do you sleep here often?" she asked.

"More, lately."

"Did anything develop on the case after we talked last night?"

"There was a reported sighting of Michael Lane in Athens yesterday that finally made it to us around midnight. I'm going to check it out today."

"I thought you were banned from working on the case."

"Until we can prove Lane is The Charmed Killer, it's a separate case. I'm still trying to find whoever blew up your car, remember."

"Athens? That's what—seventy-file miles north of Atlanta?"

"Give or take. Did you ever hear him mention ties in Athens—friends or family?"

"No. But if Michael was in Athens, he couldn't have committed the murder in Buckhead."

"*If* he was in Athens. Sightings like this are unreliable. But assuming Lane bought a car with some of the cash he stole from your house, he could've easily made the drive."

"Has the town house been processed?"

"Yeah. They're still running prints, but you and Wesley can go back when you want to." He made a rueful noise. "I assume you'll be staying with Ashford a while longer, though?"

She nodded, not hating his discomfort. "I think it's best for now. Wesley is going to install a security system."

"Finally. Speaking of security systems, have you been minding your pussy?"

She leaned in and whispered, "I blew it dry this morning."

He groaned and reached for her.

She stepped out of his grasp, then pulled the section of newspaper from her purse and extended it to him. "Rainie Stephens has a slightly different description of what happened last night."

He frowned and took the paper. "The GBI guys could've planted erroneous details in the article for their own purposes."

"It mentions my father."

His mouth tightened. "I'm sorry."

She handed him her phone. "Your crime scene photos."

"How many did you get?"

"Six—five of them are decent."

"Thanks. Are you ready for the polygraph?"

"Peter asked if I needed a lawyer to sit in. What do you think?"

"That's your call. But a lawyer would probably advise against taking the exam altogether."

"Getting a lawyer would make me look as if I have something to hide, wouldn't it?" Which she did.

"It might," he admitted, setting aside the phone and the newspaper and reaching for his dress shirt.

"Will you be watching the polygraph exam?"

"I asked, but Wick said no. Marquez will be watching, though, and it will be videotaped. And if the examiner asks a question you think is inappropriate, say so."

She nodded. Jack always made her feel better.

He winked. "Just think about having sex with me the entire time, and your heart rate will be so high, it'll throw them off completely."

Just when she thought he'd grown a sensitive muscle. "Thanks for the expert advice, Detective."

"Relax," he said. "Go cross it off the list so the state dogs will stop chewing on your ankles. I'm going to take a shower, then get on the road. I'll leave your phone with Brooklyn."

"Let me know what you find out about Michael?"

He grunted, which she took as begrudged acquiescence. "Until we can get a bead on Lane, I'm going to keep that security detail at the store. Go knock 'em dead."

She left the room and backtracked to the area where she'd seen Agents Wick and Green.

"Good morning, gentlemen."

Green smiled and stammered good morning, but Wick appeared to be preoccupied with swallowing a bagel.

"Do you still need me to take a polygraph?" she asked in an innocent voice.

Wick arched an eyebrow. "Unless you want to come clean about something all on your own."

"Nothing to come clean about," she replied easily. "Let's do this."

She pretended to be much braver than she felt when a few minutes later she was led into a small room and introduced to the polygraph examiner, a small, nervous man with cartoonish tics. Wick handed him a file, then left the room, but she could feel the agent's disapproving gaze on her from the other side of the two-way window. The examiner opened the file, which appeared to have a total of one sheet of paper inside.

The GBI agents apparently had already drafted the questions to be asked.

Irritation flashed over the examiner's face, then he looked at her and clasped his jittery hands. "I'll be asking you nine questions. Some of them will be baseline questions, like your name and age, some will be control questions to determine your general tendency toward honesty, and some will be questions relevant to The Charmed Killer case. Do you understand?"

"Yes."

He nodded. "Okay. The questions relevant to the case are questions Agents Wick and Green already asked you during your interview. If you answer truthfully and your answer is the same as before, you don't have anything to worry about." He leveled his gaze on her. "It's customary to remember details about an event after an interview. With that in mind, is there anything you'd like to amend regarding your previous interview with Agent Wick and Agent Green?"

"No," she said.

"Then let's get started."

He opened a case and removed the device and corresponding wires and electrodes. Like a prom date with a corsage, he couldn't quite figure out where to put the sensor straps around her chest, but with much sweating and fumbling, he finally got her hooked up, then slid sensors on two fingers on her right hand.

He removed a handkerchief and dabbed at his forehead, then flipped a few switches on the machine with floating needles that scrawled marks across a roll of paper. The lie detector hummed to life and the needles danced. She imagined them writing in script "You are a big fat liar."

"Okay, Ms. Wren—"

"Call me Carlotta," she said with a smile.

His ears turned scarlet. "Uh…okay…Carlotta. I'll ask a question and you should respond either yes or no. Ready?"

She nodded and swallowed hard. And thought of Jack, damn him. The needles on the machine jumped. Jack, naked and holding himself over her…

"Is your name Carlotta Wren?"

"Yes." Lowering his body onto hers…

"Do you have brown eyes?"

"Except when I wear my colored contacts."

"Just answer yes or no, please."

"Yes." Thrusting into her like a piston, taking her breath away…

"Are you right-handed?"

"Yes." Kissing and biting her nipples until they sang…

"Have you ever taken something that wasn't yours?"

She yanked her attention back to the question. According to Angela Ashford, yes. And then there were all the parties that she'd crashed. And the clothes she'd borrowed from the store to wear to an event, although technically she'd returned them afterward. Most of them.

"Ma'am? Have you ever taken something that wasn't yours?"

She exhaled. "Yes." But memories of Jack pulled her away from the moment. He always made sure she got off first…

"Did you place a charm in the mouth of murder victim Shawna Whitt?"

"No." And last…

"Do you know the whereabouts of Randolph Wren?"

Carlotta bit down on her tongue. "No."

"Have you had a romantic relationship with Detective Jack Terry?"

She blinked, but then realized that romance had never entered into her relationship with Jack. "No."

"Have you ever told a lie?"

She hesitated. "Yes."

"Do you know the identity of The Charmed Killer?"

Did it count if she suspected Michael? She shifted in her chair. "No, not for sure."

"Yes or no, please."

"No."

He made a mark on the paper, then flipped off the machine. "That's all. You can remove the sensors."

Carlotta slipped the devices off her fingers and began to remove the straps around her chest. "Did I pass?"

The man looked up, his eyes noncommittal. "I'm sorry, but I can't divulge the results to you. You'll have to talk to Agent Wick."

"So I can leave now?"

"Yes, ma'am. We're done."

She pushed to her feet and walked out of the examination room. At the sight of the closed door next to the room she'd been in, she rapped lightly, then opened it.

Agents Wick and Green and Detective Marquez had their heads together, but turned toward her at the interruption.

"You shouldn't be in here," Agent Wick said.

"When will I know the results of my polygraph?"

"When I want you to know," he replied.

Carlotta angled her head. "You're kind of a dick, aren't you?"

"Carlotta," Maria warned.

"Instead of getting out there trying to figure out if these victims are connected and what the charms mean, you're wasting time giving *me* a lie detector test."

Wick crossed his arms and smiled. "Who said it was a waste of time? We'll be in touch, Ms. Wren."

Carlotta blanched. Had she failed? Was that why they'd been huddled together when she'd come into the room?

She backed away and exited to the lobby, picked up her phone from Brooklyn and hurried outside to her scooter. Had she just corroborated some piece of evidence that she didn't know they had?

With her brain ticking away, replaying the questions and her responses, Carlotta rode to Coop's home in Castleberry Hill, a refurbished two-story car-repair shop. She knocked and knocked, but he didn't answer. She cupped her hands and looked through the glass into the living room-slash-garage and saw that his van was gone. She called his cell phone but he didn't answer. At the beep she left him a message.

"Coop, hey, it's Carlotta. I came over to say hello, but you're not home. Give me a call when you get a chance. I miss talking to you."

She disconnected the call, thinking he was probably at the morgue lab, that The Charmed Killer had managed to infiltrate all their lives in one way or another. She backtracked and rode the Vespa to Lenox Square Mall. She was careful to park near a light and in an open space, just as she'd promised Jack after her car had been blown to bits. While she was putting her purse in her locker, and getting ready to take her place on the floor, her mind reeled over all the loose ends that the GBI should be following up on.

Walking through the store, she glanced around, wondering if her coworkers had read the bit in the paper about her father being named a person of interest in The Charmed Killer case. Granted, many of them hadn't been around when Randolph had made headlines all those years ago, and wouldn't make the connection to her even if they'd seen it. But Patricia Alexander knew that Randolph was her father, as did many of the store's clientele. And nothing tasted as good to Atlanta high society as a nice juicy scandal.

When she reached her designated department, her bodyguard, Herb, was already there, loitering between a rack of Tory Burch tunics and Chetta B floral skirts. He might as well have been waving a flag. He nodded and she smiled back, glad that customers were waiting so she could forget about everything else for a while. Coop had challenged her to do more with her life than work retail, but there was something to be said about transforming a mousy wallflower into a vivacious name-taker with a single killer suit.

For the most part, selling clothes was a pretty cheery business to be in. The worst-case daily scenario was not having the right color or size of a particular gorgeous thing. Which was usually softened by the availability of the right color or size of any one of several *other* gorgeous things. The people on both ends of the transaction usually walked away happy. And retail therapy was exactly what she needed to forget that she knew too much about the layout of the midtown APD precinct.

Not to mention the layout of Detective Jack Terry.

Still, as much as she tried to forget about the polygraph exam and the fact that The Charmed Killer was probably out there right now circling his next victim, her mind kept going to those dark places. Was the killer eyeing an innocent woman, savoring how he was going to snuff out her life? Fingering a charm in his pocket that he would cram down the woman's throat afterward?

A chill crawled over her shoulders, as if someone had just walked over her grave. She could swear the temperature had suddenly dropped a few degrees.

"Well, well, well."

Carlotta swung around to see Tracey Tully Lowenstein standing there, her eyes heavy lidded and her mouth tightened in a little knot. She was sheathed head to toe in St. John and sporting over-size Versace sunglasses. Carlotta armed herself with a smile.

"Hi, Tracey. I take it you came in for our sale."

Tracey frowned. "I don't shop sales."

"Okay. How can I help you?"

"Actually, I'm here to help you."

Carlotta blinked. "Excuse me?"

Tracey slowly removed her sunglasses. "Some of the members of the club are…concerned."

"Concerned?"

"About your relationship with the woman on the wait-staff."

"Hannah?"

"The tattooed one, yes."

"Hannah and I have been friends for a long time. She's a good person."

"She's a thief."

Carlotta set her jaw, then leaned in to speak in low tones. "You have no right to say that."

A smug expression settled on Tracey's face. "Just because no one saw her take Bebe's purse doesn't mean she's innocent."

Carlotta crossed her arms. "Actually, it does. And I resent you blaming her simply because you don't like the way she looks."

Tracey made a dismissive gesture. "I didn't come here to talk about your delinquent friend. I've already arranged for her to be fired."

Carlotta gasped as anger barbed through her. "You what? How dare you?"

"You should know that your friend had worked every event where purses were stolen."

"That doesn't prove anything!"

Tracey's mouth flattened into a hard line. "What's done is done. I'm here because I was designated by some of the ladies of the club to talk to you about…your future."

"Designated? You and your friends have been discussing me?"

"We just want what's best for you," Tracey insisted, her voice tinny. "And considering that your father bilked huge sums of money from several members of Bedford Manor, what's best is if you don't return to the club."

Carlotta's jaw dropped. "Is this a joke? I'm not applying for membership at the club. I was Peter's guest."

Tracey clucked. "The social committee doesn't like to abuse its power, but we do have the authority to ban guests if we deem their presence to be injurious to members."

"Injurious?" Where was her stun baton when she needed it?

"Before you take offense, Carlotta, you really should think about Peter."

"What do you mean?" she asked through gritted teeth.

"Peter has been through so much, I'd hate to see his club membership jeopardized because he was keeping the wrong company. And if he left the club, he'd lose social contact with so many of his clients, I can't imagine what that might do to his career."

Carlotta's face burned and her throat ached from pent-up rage.

"I feel sorry for you, really I do," Tracey cooed, pushing her sunglasses back in place. "First your father embezzles from his company and friends, then he abandons you and your brother, and now you find out that he might be a serial killer. I swear, how do you sleep at night?"

Carlotta blinked back tears. She refused to let the woman get to her.

"Ms. Wren, is this lady bothering you?"

She looked up to see Herb peering at Tracey.

"It's you!" Tracey said. "No wonder you took Carlotta's side at the club. You know each other!"

"The lady was just leaving," Carlotta assured Herb, then gave Tracey a pointed look.

Thankfully from her jacket pocket Carlotta's cell phone rang. *Atlanta Police Department* scrolled onto the display screen. Carlotta turned her back on Tracey and connected the call, craving the sound of Jack's voice. "Hello?"

"Carlotta, this is Maria Marquez."

Disappointment shot through her, but she inhaled to steady her voice. "What can I do for you, Detective?"

"I was told to call and give you the results of your polygraph."

Carlotta touched her forehead. "Lay it on me."

"The results were D.I."

"What does that mean, D.I.?"

"It means…deception indicated."

17

"Hand me that wrench," Wesley said from the top of a ladder.

Chance looked at the toolbox open at his feet and scratched his head. "Which one is that?"

Wesley rolled his eyes. "The shiny silver thing on top."

Chance picked up the tool and handed it to Wesley. "Have you ever put in a security system before?"

"No, but it's just a lot of wiring, basic electrical stuff."

"Dude, why didn't you hire it done?"

"I barely had enough cash to pay for the system. I couldn't afford to pay someone to install it, too."

"What happened to the ten grand you won in the card game the other night?"

Wesley frowned. "The crazy fuck living in our guest room took it."

"Wow, that sucks." Chance looked around the living room. "Damn, the police made a mess of your place, didn't they?"

"Well, it always looks this way, more or less. But yeah, the fingerprint dust doesn't help." But the CSI team must've been rattled by Einstein because the extra Oxy Wesley had stowed in his python's aquarium hadn't been touched.

Chance nodded to the corner of the room. "What's up with the scrappy Christmas tree?"

Wesley glanced down at the sagging, metal fringe tree that kept vigil over the unopened gifts beneath its tarnished branches. He wasn't about to admit that he'd pitched a fit every time his sister had wanted to take it down over the years. "My mom put up the tree a couple of weeks before she and Dad had to leave. Carlotta won't take it down until they come home."

"So those gifts have been under the tree all this time?"

"Yep."

Chance whistled low. "Dude, your sister is one smokin'-hot babe, but that sounds a little wackadoodle, don't you think?"

Wesley frowned. "No. And it's none of your business." He tried to focus on the sensor he was trying to install, but the Oxy was messing with his concentration.

"So for the love of God, when are you going to fix me up with your sister's friend Hannah?"

Wesley's hand slipped and he dropped a bolt. He sighed and rubbed his eyes. "I'm just waiting for the right time. Be patient, all right?"

"So with your lawyer out of town, who's polishing *your* knob?"

"Nobody." Meg's face popped into his mind, then detonated. She'd ignored him this morning at the office, while lavishing Ravi and Jeff with smiles and cleavage.

"Dude, I heard that if men don't get off at least three times a week, all that come backs up and leads to prostitutionitis. That's an actual disease."

Wesley squinted. "I think you mean prostatitis. And if

not getting off makes guys sick, the hospitals would be overflowing with horny losers."

"See, there you go again. Man, I wish I was smart like you. My dad would probably like me a lot more."

"At least your dad is around." Wesley wiped his forehead with the hem of his T-shirt. "Hand me the bolt that fell, will you?"

The theme of *The Mickey Mouse Club* chimed from his backpack on the floor. He winced inwardly—that would be Mouse calling. They weren't collecting this afternoon because Mouse had to attend a "staff meeting." Somehow Wesley doubted The Carver rallied his employees with motivational speeches. More likely, he stood at the end of a boardroom table wielding an ax.

He ignored Chance's raised eyebrows and climbed down to retrieve the red phone and connect the call. "Yeah, what's up?"

"Hey, little man," Mouse said. "I got some good news for you."

"You gonna make me guess?"

"The boss is real happy with our collections. He said I could start cutting you in."

Surprised, Wesley pursed his mouth. "Great, I could use the cash."

"Yeah, and this way, you won't have to keeping skimming off the top."

Wes almost swallowed his tongue. "I don't know what you're talking about."

"Look, Wes, you can't con a con. Don't worry. I didn't rat you out. But don't be trying that shit now that you're on the payroll, *capiche?*"

"*Capiche,*" Wesley muttered.

"See you tomorrow."

Wes disconnected the call, a little shaken. The fathead was more astute than Wes realized. He'd have to be more careful on this undercover gig.

"Did you get a new phone?" Chance asked, nodding to the red pay-as-you-go model.

"It's for my new job," Wes said.

"*Another* job? Dude, you work too hard."

From his backpack, Wes's other phone rang. "Tell me about it," he said, rummaging for his regular phone. It was Kendall Abrams. Wesley grimaced, but answered.

"This is Wes."

"Wes, it's me, Kendall. I got a couple of pickups iffen you can go."

Wes glanced up at the security system that was little more than naked wires coming out of the wall. The installation was turning into a bigger job than he'd planned and the Oxy was making him antsy…or was it the lack of Oxy? He couldn't remember.

Regardless, he could finish installing the system later. "Uh, sure." He gave Kendall the town house address, then ended the call.

"That's it for the day," Wes said to Chance.

"Good, I need a nap. Who was that?"

"My body-moving partner. Guy's a full-on redneck."

"I thought you worked with your boss."

"He's been busy lately," Wesley muttered.

Chance walked out with him and climbed into his black BMW. "Let me know when you need a hand finishing up the security system. I'll bring my tool belt next time."

"Sure thing," Wesley said with a wave. His friend meant well, but he was inept when it came to almost everything.

Wesley sat down on the stoop to wait for Kendall and fought a groan when Mrs. Winningham emerged from the house next door, holding her fugly dog, Toofers.

"Hi, Mrs. Winningham."

"Your yard needs to be mowed," the woman announced.

"I know. I'll get to it as soon as I can."

"There have been a lot of police officers going in and out of your house."

"We had a break-in."

The woman's hand fluttered to her chest. "You were robbed?"

"Yeah. It blows."

The woman frowned. "Did the police catch the robber?"

"Not yet. I'm installing a security system. But in the meantime, my sister and I are staying with friends."

His neighbor shuddered. "What is the world coming to? That Charmed Killer is running around murdering women in their own homes."

He started to tell the woman that, because of her age, she was safe. But frankly, the serial killer hadn't shown any kind of pattern in the selection of his victims other than the fact that they were all female. "Do you have a gun for protection?"

The woman blanched. "I have my dead husband's revolver in a trunk, but I'd never use it."

"Just keep your doors locked, Mrs. Winningham. Toofers will protect you."

Her expression softened. "Yes, he will." The woman went back inside, nuzzling her teacup pet.

He shook his head and when he looked back to the street, the black SUV with tinted windows was rolling by.

He sprang to his feet and ran to the edge of the curb to get a look at the license plate. But the plate was obscured by mud…on an otherwise pristine vehicle. It disappeared around a corner, and Wesley cursed under his breath. What the hell was going on?

A horn blared, nearly sending him out of his skin. He turned to see the morgue van and Kendall behind the wheel waving like a goober. Wesley jogged around the front and climbed into the passenger seat.

"Scare you, man?" Kendall said with a laugh.

"Just drive," Wesley said, picking up a clipboard from the dash. "What's on the schedule?"

"A residential call—a woman suffocated."

He swung his head around. "The Charmed Killer again?"

"Nah. The M.E. says she was drunk and accidentally suffocated. After that, we have to go by a nursing home to pick up some old lady." Kendall made a face. "That could be nasty."

"Not usually," Wesley said. "With the older ones, it's like they're ready to go, you know? It's more quiet."

Kendall gave a little laugh. "What are you, some kind of poet?"

Wesley frowned. "Forget it." He glanced at the side mirror to see if the black SUV was following them, but he didn't see it.

The residential pickup was unexpectedly rough. Wanda Alderman's teenage son had found her facedown on the couch when he'd come home from school, an empty bottle of gin on the floor next to her. It looked as if she'd simply passed out and accidentally suffocated in the pile of pillows—adult SIDS.

Seeing the face of the distraught boy flanked by some distant relative triggered flashbacks for Wesley. Fractured images of his mom "sleeping" on the chaise by the pool or on the settee in the den, always with an empty highball glass curled against her chest. He wondered briefly if his mother still drank…if she ever thought about him…if she was still alive.

Medical Examiner Pennyman, a guy Wes recognized from previous scenes, nodded a greeting. The man shepherded the family into another room so the body could be removed in privacy, then returned. "She's in full rigor— are you guys okay?"

"We got it," Wesley assured him. After the M.E. left, Wes directed Kendall every step of the way—the guy was eager enough, just clumsy as hell.

"Easy, man," Wesley said when the guy dropped his end of the body—for the second time.

"Sorry," Kendall said. "This is totally different than moving a dead deer."

"You a hunter?"

"No. I worked for the Department of Transportation, removing dead animals from the highway."

Wesley pursed his mouth, half-impressed, half-disgusted. "What's the weirdest animal you ever had to scoop up?"

"Armadillo."

"There are armadillos in Georgia?"

"Freaky, huh?" Kendall grunted as they lifted the victim to the gurney. "She's all stiff. Will they have to break her arms to get her in a casket?"

"Keep your voice down," Wesley said, carefully zipping the body bag. "The rigor will go away."

"Are you in med school?"

Wesley smiled at that. "No." He pulled the gurney straps securely over the bag.

"You seem to know a lot about this stuff."

"Coop is a good teacher."

"I don't think he likes me," Kendall said.

"Coop likes everyone."

"My uncle said Coop's a drunk."

Wes bit down on the inside of his cheek and pushed the gurney toward the door. "He's a recovering alcoholic. Big difference."

"All I know is somebody at the top pulled strings to get him back in the morgue lab, and not everybody's happy about it."

"With The Charmed Killer case ongoing, I'd think that Dr. Abrams would be glad to have an extra pair of hands."

"That's the point. He can't afford any screwups on his watch. His words, not mine."

Wes bit his tongue to keep from saying something that might get back to Dr. Abrams. He was quiet as they loaded the body and drove to the morgue. His mind jumped around, but he couldn't forget the face of the victim's son. What a stupid way for the woman to die… What a cruel last memory to leave with one's child. Addicts were selfishly blind to the hurt they caused loved ones.

A sudden headache flowed over his scalp. He needed a hit of Oxy.

He glanced sideways at Kendall and when the guy was sufficiently distracted by the god-awful country music on the radio, Wesley slipped a tablet into his mouth and chewed. Nirvana seeped through him, erasing all the unpleasant thoughts about his mother and her weakness for alcohol. By the time they reached the morgue, he was feeling happy and magnanimous. His spirits were further lifted by the sight of Coop's van in the parking lot. After dropping off the body at the crypt, he said to Kendall, "I'll meet you back at the van in ten minutes."

"Cool. I'll say hello to Uncle Bruce."

Wesley walked to the lab and pushed open the door. Coop was in a corner, studying a computer screen.

The tall man looked up and smiled. "Hey, Wes, what's shaking?"

"Uh…just helping Kendall with a couple of pickups."

Coop looked back to the monitor. "What do you think of him?"

"He's okay, I guess. What are you doing?"

"Experimenting with a program I found online."

"What does it do?"

"Takes a blurred or faded image and uses an algorithm to try to recreate the original image."

"What's the application?"

"Still trying to identify our headless John Doe."

Wes tried not to react as he walked closer. "Really?"

"Yeah. I found a spot on his shoulder where the guy used to have a tattoo, but had it lasered off. That's what I'm trying to recreate. It might be an identifying marker that could be publicized. Stick around for a few minutes if you want and you can see the results."

"Has this kind of thing been done before?"

"Somewhere, I'm sure. We've never had the tools or the time to follow up on stuff like this."

Wes tried to sound nonchalant. "Why are you so keen on identifying this guy?"

Coop turned his head toward Wes. "Because even if he

was the biggest lowlife on earth, somewhere, someone who cared about him is worried sick—his mother, a sister, a son. They deserve to know the truth."

Wesley nodded, then stopped when the scent of alcohol hit him. He looked at Coop and realized that the man's eyes were a little glassy. "Have you been drinking?"

Coop frowned and straightened. "What business is it of yours?"

Wes lifted his hands. "I'm just saying you could get into a lot of trouble—"

"How about you keep your mouth shut, and I don't tell anyone that you're high right now?"

Wesley blinked. "Me, high?"

"As a Chinese box kite."

They stared at each other and tension whipped through the air. Wesley wanted to come clean to Coop, but he didn't want to concede to another mistake. Besides, he and Coop were going through the same thing. The Oxy, like the booze for Coop, was just a small indulgence to help ease him over a rough spot. A temporary prop. A helping hand.

The phone in the lab rang and Coop strode away to answer it. Wesley looked to the computer screen where each pixel of the image was being filled in. A picture began to emerge. Wesley squinted. It looked like some kind of ornate cross with extra graphics out to the sides…angel wings maybe?

A message popped up on the screen to indicate that the process was complete and asked, "Do you want to print the image?"

He looked over his shoulder to see that Coop was still on the phone and flipping through records in a file cabinet.

Wes turned back and hit *Y* on the keyboard. A few seconds later, a nearby laser printer hummed to life and churned out a piece of paper with the design printed on it. Wesley removed the paper, folded it and slipped it under his shirt.

Across the room, Coop dropped the receiver back to its cradle. "Did the program finish?"

"I think so," Wes said, then gestured to the door. "But I gotta go, man."

"Okay. You take care of yourself," Coop said, giving him a meaningful look.

Wes dipped his chin. "You, too."

He walked out of the lab and exhaled. When it came to puzzles, Coop was like a hound with a scent. He'd keep digging until he found out who the guy was and dig even deeper to find out what had happened to him. But if Wes could identify the man first and call in an anonymous tip to the police along with some story about how the guy had died, it might be enough to convince the police and the M.E. to drop the case… Or at least, it could send them on a wild-goose chase that would drain their enthusiasm.

Under his T-shirt the piece of paper crackled, and on the way to the parking lot, an idea came to him. Wes pulled out his cell phone and punched in a number.

"What do you want, shithead?" Hannah asked on the second ring. "Are you in trouble again?"

"No," Wes assured her. "Nothing like that. I was calling to see if you were ready to have that tattoo on your back finished. My buddy Chance is still willing to pick up the tab."

"I told you I'd think about it."

"Come on. My man is loaded and he wants to spend money on you. What's to think about?"

Hannah sighed. "Does doughboy still want to watch?"

"Yeah. Is it okay if I come along, too?"

"On one condition," Hannah said finally. "If you tell Carlotta, I'll tattoo your balls, got it?"

Wes smiled into the phone. "My lips are sealed."

18

Deception indicated.

It meant, Detective Marquez had explained, that Carlotta couldn't be cleared of involvement in The Charmed Killer case unless she wanted to retake the polygraph. If she elected not to retake the test, she would be under heightened scrutiny, even surveillance. Which, after Carlotta thought about it, wasn't such a bad thing. She knew she was innocent. And if Michael Lane decided to come after her, she wanted as many eyes on her as possible.

A horn sounded, jarring Carlotta back to the present. She goosed the gas on the scooter and zoomed ahead.

Still…Detective Marquez could've at least told her which questions she'd failed.

Never mind. She'd get it out of Jack…assuming he could get it out of Marquez.

That made her frown.

But if Jack had been spending most of his nights at the police precinct, he hadn't been spending them with Maria.

That made her smile.

She spotted a grocery ahead and put on her blinker. Thirty minutes later her storage compartment was full of cat food, in case they couldn't find the feline's owner right away. On a whim, she'd also picked up a couple of salmon fillets, thinking she'd prepare dinner for Peter.

Deception indicated.

When she pulled up to the Martinique Estates security gate a few minutes later, she had a brain blip and couldn't recall Peter's access code. The harder she thought about it, the more clearly she saw Tracey Lowenstein's face telling her that she was an embarrassment to Peter.

"I got it, miss," the guard called from the shack. "I recognize the scooter. Not many of those in this neighborhood."

She lifted her hand in a wave, but her face burned. Obviously, no other full-grown women in this neighborhood rode around on a pink scooter.

As she wheeled toward Peter's house, she glanced at the expansive homes on either side of the street and wondered if people were looking out their windows, watching her, laughing at her…laughing at Peter.

A few minutes later, she pulled in to Peter's garage, disappointed that he wasn't home yet, and a little nervous about going into the house alone. The garage door hummed down as she lowered the Vespa kickstand. She loosened the chin strap on the helmet and climbed off the scooter, then stood back to look at it objectively.

Maybe it was a little…youthful. And the color a little… frivolous.

But God help her, she loved it.

Carlotta gave the gas tank a little pat, then removed the bag of groceries and walked to the door leading into the mudroom.

The cat had obviously heard her arrive and was

meowing frantically. Carlotta opened the door and the Persian was instantly underfoot, making angry noises that sounded almost human.

Carlotta turned off the security alarm, then shook her finger at the cranky cat. "You'd better be good to me, I brought you food." She grimaced at the contents of the cardboard box, but took it as a further sign that the cat was house-trained.

The Persian followed her into the main part of the house, the combination keeping room/kitchen/casual dining area. Carlotta was conscious of the echo of her footsteps as she walked into the spacious kitchen. The electrical whine of the commercial-grade appliances vibrated in the air. Everything felt very sterile, especially when she thought of her and Wesley's cluttered, homey kitchen.

She smiled as she stored the groceries. Was it possible she was a little bit homesick? Carlotta closed the refrigerator door and leaned into the counter, glancing around at the cavernous space. She could see how being alone in a house like this would be achingly lonely for Peter. And how Angela would have resented Peter working late or going to business dinners.

She glanced over to see that the cat had either climbed or jumped onto the lowest bookshelf and was sniffing around the items placed there.

"Get down," Carlotta said, hurrying toward it. The last thing she needed was for the cat to break something of Peter's. The Persian ignored her, rubbing her face on the corners of the framed black-and-white photo of Angela. The animal purred like a little engine, obviously happy to have an itch scratched.

"You can't be climbing on things," Carlotta said, reaching for her.

The cat's ears slid back and it hissed at her.

She retreated, hands up. "Okay." Trying another tactic, she backtracked to the kitchen and noisily opened a can of the expensive cat food, emptied it onto a saucer and set it on the floor.

The ploy worked. The cat jumped down and ran to the saucer. But instead of diving in, she sniffed the food, sat on her haunches and looked up at her. *Meow.*

The cat sounded…disappointed. Carlotta frowned. "Okay, so it's not sardines. But it's what you're supposed to eat."

Its whiskers twitched.

"Or not," Carlotta said, throwing up her hands. "It's up to you, Miss Priss."

Her cell phone rang and she reached for her purse. A glance at the caller-ID screen revealed that Peter was calling. She smiled and connected the phone. "Hi."

"Hi, yourself. Are you home?"

Home. "Uh…yeah. I'm feeding the cat. And I bought us salmon fillets for dinner."

"That sounds wonderful, but I'm afraid I'm going to be working late."

Carlotta frowned. Something in Peter's tone sounded… off. Was the GBI there again, asking about Randolph? Had her failed polygraph triggered another round of questioning? "I can wait for you," she offered.

"No, go ahead and eat," he said, his enthusiasm sounding forced. "But I don't like the idea of you being there alone. I thought maybe you could call your friend Hannah to come over."

"Do you trust her to be in your house?"

"Where's that coming from?"

She sighed. "Sorry, I'm not mad at you. Tracey Lowenstein came to see me today at work. She had Hannah fired from the catering company that services the country club."

"Oh. I'm sorry, Carly. Tracey is…well, we both know what she is. It's not fair that your friend lost her job, but even if Hannah had stayed on, Tracey and her cronies would have made things difficult for her. She's better off finding another gig."

"I suppose," Carlotta muttered. "I think I will call Hannah and see if she'd like to come over for a swim."

"Good idea. There are extra swimsuits in the guesthouse. Help yourself. Hannah can have my salmon. It might be late when I get home, so keep the alarm on."

"Okay."

"Oh, I almost forgot. How did the polygraph go?"

"Fine," she lied…again.

"Good. See you later."

She disconnected the call and looked down to see the cat staring up at her with…*recrimination?*

Deception indicated.

"Oh, go lick yourself," she said to the beast, then dialed Hannah's number. She was relieved when her friend answered.

"Hey."

"I'm sorry that witch Tracey Lowenstein got you fired," she said without preamble.

"How did you know?"

"She came in to the store to tell me. And to let me know that I'm not welcome back at the club."

Hannah snorted. "Can she bar you from the club?"

"If she wants to."

"Just because you and I are friends and she thinks I'm a thief."

"That's not the only reason. This goes way back and much deeper than anything you did or didn't do."

"Didn't," Hannah said.

Carlotta closed her eyes briefly. "I know you didn't steal those purses."

"Plural?"

"Apparently another purse was stolen last night besides Bebe Plank's."

"Damn. Someone's got a good gig going."

"And when another purse is stolen, they'll know it wasn't you."

"It doesn't matter," Hannah said, but her voice sounded strained. "There are lots of other catering companies to work for."

"Why don't you come over," Carlotta asked.

"To Peter's?"

"Yeah. He's working late, and we'd have the pool to ourselves. I'll make dinner." She waited a beat. "Or not, whichever sounds more appealing."

There was silence on the other end for a moment. "I don't think so," Hannah said finally.

Carlotta could've played the "I don't want to be alone" card and her friend probably would've given in, but she understood how Hannah must be feeling. Right now, she hated Tracey Lowenstein and all the woman stood for. If she were Hannah, the thought of coming to Peter's mansion would probably feel as if she were fraternizing with the enemy. "Maybe some other time?"

"Sure," Hannah said. "I gotta go."

Carlotta said goodbye and disconnected the call, nursing a pang of guilt. If it hadn't been for Carlotta, Tracey probably wouldn't have pursued Hannah so vigorously. She liked to think that people like Tracey would get theirs in the end, but she knew that wasn't always the case. Some people just steamrolled through life getting what they wanted, and everyone else be damned.

Carlotta sighed at the cat. "Looks like it's you and me, kitty."

The cat, utterly disinterested in the cat food and in her, began exploring the room. Carlotta turned to the sliding glass door and looked out to the aquamarine pool, but conceded that swimming alone didn't hold much appeal. She'd only be thinking about Angela the entire time. Besides, it read like the beginning of every horror movie she'd ever seen—the heroine knows a madman is on the loose, but decides to go skinny-dipping anyway.

No, thanks.

She unwrapped the coral-colored salmon fillets and bit her lip. Wesley made salmon all the time. Maybe she should've paid attention a time or two. She picked up her cell phone and dialed his number.

"Hey, sis."

She frowned. His voice sounded a little slurred. "Are you busy?"

"On a body run to the nursing home."

"With Coop?" she asked hopefully.

"Uh, no, with Kendall. I saw Coop earlier, though, at the morgue lab."

"How did he seem to you?"

"Fine. He's busy working on cold cases."

"So he's not involved in The Charmed Killer investigation?"

Wesley cleared his throat, then lowered his voice. "I get the feeling he's being kept away from high-profile cases."

"Oh. Abrams's nephew is listening?"

"Yeah."

"Are you okay? You sound like you've been drinking."

"No…I'm just tired," he said, but she could tell he was speaking with more deliberation. "Where are you?"

"In the kitchen."

He laughed—too hard. "Good one. Seriously, where are you?"

"I'm in Peter's kitchen."

"Just to be sure…do you see a big metal box with fire coming out of it?"

"Very funny. I called for advice on how to prepare salmon fillets."

"Ah, that's easy. Season with a little lemon juice, salt and pepper, and sprinkle a little brown sugar on top. Add some oil to the pan and cook it on medium heat. You can't mess it up." He made a rueful noise. "I take that back—don't undercook it."

"Sounds doable," she said, then wet her lips. "How's everything else?"

"I started installing the security system in the town house."

"Where did you get the money?"

"From my job."

"So your courier job must be going pretty well."

"Yeah. Listen, we just pulled up to the nursing home. Don't burn the house down."

She gave a little laugh, then disconnected the call. Uneasiness curled in her stomach. Wesley didn't sound right. Could he be high? She thought back to the pill she'd found in his bathroom floor—generic OxyContin. He'd told her that he'd taken only a few of the pain pills after that animal The Carver had used him as a whittling stick. Those and the two Percocet-tablet refills that he'd taken from her purse.

But what if he'd lied?

She chewed on her thumbnail until she remembered his probation meetings. The guidelines required him to stay drug free, and he had to supply urine samples on demand. She'd met Wesley's probation officer—Eldora Jones seemed like the type to make him toe the line.

She relaxed and turned on the flat-screen television mounted under the kitchen cabinets to listen to as she prepared dinner. No surprise, the local news was all about The Charmed Killer and his latest victim. But there were no official comments from the APD or the GBI, only a lot of conjecture and unsubstantiated rumors. Michael Lane's photograph flashed onto the screen.

Carlotta's heart squeezed. Michael was a handsome guy, with charm to spare and a big personality. How had things gotten so twisted in his mind?

"Fugitive Michael Lane," the anchor said solemnly, "is the most wanted man in the state of Georgia. Aside from his involvement in the deaths of two women in an identity-theft ring, Lane is reportedly the number-one suspect in The Charmed Killer case. The public is advised that Lane could be armed and is considered extremely dangerous. If you see him, do not approach him. Repeat—do not approach him. Call 911 immediately."

Fear washed over her as the extent of what Michael

might have done began to sink in. Five more lives lost... that they knew of. What if Peter was right? What if Michael was killing these women out of some perverted game he was playing with Carlotta?

The lights around the pool kicked on, sending alarm stabbing through her. Then she realized they were on the timer Peter had told her about. Still, she was suddenly aware of how open the house was, especially on the side that faced the pool. She hurried to close the blinds, then switched the TV channel to a sitcom.

The scent of salmon caught the attention of the cat, who made a pest of herself underfoot as Carlotta stood at the stove cooking the fillets in a pan, one seasoned for her, one unseasoned for the cat. She pulled ingredients for a small salad from the refrigerator, but acknowledged that she didn't have much of an appetite when she sat down at the table...alone.

It was just her and the cat, who seemed more pleased with the cooked salmon than with the plate of cat food that sat uneaten on the floor. The feline gobbled it down, then jumped up on the table.

"Get down," Carlotta admonished.

But the cat ignored her, seemingly fascinated by the lidded Oriental-design vase that sat in the center of the table. While Carlotta ate, she idly wondered what Peter had done with the much-hated designer silk flower arrangement that had once sat here, the one that seemed to represent everything that was wrong with his and Angela's relationship. Maybe he'd put it on Angela's grave, she mused. Or maybe he'd simply tossed it, along with the bad memories. Regardless, she was in agreement that the tasteful vase was a better choice for a centerpiece.

The cat purred and rubbed itself against the raised surface of the vase until Carlotta waved her hand and shooed the animal off the table. The cat swiped at her and even though she missed, Carlotta snapped.

"That's it," she said, pushing to her feet. She carried her empty plate to the dishwasher. "I'm making up flyers tonight to find your owner, the sooner the better. That's assuming someone wants you back, you hateful beast."

The cat came to stand at her feet, meowing at her as if in rebuttal. Carlotta squinted at the animal, again struck by the sense that she was trying to communicate her mutual dislike of her. Then suddenly the cat started hacking, its mouth jerking open in spasms.

Carlotta's eyes widened—maybe she'd poisoned her. Weren't cats supposed to eat fish? Maybe not that much. She watched in horror as the cat looked to be lapsing into some kind of seizure. "Omigod, omigod, omigod."

Then with a wrenching heave, the cat expelled something from its throat and walked away as if nothing had happened, its tail held high.

Carlotta looked down to see a wet, blond hairball on the toe of her favorite Mui Mui cream-colored slides.

She grimaced in disgust. Minus twenty.

19

Carlotta typed as she spoke aloud. "Found…one ill-tempered female Persian cat, blond hair, green eyes."

She turned to glare at the cat who had curled up on top of a pair of Peter's house shoes, looking deliriously content.

"Maybe I should offer a reward, just to make sure someone claims you," Carlotta said.

The Persian gave her a slow blink and looked away as if to stay, "Please stop talking."

Carlotta frowned and looked back to the computer screen. It had taken a while to figure it out, but she'd managed to download the picture of the cat she'd taken with her phone into a word-processing document. To the tart description she added her cell-phone number as the contact, then printed twenty-five flyers.

While the machine churned out pages, she sat back and glanced around the home office. It was another beautifully furnished room, this time equipped with a state-of-the-art computer and accessories. It was a luxury to have access to a computer again. When Wesley had been arrested for hacking, all of his equipment had been confiscated. Under the conditions of his probation, they weren't permitted to have a computer in the house. She'd resorted to going to the public library to look up things when she needed to.

It was on a research trip at the library that she'd discovered that the first presumed victim, Shawna Whitt, had posted info to the Charmers Web site community, a site established for the fans of the charm bracelets promoted by Olympian Eva McCoy. Charmers could post first-person accounts about their experiences with their own charm bracelets and whatever bits about their lives they wanted to share. It was possible that Shawna Whitt had shared too much, posting that she lived alone and had joined an online-dating service.

Carlotta had given the contents of the postings to Jack and Maria, but she hadn't heard any more about it. Both detectives had been skeptical, simply because at the time, they weren't convinced that Shawna Whitt had been murdered. It was true that the autopsy results had indicated death by natural causes, but that had been before the next victim had been found with a charm in her mouth. By that time, Shawna Whitt's body had been cremated, rendering a more in-depth autopsy impossible.

Carlotta had been confident that Jack would follow up on the Web site connection, but he'd been taken off the case. And how much credence would the GBI agents give to clues that she'd found when they considered her father to be a suspect, and her to be a liar?

But sitting in front of the hi-res, flat-screen computer monitor, it occurred to her that she could do a lot of investigating in the privacy of her own home.

Er, make that Peter's home. And he probably wouldn't be too thrilled to know she was using his computer to delve deeper into The Charmed Killer case. But considering that she, as Agent Wick had pointed out, had a direct or indirect connection with most of the victims, didn't she owe it to them to try to figure out if she was simply in the wrong place at the right time, or if the killer was trying to communicate with her? If it was Michael, maybe she could figure out what he wanted, or what his next move might be.

And if it was her father—

Carlotta stopped and blinked back sudden tears. How could she even think such a thing?

Because he abandoned you, and took your mother...

Because he chose himself over his family...

Because he threw you to the sharks to fend for yourself...

Maria had described the perfect psychopath as a narcissist to the nth degree, a person who discarded those who didn't suit him and would destroy anyone who stood between him and what he wanted.

A narcissist to the nth degree...that was Randolph Wren.

A coldness seeped over her. She'd been trying to make up for her father's sins her entire life. If Randolph was responsible for these horrible acts, if he was The Charmed Killer, then it was up to her to reveal him for the murderer he was.

She found a notebook and began to write down all the details she could remember about each victim, every conversation she'd had with Jack, Maria, Coop, the agents. Then she pulled up a search engine.

Since she'd tracked down Shawna Whitt through the Charmers Web site community, it seemed like the obvious place to start looking for the names of other victims.

Except the Web site had been suspended…no doubt because of the publicity surrounding The Charmed Killer case and the rumors circulating that he was picking his victims based on the fact that they were wearing charm bracelets.

She sighed in frustration at the quick dead end. But she rolled up her sleeves and tried again…and again… and again. There were thousands of repetitive entries about the killing spree, most of them regional, but not all. She waded through entry after entry, noting any new detail she could find, but it was a tedious, imprecise process.

The theories concerning the charms themselves ranged from reasonable to ridiculous—that the killer was a jeweler, that he was dismantling the charm bracelet of a woman he'd lost, that he was a frustrated cross-dresser. Jack had mentioned at one point that charms could be clues to the killer's identity, or to his motive.

She made a list of the charms that had been recovered: a chicken/bird, a cigar, a car, a gun, and most recently, a pair of handcuffs.

Only one matched the M.O. of the murder—the gun found in the mouth of A.D.A. Cheryl Meriwether, who had been shot. To her knowledge, Randolph hadn't owned a gun. But the unidentified couple who had robbed the hotel in Florida where her father's fingerprints had been found had used a gun.

The bird charm had already been linked to her father by virtue of his nickname, The Bird. As far as the cigar charm, Randolph had certainly enjoyed his stogies. The car was pretty generic and could apply to almost anyone. And the handcuffs…well, the image of her father being led away in handcuffs was branded on her brain. It had been a widely publicized photo in the *AJC*.

While the charms could loosely fit her father, they skewed masculine in general. And it was highly possible that the charms meant nothing whatsoever.

The cat suddenly jumped up and shot out the door. Carlotta froze, then realized the distant sound of a door closing, then opening, meant that Peter was home. She glanced at her watch, shocked that the entire evening had disappeared.

"Carly?" he called. "Where are you?"

"I'm coming." She hurriedly shut down the computer and closed the notebook, then put the flyers on top and stood up just as he appeared in the doorway. The cat rubbed against his legs, energized.

Peter smiled. "Using the computer?"

She patted the papers she held. "I made flyers for our runaway."

He leaned in and dropped a kiss on her mouth. "Where's Hannah?"

"Uh…she had other plans."

"Don't tell me you've been alone all evening."

"Oh, no, it was fine, really. Other than the hair ball."

"Hair ball?"

She gave a dismissive wave. "Never mind. Did you get everything done at the office?"

Peter's expression changed and he nodded toward the great room. "Carly, can we talk?"

Her stomach clenched. "Sure…what's going on?"

He clasped her hand and led her into the den, then pulled her down to sit next to him on the couch.

"Does this have something to do with my father?"

"As a matter of fact, it does. When the GBI agent interviewed me yesterday about Randolph, something stuck in my mind."

"What?"

"When we were dating, your father took me to work with him one day. Do you remember that?"

She squinted. "Vaguely."

"It was my senior year. He knew I wanted to be a broker, and he was nice enough to give me a glimpse of what it was like."

"Okay. Where is this going?"

Peter pressed his lips together. "When I was in his office, a woman came in who delivered mail for several companies in the building. I remember her because she was really pretty and she had a great figure…"

"And?"

"And she seemed…familiar with your father."

"In what way?"

He looked uncomfortable.

"Oh." She flushed with shame.

"Anyway, the circumstances were awkward enough that I remembered her first name. I stayed late tonight to go back through old security records to confirm my suspicions. Her name was Alicia. Alicia Sills."

Her burning cheeks cooled as the blood drained from her face. Alicia Sills—The Charmed Killer's second victim. And apparently, one of her father's old flings.

20

"You're awful quiet, little man."

Wesley winced against the pain pulsating between his ears. "Headache."

Mouse gave a little laugh. "Why don't you just pop one of those little pills of yours?"

"Why don't you be quiet for two minutes?" Wesley barked. Then he exhaled and held up his hand. "Sorry, man. That was out of line."

"I don't mind the attitude when it brings in the kind of cash you collected today."

Wesley turned to look out the window. Today was the first day he'd hit something with the baseball bat other than appliances. It had felt good at the time to work out some of the frustration that had him on edge. Meg had barely spoken to him this morning, but she'd smirked at his shaking hand when he'd handed her a highlighter. He gritted his teeth. She was so self-righteous. He wanted so bad to prove her wrong, that he could kick the Oxy anytime. His body screamed for a hit right now, but he was trying to resist…and the baseball bat was helping.

"It's gotta be a woman," Mouse said.

Wesley started to protest, then caught sight of the black

SUV in his side mirror. "Do me a favor, man. Pull over to the curb before you get to the light."

"What's up?"

"Just do it."

Mouse did what he asked. Wesley waited until the black SUV passed, then tried to get a look at the license plate. It was covered with mud. Which meant that this was the same fucker who'd been tailing him for weeks.

"Cover me," Wes said. Then he pulled the baseball bat out of the backseat and jumped out of the passenger-side door. Adrenaline pumped through him as he strode up to the SUV, now stopped at a red light. He swung fast and hard, bashing in the driver's side window. Glass showered him, but the driver got the worst of it.

The stocky man on the inside was holding his hands over his head. "What the fuck, man?"

Wesley pushed the bat against the man's throat. "What the fuck is right. What the fuck are you doing following me?"

"Whoa, whoa. No harm, no foul."

Wesley swung the bat again and bashed in the windshield.

"Hey! Not my windshield!" the man yelled.

"Start talking, dude."

Horns were starting to sound from cars backed up behind the SUV.

"We've met before," the man said. "I'm a private investigator—Gregory Young. I worked on the Kiki Deerling case."

"That case is over. Why are you following me?"

"Someone hired me to…watch you."

Wesley frowned. "Who?"

The man's mouth turned down.

Wesley swung again and took out the rest of the windshield.

"Okay, okay! Jesus. The guy's name is Harold Vincent."

"Who's that?"

"That's all I know. Dude's a doctor. He asked me to find out where you go, what you do, who you hang out with."

Vincent…Meg's last name was Vincent…and her father was a doctor.

"You must've done something to piss the guy off," Young offered.

His mind raced. Why would Meg's dad have him followed? Unless…he thought his little princess was interested in Wesley?

Wes didn't have time to revel in the moment because sirens sounded in the distance. He looked at Young. "You know what kind of people I hang out with, so if you know what's good for you, you won't report this—to the police or to Vincent."

Young lifted his hands. "You got it."

Wesley sprinted back to the Town Car and jumped in. "Let's get out of here."

Mouse didn't ask questions. He drove the Town Car up on the sidewalk to bypass traffic and made a right down a side street. It was only after they were several blocks away that Mouse said, "What the hell was that all about?"

"I don't know," Wesley said. "But I'm going to find out."

21

Carlotta was numb. Oh, she was conscious of the air hitting her face as she steered the Vespa up a hill, but she didn't feel it. Because if she felt the really good sensations so acutely, she'd have to feel the really bad sensations just as acutely. And she didn't want to go there.

She was still reeling over the fact that her father had not only known Alicia Sills, but he'd probably had a fling with her, if Peter's long-term memory could be trusted. And she certainly trusted a high-school senior boy to sense when sex was in the air.

Peter had said it was her decision whether or not he reported what he remembered to the GBI. On the one hand, it could be a harmless coincidence. On the other hand…

It was a good thing she had the day off because she'd gotten next to no sleep. In addition to tossing and turning over yet one more dilemma her father had managed to implicate her in, the cat who hated her also insisted on sleeping with her.

On her head, on her stomach, on her feet.

She stifled a yawn and stopped the scooter. After lowering the kickstand, she removed the stapler and one of the remaining flyers from the storage compartment. She walked over to a tree next to the sidewalk to attach the Found Cat ad. When she got back to the scooter, her phone was ringing. She checked it to see if it might be someone calling already about the cat, pleasedearGod. But instead, it was Jack.

She closed her eyes briefly, then hit the silence button and restowed the phone. She'd avoided his call last night because she hadn't been in the mood to be flirted to sleep… Not while she'd debated whether or not to rat out her ratty father.

Within another twenty minutes, she'd posted all but one of the flyers. The last one she'd saved for the community center so she could eat a late lunch at the café inside. She parked her scooter outside the sprawling white building that served as the hub of the neighborhood—an enormous community pool, loads of tennis courts, meeting facilities and a day care. It was busy on a Friday summer day, with the kids out of school and moms getting an early start on the weekend. She felt like an outsider, but the activity made her feel safe. It was a welcome distraction from her own thoughts.

She walked inside and found a public bulletin board. There were no ads for lost cats, so she posted the last flyer and crossed her fingers. She went to the café and found a seat at a table with partial shade that overlooked the pool, and ordered a chicken-salad sandwich with fries. She saw Sissy Talmadge, Peter's nearest neighbor, having lunch with someone. Carlotta waved, but when Sissy's companion turned around and Carlotta saw it was Bebe Plank, her hand froze midflutter.

Bebe turned back and the women were instantly

involved again in deep conversation over their martinis—
no doubt about her. Carlotta dropped her hand. She was
starting to regret her decision to infiltrate the upper ranks.
She wondered if Tracey could have her banned from the
community center, too.

Her food was delivered quickly and while she ate, she
enjoyed the summer scene that was worlds away from the
ugliness of The Charmed Killer. From the pool, screams
of children's laughter rode the air. In the distance, sprin-
klers fanned back and forth over green, green lawns. The
air was thick with the smell of fresh-cut grass.

A wave of nostalgia washed over her. This was how
she'd spent her childhood. A happy cocoon of summer
camp, tennis practice and endless birthday parties. If she
married Peter, this was how their children would grow up.
Carefree summers…private school…the best of everything.

The thought had slipped into her head, catching her
unawares. Did Peter even want children? Did she?

"A penny for your thoughts."

She looked up just as Jack settled into the empty seat
across from her. In his dark suit and tie, he stuck out like a
sore thumb. And he had the eye of every female in the
vicinity.

"How did you know I was here?" she asked with a
frown.

He snagged a fry from her plate. "I followed the trail
of flyers, and I saw your Pinkie Tuscadero scooter parked
out front."

"You just happened to be in the area, Jack, or do you
live around here?"

"Neither. Is your phone dead?"

"Yes."

He pulled out his cell and punched in a number. When her phone started ringing inside her bag, he snapped his shut. "Liar, liar, pants on fire."

She rolled her eyes. "So I'm not answering my phone."

He chewed the fry, then snagged another one. "I was worried. When you didn't answer last night, I thought you might have been kidnapped."

"By Peter?"

"It's called the Stockholm syndrome, where you become brainwashed by your captor."

She leaned forward. "Jack, if you're jealous, just say so."

"Of Ashford? Please. The guy is rich and works in a nice air-conditioned office all day while I grub around in a cubicle and get shot at. What's to be jealous of?"

"Me?" she asked, angling her head.

He looked under the table and frowned at her shorts. "I thought you'd at least be wearing a bikini."

She sighed. "Sorry to disappoint you. I came for lunch. Do you want something?"

He gestured to the half of the sandwich she hadn't eaten. "Are you through? If so, I'll just finish this."

"Knock yourself out. Any updates on Michael?"

He flagged the waiter and asked for a soda, then tore into the sandwich. "The sighting in Athens was bogus. We're back to square one. Can you think of anyplace he might be, or what he might be doing?"

"With ten thousand dollars, he's probably shopping," she said wryly. "Michael had an affinity for things he couldn't afford…which probably explains why he started stealing people's identities to begin with."

"It's something," he said. "I'll have uniforms recirculate Lane's photo to all the shop owners at Lenox Square and Phipps Plaza."

"Did you hear I failed the polygraph?"

He nodded and grinned. "So you thought about me during the test, huh?"

"No." She tossed her napkin at him. "Maria wouldn't tell me which questions I failed."

He frowned. "Let's just say you weren't forthcoming about the men in your life."

Meaning Jack and Randolph. She shifted in her seat. "Does this mean the state guys are going to bring me back in for questioning?"

"I don't know. Nobody will tell me anything."

"Not even Marquez?"

"Not even her."

She pressed her lips together. "Jack, I'm sorry if they took you off the case because of me."

He shrugged his big shoulders. "Doesn't matter. Those guys would've found another reason to take me off the case. Happens all the time. Big case like this, they want to run the investigation."

"Do you think they'll solve it?"

The waiter set the soda in front of Jack and he took a deep drink before answering. "Eventually."

"But?"

"But bureaucracy is slow. And sometimes when the state and federal agencies step in, the perp escalates."

"Because the case is more high profile?"

He nodded. "All serial killers are egomaniacs at heart."

She looked away. Randolph certainly was an egomaniac.

"So…are you going to tell me why you've been avoiding my calls?"

She looked back and found Jack studying her. She considered telling him about the connection Peter had made between her father and Alicia Sills. But even if Jack wasn't officially on the case, he'd be honor-bound to share that tidbit with the state agents.

Before she could manufacture a response, her cell phone rang. She pulled it out and saw Wesley's name on the caller ID. "It's Wes, I should get it."

Jack nodded and tackled the rest of the sandwich.

She connected the call. "Wesley? What's up?"

"Thought you might want to know—there's another victim of The Charmed Killer."

She reached forward to touch Jack's arm. "Another victim? Where? When?"

Jack's expression hardened.

"It was a run I made yesterday with Kendall in College Park. The M.E. thought the woman had passed out and suffocated, but the charm was found in her stomach during the autopsy."

"She'd swallowed it?"

What kind? Jack mouthed.

"What kind of charm was it?"

"Kendall said it looked like a keg, or maybe a barrel."

"A keg or a barrel."

Jack took out his pen and wrote on a napkin. NAME?

"Wesley, do you remember the victim's name?"

"Alderman was the last name, I don't remember the first name."

"Last name Alderman," she repeated, and Jack wrote it down.

"She was a middle-school teacher," Wesley offered. "Her teenage son found her at home."

She made a mournful noise. The situation must've affected Wesley if he was bringing it up. He sounded different. Yesterday he had slurred his words, but today he sounded antsy, and a little out of breath.

Jack wrote ADDRESS?

"Do you remember the street address?"

"Yeah—it was Rever, or Revere, one or the other."

"Rever or Revere."

"Are you with somebody?" Wesley asked.

Since Jack wasn't supposed to be on the case, she decided it was best not to say anything. "No...just me. I'm keeping track of as many details as possible."

Jack indicated that was all he needed for now.

"Thanks for the heads-up," she said. "Let me know if you hear anything else."

"Sure thing. Tell Jack hello for me."

She frowned into the phone and disconnected the call. "He said they picked up the body yesterday. It looked as if the woman had passed out and suffocated, but the charm was found during the autopsy."

"That's different," Jack said. "It means she was alive when he put it in her mouth, poor thing."

Jack flagged the waiter for the bill, then handed him cash and pushed to his feet. "Come on, I'll follow you back to Ashford's."

She gave him a wry smile. "Yes, I'm ready to leave, thank you for asking."

Jack gave her a pointed look. "And Carlotta—whatever you're keeping from me? Eventually I'll find out."

She wet her lips, thinking how secretive Jack could be when it came to personal details. "Right back at you, Jack."

22

"I'm nervous, dude. What if she doesn't like me?"

Wesley pulled his thoughts away from his own problems and turned his head to look at Chance, who was holding the steering wheel of the BMW like a driver's ed student.

"Relax, man. Hannah can't stand you. Which means you can only improve in her eyes."

Chance pursed his mouth and nodded. "I never thought about it like that."

"Besides, how can she resist the shirt?"

Chance smoothed a hand over his All This and a Big Dick, Too T-shirt and grinned. "You're right."

Wesley shook his head and looked back to the road. "There's the tattoo parlor on the left. And that's Hannah's van in the parking lot." They watched as Hannah, tall and solid and wearing more leather than a cow, emerged from the van.

"Just look at her," Chance said in awe. "I'm already sporting wood."

"Down, boy. You're going to have to work for this one."

Chance's chest puffed up. "I'm the man for the job."

Wes smothered a smile. This ought to be good.

Chance parked the car next to the van and they got out.

Hannah stood, arms crossed, glowering at them, her eyes ringed with kohl, her lips bloodred. "You're late."

"Five minutes," Wesley said. "Is that a new eyebrow piercing?"

"Yeah. Come on, I don't want to miss my appointment." She headed toward the entrance of the tattoo parlor.

"Hannah, you remember my buddy Chance Hollander," Wesley offered, following her.

"Hi, Hannah," Chance said, his face shiny and hopeful.

Without breaking stride, Hannah looked him over, then snorted at the shirt. "Better watch out. Someone will arrest your fat ass for false advertising."

Undaunted, Chance trotted to keep up with her. "So this is where you get your tats?"

"Inkwell is the best tattoo parlor in town," Hannah said. "My artist, Axle, has tattooed Tommy Lee."

"No shit?" Chance said. "How many tattoos do you have?"

"I don't know. After a while they all kind of run together. But he's been working on my torso for over a year now."

"I can't wait to see it," Chance said.

Hannah glared. "Axle doesn't work cheap. Are you sure you can pay for this?"

Chance pulled out a wad of cash rolled with rubber bands. "Will this cover it?"

Hannah nodded, her mouth pursed. "Carlotta said you traffic porn, is that right?"

"That's one of my businesses."

"Cool," she said.

Chance grunted and Wesley wondered if his friend had just come in his pants.

They walked into the tattoo parlor, a converted Victorian house that was rife with dark brocade wallpaper and chandeliers. The female receptionist sat behind a rolltop desk, reading *Prick* magazine. She was bald, with yellow cornrows tattooed onto her head. She looked up and smiled.

"Hi, Hannah."

"Hi, Sela."

"You're here to see Axle?"

"Yeah, I have an appointment." She gestured to Wesley and Chance. "I know these weirdos. They're going to sit in."

"You guys looking to get inked?" the girl asked.

"Uh, maybe," Chance said.

Wesley rolled his eyes. He didn't think so. Chance was a wuss when it came to pain.

"Go ahead," Sela said.

Hannah led the way up a wide wooden stairway, her boots clomping on every step. The landing on the second floor was filled with T-shirts and tattoo lore. As they walked down the hall, Wesley looked around. The rooms retained high ceilings and original moldings, but had been converted into spaces that resembled doctors' examination rooms, with barber chairs and tables for clients to accommodate whatever part of the body was being worked on, and glass cabinets of supplies like antiseptic and gauze.

Inside one room, a tattoo artist was working on a guy's beefy arm. In another, a woman was having her ankle tattooed. About halfway down the hallway, Hannah walked into a room and high-fived a stocky guy she introduced as Axle. Axle wore jeans and a polo-style shirt, and his only visible tattoo was the wraparound black text on his neck. Wesley squinted to read it. *Say something nobody understands and they'll do practically anything you want them to.* He recognized it as a quote from one of his favorite books, *The Catcher in the Rye.*

"Hannah, good to see you," Axle said. "I'm glad you decided to finish your back before the rest of the art faded."

"Tattoos fade?" Wes asked.

Axle nodded. "Over time, and faster if they're exposed to the sun."

"This is Wesley…and his helper," Hannah added in a bored tone. "I told them they could watch."

"Nice to know you," Axle said. "I don't mind an audience if Hannah doesn't. Let's get started." He looked at Wesley. "Will you get the door?"

Wes closed the door and looked around the room at pictures of tattooed individuals, some of them celebrities, obviously clients of Axle's. Axle moved to his tattooing machine, which looked like a mobile vacuum. At the end of a long plastic tube was the needling tool. Chance hovered close to Hannah, who had her back to Wesley. She shrugged out of her black leather vest, then lifted the hem of her tank top and pulled it off, revealing her bare back, partially tattooed.

Chance was standing in front of Hannah and stared openmouthed.

"Whoa," Wesley said, then spun around to face the door. "Uh, no offense, Hannah, but I don't want to see you naked."

"Then you'd better get out, squirt."

He didn't have to be told twice. He slipped out the door and into the hallway, then walked to the room at the end which had once been a living or dining room but was now a waiting room with vending machines and a television. A long coffee table featured thick photo albums of customers in all their tattooed glory. He flipped through the gallery, morbidly fascinated by the people who went to such great lengths to turn their bodies into canvases, billboards and soapboxes. Some of the results were winceworthy, some were comical, and some, stunning.

There were also tattoo-design books that looked like clip art. He flipped to the religious-symbols section of several books and perused pages of cross patterns, but didn't see one that matched the image on the paper in his pocket. Notes printed in the page footers stated the designs were merely suggested images, and that each tattoo artist owned the copyright to the unique designs they tattooed onto a person's body. Which meant he might not be able to match the design from the headless corpse that Coop had recreated unless he stumbled across the exact artist who'd inked the tattoo.

A proverbial needle in a haystack.

A spike-haired guy in skinny black jeans and a T-shirt walked in and fed coins into the soda machine. "Are you being helped?" he asked.

Wesley scratched his temple. "I'm trying to find a guy based on his tattoo."

Spike retrieved his soda and cracked it open. "That could be a bitch. What kind of tat?"

Wesley pulled out the piece of paper with the printed design and unfolded it. "He had it lasered off."

The guy took the paper and squinted. "If you don't know the guy, how did you get a picture of his tat?"

"Um…the guy's a John Doe in a coma."

"So you're working for the hospital?"

"Yeah."

Spike frowned and handed back the paper. "Get a better story, dude."

Wesley sighed and looked around to make sure no one else was within earshot. "Okay, look—you don't want to know the details, trust me. I got two hundred bucks in my wallet. It's yours if you can find out anything."

The guy considered Wesley, then took a sip of his soda. "Is the guy going to come after me?"

"Negatory. He's dead."

Spike nodded. "Three hundred."

"Two hundred now, another two if you get me a name."

"All this for a dead guy? Why do you care?"

Wesley set his jaw. He'd do anything to make the nightmares go away. "Do we have a deal or don't we?"

"Okay. It's your coinage."

Wesley nodded. And his sanity.

23

At the end of her shift, Carlotta waved goodbye to Herb the security guard and called Hannah's number as she left the employee break room. She frowned when she got her friend's voice mail…again. She conceded Hannah could've had a dozen things to do on a Saturday afternoon, but she hoped her friend wasn't ignoring her because she blamed Carlotta for getting her fired from the catering company.

Giving in to another growing concern, she punched in Coop's number. When his phone also rolled over to voice mail, she sighed. Two for two.

Frustration welled in her chest. Wesley and Jack said that Coop was fine, but it bothered her that he hadn't returned any of her calls. On their last body run together, she'd found a pint of vodka under the seat of Coop's van. She hadn't mentioned it to him—or to anyone—hoping that he was the kind of recovering alcoholic who needed to keep temptation within reach to prove to himself that he could resist.

That was the night they had been called to the home of Shawna Whitt, the first-known victim of The Charmed Killer. Coop had been the first to notice the foreign object in the woman's mouth. He had asserted the charm had been placed postmortem, but no one had believed him... until the second victim was discovered.

Carlotta bit her lip. How maddening would it be to possess so much knowledge, but be dismissed due to past mistakes? Is that why Coop had fallen into a funk? When she'd seen him at the memorial service for A.D.A. Cheryl Meriwether, he'd seemed a bit unkempt and withdrawn. Even before that, when she'd sought his help in uncovering a conspiracy against Olympic marathoner Eva McCoy, he'd made a strange comment to her.

No matter what happens to me, no matter what I might do or say, I don't regret a minute I've spent with you.

At the time, she'd pressed him to tell her what was wrong, but he'd sidestepped the question by saying it was nothing she'd done. Only days before that, he had stopped by the town house after midnight to talk to her. He had seemed desperate, but it was the same day the police had learned that Michael Lane had escaped, and Jack had been playing bodyguard in her living room. Coop had acquiesced to her request to spend the night in Wesley's vacant bed, but whatever he'd been on the verge of telling her had gone undisclosed.

On a whim, Carlotta called Moody's Cigar Bar and asked for June, the owner. A few minutes later she came on the line. "Hello?"

"June, hi—it's Carlotta. Have you by chance seen Coop?"

"It must be fate."

Carlotta frowned. "What?"

A sigh sounded over the phone. "I've been wanting to call you for days, but Coop wouldn't let me."

Alarm shot through her. "What do you mean?"

"I mean that Coop is drinking again. Not a lot, but I'm worried. He asked me not to say anything to you and I went along with it because I didn't want him going somewhere else to drink. At least here, I can keep an eye on him."

"Is he there now?"

"Yes, he's upstairs in the lounge. I don't suppose you could stop by and make it look unplanned?"

"I could arrange to meet a friend there."

"Please do. My son Mitchell is here, too, and Eva."

"Eva McCoy?"

June made a happy noise. "That's right. I wish Mitch could extend his leave from the Army—I think something could develop between them."

"Good for them."

"So I'll see you later?"

"I'll try to be there within the hour," Carlotta promised. "If Coop leaves, will you call me?"

"Absolutely."

"Thanks, June."

Carlotta disconnected the call, then pressed her lips together hard. Jack had warned her not to take ownership of Coop's problems, but she felt like a failed friend for not being there at the time Coop might have confided in her.

She called Peter and he answered on the first ring.

"Hey, I was just thinking about you," he said. "What do you want to do tonight?"

Irritation niggled at her that he'd expected they would spend the evening together, but she tamped it down. She was living in his house, after all.

"I'm just leaving work. Want to meet me at Moody's for a drink? We can get dinner afterward if you like."

"Sounds good. Why don't I pick you up. We can put your Vespa in the back of the SUV."

Except she was hoping to talk to Coop before Peter got there. "I have an errand to run near the bar," she lied. "Why don't I meet you there, and we'll ride home together." She winced when she realized she'd used the word *home* to refer to his house.

"Okay," he said happily. "See you in a few."

She closed her phone and waited for a break in foot traffic to step off the sidewalk. Two immaculately dressed women walked by her, deep in conversation.

"The Charmed Killer could be anywhere. I'm scared all the time."

"You should buy a handgun," her companion said. "David bought one for me and I keep it by my bed."

"That's not a bad idea. I wonder if you can buy a gun at the mall?"

Carlotta watched them walk away, acknowledging that fear had truly permeated the city if socialites were talking about packing heat. Valet service at the mall had increased exponentially because people didn't want to walk to their cars alone or with their arms full of packages. And while her car explosion had been reported by police as "an isolated incident," employees and customers who'd heard about it weren't taking chances.

As Carlotta stowed her cell phone in her purse, she touched the comforting heaviness of the stun baton that Jack had given her. Spooked, she hurried to where her scooter was parked, glancing around as she unlocked the storage compartment and removed her helmet. The latest murder, which had almost gone undetected because the victim had swallowed the charm, had been splashed on the front page of this morning's *AJC* in a titillating headline: NUMBER SIX AND COUNTING.

The victim, Wanda Alderman, had been relegated to a number. Worse, Rainie Stephens's headline inferred that there were more deaths to come.

The reporter was probably right.

Carlotta drove the Vespa to Moody's Cigar Bar and pulled in to the crowded parking lot just as the sun was setting. She was relieved to see Coop's vintage white Corvette convertible parked nearby, which meant he was still at the bar.

Moody's Saturday crowd was light on the regular business patrons who came after work for a cigar and a drink, heavy on single guys and couples. She didn't see Coop around the horseshoe-shaped cigar bar on the first floor, so she headed upstairs to the lounge just as June Moody was descending. The owner of the establishment looked striking in a brown pencil skirt and a pale yellow starched dress shirt. She touched Carlotta's arm and pointed upstairs to indicate Coop's whereabouts. Carlotta nodded and continued her ascent to the second floor.

At the top of the stairs and to the right sat the bar, which was packed five people deep. Nathan, the bartender, gave her a wink hello without pausing from drawing a beer. She scanned the area for Coop, but he wasn't seated on any of the bar stools. As her vision adjusted to the low lighting, she recognized Eva McCoy waving to her from the couch where she sat next to Sergeant Mitchell Moody, June's son who was visiting on military leave. He was a big guy, good-looking, with a shaved head and the sharp edge of a career Army man. Eva was a pretty brunette with the slender build of an elite marathoner. She looked vastly different from the woman she'd been only a few days ago, racked with self-doubt and paranoia—rightfully so, as it turned out. But her stalker was now behind bars.

Carlotta walked over with a smile and leaned in close to speak to them over the noise. "Hello. How are the two of you?"

"Good," Eva said, then she and Mitchell shared a smile. His arm was settled possessively around the woman's shoulder.

"Hi, Carlotta," Mitchell offered.

She returned the greeting, telling herself that it was none of her business that Mitchell was being a hypocrite, enjoying the bar while giving his mother a hard time. He deemed owning such an establishment as inappropriate for a proper Southern woman of a certain age. Carlotta itched to tell him he was lucky to have a mother so warm and caring, but she didn't want to get in the middle of someone else's family drama.

Carlotta noticed that Eva's wrist was bare. "You're not wearing your charm bracelet."

Eva touched her arm where she'd worn the infamous bracelet that she'd credited with her Olympic win, and her smile faltered. "With all the publicity surrounding The Charmed Killer, I thought it was inappropriate."

"I told her I'd protect her," Mitchell said, giving her a squeeze.

"Still," Eva said, looking uncomfortable.

Carlotta nodded, then caught sight of Coop across the room. "Excuse me, there's someone I need to talk to."

She made her way through the crush of bodies toward Coop, her heart in her throat. He was sprawled in an oversize chair, a cigar in one hand and a drink in the other.

Dressed in holey jeans and a T-shirt, he looked relaxed with his long sideburns and his tousled hair. He wasn't wearing his glasses, which might have accounted for the reason he squinted when she walked up to him.

"Hi, Coop."

He straightened slightly. "Hi, Carlotta."

"I left you a few messages, but I haven't heard back from you."

"I've been busy," he said, then punctuated his sentence by taking a drink. She could tell from the burning scent of alcohol that there was more in his glass than tonic. And she could tell from the slight slur in his voice that it wasn't his first drink.

Her stomach clenched. "Are you sure you want to do this, Coop?"

A blonde wearing a minidress brushed past Carlotta, then settled into the chair beside Coop, draping one long leg over one of his.

He smiled at the heavy-lidded woman, lifted the cigar for a puff, then exhaled slowly as he looked up to Carlotta. "Oh, yeah. I'm sure."

The blonde twisted and kissed him hard on the mouth, and Coop didn't object.

Carlotta inhaled sharply against the pain that stabbed through her chest. Myriad emotions slammed into her, sending her stumbling backward. She caught herself, then turned on her heel and walked blindly across the room. A hand reached out to grab her and she cried out.

"Hey, it's me," Peter murmured.

She looked up and registered Peter staring down at her with concern.

"Are you okay?" he asked.

"I'm fine," she managed to say, then relaxed. "You startled me, that's all." She gently disengaged her arm from his grasp.

He lowered a quick kiss next to her ear. "Sorry. Have you ordered a drink?"

"No, not yet."

"What can I get for you?"

She said the first thing that came to mind. "A Cosmo."

"Coming up."

Carlotta touched her forehead. "Peter, I'm going to the ladies' room. I'll be right back."

"Okay, I'll meet you here."

She turned and walked into a rear hallway that led to the restrooms. The ladies' room consisted of two generous floor-to-ceiling stalls and a mirrored vanity befitting any movie star from the Hollywood glam era. The bathroom was empty, so she went into a stall and locked the sliding bolt. The toilets were dark pink, sitting atop one-inch black-and-white tiles. The wooden stalls were lacquered white with geometric moldings and louvered doors. Carlotta lowered the commode lid and sat, trying to gather her wits. She pulled out a cigarette and lit it, then took a deep drag and exhaled.

It was none of her business what Coop did and who he did it with... She'd had her chance with Coop and had allowed it to slip away so she could be with Peter. It was just jarring to see Coop in a state that was natural for other men—drinking and womanizing. With a start, she realized maybe it *had* been a natural state for Coop before she'd known him. She pulled on the cigarette and analyzed her reaction, trying to sort through what bothered her the most—seeing Coop with a drink in his hand, or seeing his hands full of another woman.

Carlotta couldn't decide.

The outer door opened, ushering in noises from the lounge. Footsteps sounded on the floor, then the woman went into the other stall and closed the door. Carlotta took another deep drag on the cigarette, thinking she should hurry, that Peter would be waiting for her.

But the cigarette tasted so good, she couldn't bear to waste any of it. She inhaled deeply and exhaled luxuriously until the cigarette was spent down to the filter. She stood and opened the toilet lid to drop in the butt, then suddenly realized that the woman in the stall next to her hadn't made a sound.

"Are you all right over there?" she called.

There was no response. Carlotta frowned, then strained to hear if the person was talking on their cell phone. Silence buzzed. A finger of alarm tickled her spine. "Hello?" she tried again. "Are you all right?"

Now that her cigarette had been extinguished, a magnificent scent reached her nose, a complicated blend of spices and fruits, plus sandalwood and other aromas she couldn't identify. Even though she felt sure she'd smelled the combination somewhere before, she couldn't place the scent. But it meant the woman was still there.

"Ma'am? Are you ill? Do you need help?"

The other stall door opened and footsteps sounded. But strangely, it seemed as if the woman had stopped just outside Carlotta's stall. She could see the person's shadow through the louvered door.

Fear swirled in her stomach. Something wasn't right. Carlotta stood stock-still, eyeing the flimsy lock on the door. Her pulse thudded in her ears. She scrambled for her purse and dug for the stun baton.

Then the footsteps sounded again and the outer door opened and closed.

Carlotta went limp with relief, chiding herself for manufacturing danger where none existed. She emerged from her stall. The rich scent of the wonderful cologne lingered in the air. She slowly washed her hands at the art deco-style vanity, hesitant to go back out there, but she'd already kept Peter waiting long enough. Trying to ignore the knot in her stomach, she touched up her lipstick, then exited to the hallway and walked back to the lounge.

Peter was waiting for her, holding their drinks. He gave her a brilliant smile that she returned. Affection rushed her chest. Since coming back into her life, Peter had been a constant, even though she hadn't given him much encouragement.

A quick peek across the room revealed that Coop—and the blonde—were gone. At least she didn't have to watch them neck. But it left her wondering if Coop had taken the woman back to his place…if the other woman had gotten the full tour of his place—bedroom included—that Carlotta hadn't received. She pushed the thought from her mind and turned her attention back to Peter. She asked about his day and once again she wondered if she should tell the GBI about the connection he'd uncovered between Alicia Sills and her father.

She concluded that Monday morning was early enough to decide, and ordered another drink. Later, as she and Peter left the bar, she scanned the room for Eva McCoy and Mitchell Moody, but she didn't see them. She hoped that June and her son made peace with each other before the man left town. And she hoped that Eva didn't get her heart broken again.

Dinner was a lush affair at a small restaurant. Peter seemed to sense that she had a lot on her mind and carried the load of the conversation, bless him. She found herself warming more and more toward him, imagining the life she would have with him, how it would be, should be, an easy decision to attach herself to Peter. A relationship with Jack was a misnomer. And as for Coop, he was wrestling with internal demons.

Peter was the natural choice.

He smiled and reached across the table to squeeze her hand. "I'm getting used to having you around."

She squeezed back. "Me, too."

When they got back to his house, the cat greeted them at the door, meowing insistently and climbing Peter's leg until he picked her up.

"Still no word from her owner?"

"No," she said. "We might have to start thinking about a backup plan."

The cat yowled at her. Carlotta drew back and narrowed her eyes. If she didn't know better, she'd swear the cat could understand what they were saying.

Peter frowned, stroking the cat's head. "Like a pet shelter?"

She shrugged. "Unless you want to keep her."

"Let's give the flyers a few more days," he said, then set the cat back on her feet. The Persian complained, winding around his legs as he loosened his tie and sorted through the mail on the kitchen counter.

Carlotta refilled the cat's water dish, frowning at the uneaten cat food. The finicky feline turned up its nose at anything other than sardines or freshly cooked fish.

"Do you have to work tomorrow?" Peter asked, setting aside the mail.

"No."

"It's supposed to be nice. How about if we relax by the pool?"

She nodded. "I'd like that."

He stretched, yawning. "I'm going to turn in. How about you?"

The cat bounded to the stairs again, as if she had understood him. Carlotta stared after her, then murmured, "I think I will, too. It's been a long day."

They climbed the stairs amiably, Peter's presence next to her warm and comforting. At the top of the stairs he gave her a lingering kiss, then thumbed her cheek, his eyes full of hunger. "Sleep tight."

Her heart was beating hard, her body aching to be touched. When he turned away from her, she sensed his hesitation. His hope that she would offer to sleep in his bed was palpable. Carlotta opened her mouth to call him back…but something made her stop. If she made love with Peter, the repercussions would be far-reaching, the implications difficult to unravel.

In the wake of her silence, Peter continued to his room, practically tripping over the cat that was underfoot. When he opened the door to his bedroom, the feline darted inside. Peter gave Carlotta one last look before closing the door behind him.

Racked with uncertainty, Carlotta retired to the room where she was sure Peter's former wife had sought solace. After getting ready for bed, she reached for the diaries she'd brought with her. Her hand touched her father's file, but she couldn't bear to open it, not until The Charmed Killer was captured.

She turned to the passages in the diaries describing how her romance with Peter had flowered. After months of petting in the backseat of his car that had left both of them dazed with yearning, she had given her virginity to Peter.

Making love with Peter was better than my girl-friends said it would be, better than the magazines described. Having him inside me was incredible—it was as if we were one person. I thought I would die from loving him so much. He was gentle and kept asking me if it felt good. When I came, so did he, and we made all these wonderful noises together. After-ward, we lay in each other's arms, and for the first time I felt like a woman, loving her man.

Carlotta smiled a bittersweet smile at the naive but heartfelt entry. It had been a magical time of sensual ex-ploration, a time that had cemented their love for each other.

At least for her.

After Peter had dumped her, years had passed before she'd slept with another man, partly because she was consumed with raising her young brother, and partly because she wouldn't allow herself to trust anyone else. Eventually nature had won out, but sex had never been the same…

Until Jack.

She frowned. If Jack knew that little tidbit, his head would blow up as big as a Macy's Thanksgiving Day parade balloon. Besides, sex with Jack was purely physical. Sex with Peter would be…meaningful.

In a moment of clarity, she conceded that she'd kept Peter at arm's length since their reunion partly because she enjoyed the power. There was something very satisfying about being pursued by the person who had so abruptly and so publicly cast her aside. Making love with Peter would mean she'd forgiven him for what he'd done to her, and their relationship would change… into what?

One thing was certain—she would never know unless she took a chance.

Carlotta pressed the diaries to her chest and resolved in her heart to take her relationship with Peter to the next level. It was time. Just making the decision seemed to calm a place deep inside her.

She closed her eyes and inhaled the scent of fresh-cut suburban grass, with undertones of organic pesticides and fertilizer, wafting through the screens of the open veranda windows. Now, *there* was a scent to be bottled…

Carlotta's eyes flew open. She suddenly remembered where she'd smelled the scent from the ladies' restroom at Moody's Cigar Bar. It was at Neiman's, at a private testing session for Clive Christian colognes, the most expensive ones in the world. And she remembered well her coworker who had coveted a tiny bottle of No.1 Pure at twenty-four hundred dollars a pop.

Michael Lane.

Her heart thumped against her breastbone at the implication that it might have been Michael who'd followed her into the women's restroom and stood next to her in a stall. Had he meant to harm her, then changed his mind?

Carlotta picked up her cell phone and punched in Jack's number with a shaky hand. He answered on the second ring, but sounded groggy. "Did I wake you?" she asked.

"Just dreaming of you, darlin'. Since you're calling at this hour, I take it Ashford hasn't ventured across the hallway yet."

Carlotta rolled her eyes. "Jack, shut up and listen. I think Michael has been shopping."

24

Wesley unzipped his backpack and a toothless head stared back, mocking him. He dropped the backpack and fell backward, jarring himself awake.

When light bounced off his retinas, pain exploded in his head. Damn, the more he tried to stay away from the Oxy, the worse the headaches got. He pushed himself up from the bed in Chance's guest room, holding both temples. The pain was almost unbearable. He felt for his backpack and rummaged frantically for the small bag of Oxy he had left. When his fingers closed around it, he popped a pill in his mouth and chewed until the crashing in his head stopped.

Sighing in relief, he stepped into the small private shower adjacent to his room and stood under the cool water until he felt more like himself. When he turned off the tap, he could hear bells pealing in the distance.

He wondered briefly if Meg was sitting in church this morning like a good little girl. He still hadn't decided what to do about the fact that her father had hired someone to follow him, but he was forming a plan. On the table next to his bed was a bulletin announcing a lecture this afternoon at Piedmont Hospital by Dr. Harold Vincent, noted geneticist, on the subject of cancer stem-cell gene therapy.

The lecture was open only to physicians and invited guests, but that didn't bother Wesley. Thanks to a digital camera, Photoshop software, a color laser printer and the lamination machine at OfficeMax, he'd fashioned a pretty convincing lanyard identifying him as Wesley Wren, M.D. It was kind of a kick.

He slung his backpack over his shoulder, then walked out into the living room and stopped. The fact that Chance was up before noon on a Sunday was enough to give him pause, but his buddy was standing at the kitchen stove wearing nothing but an apron that left his white ass hanging out. He was whistling under his breath as he used a spatula to move sizzling sausage patties around in a skillet.

Chance looked up to see Wesley and waved the spatula. "Mornin', dude. Where are you going all dressed up?"

Wesley looked down at his chinos, short-sleeve collared shirt, and hard-sole shoes. "Uh…to church."

Chance nodded. "Jesus is cool. Want some breakfast?"

"Since when do you cook?"

"Since I woke up fucking starving."

Wes was still marveling over the fact that his buddy knew how to turn on the stove, when Chance's bedroom door opened and Hannah emerged wearing Chance's All This and a Big Dick, Too T-shirt. And from the looks of it, nothing else. The funny thing was that the shirt was more believable on her than on his friend.

"Mornin', shithead," she said to Wesley, then she smacked Chance on his bare ass, leaving a red handprint. "Mornin,' you."

Chance gave her an adoring look, then blushed.

Blushed, for crying out loud.

"You're going to catch a fly if you don't close your mouth," Hannah said to Wesley. "Haven't you ever seen a man frying sausage?"

"Not that man," Wesley said. "How's the tattoo?"

"Still tender," she said, rolling her shoulders.

"But it's so damn beautiful," Chance offered.

Wesley thought his friend wiped the corner of his eye. "O-kay," Wes said, "I'm outta here."

He exited the condo and tried to squash the image of his friend riding Hannah. Of course, the more likely scenario was that she'd ridden Chance…with spurs on.

Wes's phone rang and he reached for it, happy for the distraction. It was a local number he didn't recognize. "Hello?"

"Wesley, right?"

"Yeah, who's this?"

"Bernard from Inkwell. I got the name of the guy who had his tat lasered off."

Wesley blinked. "That was quick."

"Made a few calls to tattoo-removal places I make referrals to, and I got lucky."

"What's the name?"

"Where's my cash?"

Wesley sighed. "Are you at the tattoo parlor?"

"Yeah."

"I'll be there in thirty minutes."

He disconnected the call, then unlocked his bike and took off toward Inkwell. His reflexes were a little slow though, and his mind was elsewhere. Once, he came close to being clipped by a car because he swerved out of the bike lane. He cursed and pulled over until his heart slowed, then gave himself a shake to regain focus. His inner voice whispered that maybe his baby habit was morphing into something more serious, but he refused to listen.

He climbed back on his bike and pedaled to the tattoo parlor. Spike, aka Bernard, was in the parking lot taking a smoke. He dropped the cigarette and stubbed it out with the toe of his boot as Wesley wheeled up.

"You got my cash?" the guy said.

"Give me the name," Wesley said.

Bernard dug in his pocket and removed a slip of paper.

Wesley took the scrap and scanned the words written in skinny print. *Crosby Newell or maybe Croswell Newton. Newt Crossen?* He looked up. "What the hell is this?"

"Hey, I was lucky to get a name at all. This laser tech normally does things off the books, ya know what I mean? But he remembers this guy's tat. Guess they had a conversation or something. Said the guy was a bear."

"A bear?"

"Fat. And he paid in cash."

Fat and shady—it sounded like the kind of guy who'd do business with The Carver. And it was more information than Wesley had to go on before. He pulled out his wallet and peeled off two hundreds. "Okay, thanks, man. Later."

Bernard pointed to the angry scars on Wesley's arm that his short-sleeve shirt revealed. "Come back when your scars fade some. I can camouflage them with a radical tat."

Wesley looked down at the crude C-A-R that had been sliced into his skin. "I'll think about it."

He took his time pedaling to Piedmont Hospital, nursing what was left of his buzz and hoping it lasted through the lecture. He locked his bike in front of the hospital's fitness center that was across the road from the main building. He waited until a member approached the door, then he slung his backpack to his shoulder and casually followed the man inside, bypassing the card reader.

Once inside the fitness center, he headed toward the men's locker room. Several men, chatting while they buttoned shirts and donned jackets, were easily identifiable as physicians who took advantage of the state-of-the-art facility. Wesley tried to blend in as he opened an empty locker and deposited his backpack inside.

When he unzipped the backpack, he half expected to find a toothless head inside. Instead, he removed a clean folded lab coat that he'd acquired as a prop for collecting with Mouse, and shrugged into it. Then he removed the lanyard he'd made and hung it on his neck so that his picture and name faced his shirt. No use broadcasting unless someone asked to see his ID. With the hospital name on the back, the lanyard looked legit.

He placed his combination lock on the locker, then walked out of the fitness center and joined a group of lab-coated doctors who were crossing the street to the main hospital. He mimicked their posture and stride, and somewhere between one side of Piedmont Street and the other, he actually began to feel like a doctor. He had a slight build, but his height and his glasses made him look older. Besides, what was the quote on the tattoo artist's neck?

Say something nobody understands and they'll do practically anything you want them to. Meaning, it was possible to bluff your way through life.

Inside the hospital, his chest swelled with confidence as people gave him admiring glances, stepped out of his way or opened doors for him. They really thought he was a doctor, all because of a lousy lab coat. If he bought a stethoscope on eBay, he could probably talk his way onto the E.R. staff.

He stopped to consult a hospital directory and took the elevator to the floor with the meeting rooms and lecture hall. On the way up, a tall salt-and-pepper-haired man nodded to him. "Are you headed to the gene-therapy session, son?" he asked in a booming voice.

Wesley's back stiffened. He hated it when older men called him "son," as if they were a father figure to him. But he squashed his anger, reminding himself of his reason for coming. The key to getting into secure areas is to act as if you belong there. He pushed up his glasses. "Yes, sir, as a matter of fact, I am."

"Me, too," the guy boomed. "See you in there, son."

Wesley gritted his teeth and let the man stride off the elevator ahead of him, not wanting to attract any seat companions who might want to talk medicine. Following signs displayed on easels, he fell in with a group of doctors who were heading toward the auditorium. At the check-in table, attendees simply picked up their printed name tags and waved them in front of the accommodating registrar. Wesley followed suit and nabbed the name tag of Wilson Wendt, Pharm D If he was questioned, it would be easy to say he picked up the wrong one by mistake.

He clipped the name tag onto the collar of his white lab coat, then entered the lecture hall and took a seat in the rear next to nobody. As the hall filled with doctor types, Wesley studied them, exchanging waves and shaking hands—the brotherhood of the elite. Something akin to envy washed over him. Their heads were full of knowledge that could heal people…stuff that could change the world. Things might've been different for him if he was the college type, but he couldn't picture himself sitting in class, pledging a fraternity, tailgating at football games.

The front of the hall filled first, probably because over-achievers liked to sit up front. He'd hoped to sit alone, but a dark-haired man dropped into the seat next to him and nodded hello.

The man looked familiar and Wesley panicked, trying to jog his memory. The Oxy was working on him. His brain chugged along as if it were underwater. He glanced at the guy's name tag: Frederick Lowenstein, OB/GYN. It didn't ring a bell, although he was sure he knew the man's face. Wesley stared straight ahead, but he felt the guy studying *him.*

Crap.

"I'm sorry, have we met?" Lowenstein asked.

Wesley glanced at him for a split second, then shook his head.

"You look familiar to me," the man insisted, then leaned forward to look at Wesley's name tag. "Dr. Wendt." He stuck out his hand. "Freddy Lowenstein. Are you from Atlanta?"

"Uh…no," he said in his best Germanish accent. "Vis-i-tor."

"Ah, I see. *Velcome,*" Lowenstein said, then chuckled at his cleverness.

What an asshole. Suddenly Wesley had a flash of seeing the man holding a glass of wine and a cracker of caviar…

Screen on the Green, he realized. The man and his wife— Tracey Tully, the daughter of one of his father's former partners—had been sharing Carlotta and Peter's blanket when Wesley had come to get Carlotta for a body-moving job.

From the stories Carlotta had told him about Tracey, the woman would be delighted to catch him impersonating a doctor.

Which, now that he thought about it, was a federal offense.

Sweat trickled down his temple, but he brushed it away, estimating the distance from his seat to the door in case he had to make a run for it.

A bookish man came onto the stage and introduced himself as some sort of administrator of the hospital, then introduced Dr. Vincent. The speaker's professional credentials in research and clinical trials were long and impressive. At the end of the introduction, a man from the front row stood and walked up the steps on the side of the stage to the podium to enthusiastic applause.

Wesley's mouth went dry. It was the salt-and-pepper-haired guy from the elevator. Anger whipped through him. Harold Vincent was having him followed like he was some kind of lowlife, but had been downright chatty when he'd thought Wesley was a doctor. He'd even called him "son." Wesley's hand tightened on the armrest.

The lights lowered and Dr. Vincent led the audience through a slide show. Wesley had to force himself to concentrate and was sweating profusely. He conceded that the presentation had its merits—parts of it were fascinating. And even though some of the terminology was over his head, he followed the gist of identifying tissue-specific cancer stem cells as the targets for therapy. By honing in on the cancerous cells, fewer healthy cells would be sacrificed in the treatment, meaning treatments ultimately would be not only more effective, but the patient would also suffer fewer side effects throughout the healing process.

"What we're talking about here," Dr. Vincent said, "is creating patient-specific cancer treatments—designer oncology, if you will. Hopefully, some of the new devices my research team is developing, devices that are being tested right here at Piedmont Hospital, will streamline the cell-targeting processes to the point that these couture treatments will be affordable for anyone who needs them."

The lights came up and applause filled the auditorium. Wesley glanced around at the respect and admiration on the faces of the attendees. Sweat trickled down his back and his left eye was twitching. But even plummeting from his Oxy high, Wesley recognized this as a watershed moment for him. At the end of Dr. Vincent's life, much would be said and written about his mark on the world.

At the end of Wesley Wren's life…would anyone even know he'd existed?

Wesley pushed to his feet and sidled past Lowenstein.

"Nice to meet you," Freddy said.

"Dankeshein," he muttered, effectively exhausting his German vocabulary.

Wesley left the auditorium feeling antsy and frustrated, but he managed to smile at all the people who looked at him with reverence. It was a heady feeling to be treated as a physician. He rode to the first floor, lifted a pair of thin latex gloves from a cart, put them on and walked up to a sign-in desk.

"Excuse me."

A woman turned his way. "Yes, Doctor, what can I do for you?"

"Uh…I was wondering if I could get an envelope with the hospital's return address?"

"Certainly, Doctor. Here's a self-sealing envelope. Do you need a stamp?"

"Uh…sure. And a pen?" He took the items she handed to him and thanked her, chalking up another one to the power of the magic lab coat. He walked away from the desk, then reached into his pocket and withdrew the scrap of paper listing the potential names of the man who'd had his tattoo lasered off.

Wesley turned over the paper and wrote "Decapitated man in county morgue," purposely altering his handwriting. Then he stuck the piece of paper into the envelope, sealed it and addressed it to Atlanta Police Department, Homicide, Atlanta, Georgia. When he exited the hospital, he stopped at a blue mailbox and hesitated, trying to think if there was any way the envelope could be traced back to him. His mind chugged along, turning over all the pieces, but he couldn't think of one.

He dropped the envelope into the mailbox, and instantly felt relieved. Coop was right—no matter who the guy was, his family had a right to know what had happened to him. He would want someone to do the same for him if the tables were turned.

He turned around to head back to the fitness center across the street, but came up short. As if he'd conjured up Coop, the man himself was striding toward the front entrance, wearing holey jeans, T-shirt and tennis shoes. Wesley turned his back until Coop had passed, then he frowned after his boss.

If Coop was at the hospital for a body pickup, he

wouldn't come through the front door. And he wouldn't have dressed so casually.

Curious, Wesley backtracked into the hospital lobby in time to see a flash of Coop's T-shirt as he got on the elevator servicing floors one through nine. When the elevator doors closed, Wesley watched the numbers light up to see where it stopped—on floors three, eight and nine.

Wesley got his own elevator and a few minutes later, stopped on the third floor. He asked a security guard if he'd seen a man matching Coop's description, and the man shook his head. Wesley got back onto the elevator and rode to floor eight. After hearing Wes's description of Coop, the security guard on that floor pointed down a hallway. Wesley explored carefully, peeking through the glass and frosted-glass doors into the waiting rooms of individual doctors. He relaxed some, thinking that Coop might be getting his eyes checked, or having a routine physical. In fact, when he spotted his boss sitting in one such waiting room, reading a magazine, Wesley exhaled in relief…until he glanced at the practice specialty lettered on the door.

Department of Neurological Disorders and Diseases.

Wesley's throat convulsed as he remembered all the validated parking receipts for Piedmont Hospital that he'd spotted in Coop's van. Carlotta had been worried about Coop, had said he was acting strange and was convinced something was wrong, something he wouldn't share. Carlotta was right.

Coop was sick.

25

Carlotta sighed, wondering what all the poor people were doing while she floated on a chaise lounge in an aqua-marine pool on a perfect sunny day sipping a frozen pink drink.

With a little umbrella and everything.

"What are you thinking about?"

Carlotta lifted her head and shielded her eyes from the late-afternoon sun to watch Peter swim up. He stopped to hang on to the edge of the chaise, grinning up at her.

Her breath caught in her chest. With his hair slicked back from his face, his skin glowing with sun and health, and his dark blue eyes dancing, he was the handsome teenager she'd fallen in love with. A pang of desire struck low in her abdomen.

"I...I was thinking about you," she said. "About us, actually."

He looked surprised. "Is that good?"

"I think so," she murmured, reaching out to stroke his tanned forearm. Since her decision last night to take their relationship to the next level, she'd thought of little else.

From the patio came a yowling sound, the cat express-ing her displeasure at being ignored. The Persian slunk around the pool, eyeing her and Peter warily, but staying well away from the edge.

"Your girlfriend is jealous," Carlotta teased, nodding at the cat.

He shook his head. "I have no idea why that cat has taken to me. I've never liked cats."

"Then you'd better hope that someone claims her."

"I noticed this morning when I went out to get bagels that the flyers are still up."

"Maybe her owner is on vacation," Carlotta mused. "Or got tired of buying salmon and sardines to feed her."

Peter laughed. "One thing's for sure, the cat's not sleeping in my room anymore. I couldn't keep her out of my bed and I got no sleep last night."

At the mention of his bed, their gazes locked and her thighs tingled.

"You don't like having your sleep disturbed?" she asked.

"I don't mind losing sleep," he said with a sexy smile, "as long as it's for a good reason."

Her breasts tightened. "I agree."

Hope sparked in his eyes. Knowing that he wanted her so badly was a powerful aphrodisiac.

"Peter, I appreciate you giving me time and space to sort things out in my head."

He reached up to curl his warm hand around her leg. "I know I hurt you, Carly. The least I can do is let you set the pace for where our relationship might go from here." He wet his lips. "But I have to admit that having you here and keeping my distance has taken a lot of willpower...and a lot of cold showers."

She laughed, her body responding to his touch. And to

his devotion. And to both of them being half-naked in the sun.

In that moment, being with Peter seemed so right.

Carlotta leaned over to kiss him, a slow exploratory kiss full of apologies and possibilities. He pulled her off the chaise into the water with him, sliding her against his lean, muscled body. The frozen drink was forgotten, spilling into the water as hands were freed for roaming.

She ran her fingers over his shoulder blades and down his spine. He slid his hands down to her rear and pulled her sex against the bulge in his trunks, all while kicking to keep them afloat. He groaned into her mouth and deepened the kiss, his desire for her obvious in every fevered movement. But she didn't want their reunion sex to be in the pool, especially when Sissy Talmadge might have her binoculars trained on them this very moment.

Carlotta lifted her head. "Let's go inside."

He didn't argue, just used one hand to swim them to the ladder. She climbed out, feeling sexy and uninhibited as water sluiced off her turquoise bikini. Peter pushed himself up on the pool ledge and climbed out next to her. He grabbed her hand and pulled her toward the sliding glass door leading to the house.

"But we're dripping," she protested. "We'll get water everywhere."

"Who cares?" he said, pulling her along.

She laughed and gave in to his enthusiasm. They hurried into the house, through the great room, then up the stairs to his bedroom. Peter flung the doors open, then practically launched them onto his bed.

Happy their first time together again would be fun and spontaneous, Carlotta wrapped her arms around his neck and kissed him hard, pulling him on top of her. His body was more muscular than it had been when he was young, more mature, the mat of light hair on his chest thicker. But she knew this body and this body knew hers.

He broke the kiss to nuzzle her neck and untie the string holding up her bikini top. When her breasts fell into his hands, his eyes grew hooded and he sighed against her skin. "You're so beautiful, Carly. I've never wanted a woman the way I've always wanted you."

He licked circles around her stiff nipples, then suckled her, sending shards of pleasure coursing through her body. She urged him on, arching into his mouth. He was like a starved man, making little hungry noises as he slid his hands into her bikini bottoms and pushed them down over her wet legs. She lifted her hips to help him while rolling his trunks down to free his powerful erection.

His urgency to be with her seemed to border on desperation. She felt the same way, impatient to right a wrong, keen for things to return to the way they'd been before all the ugliness in her life had unfolded. Peter was the first man she'd ever loved. This was how things should've been…how things should be.

Carlotta reached down to grasp his thick cock, eager to have him inside her. Suddenly Peter's eyes flew open and he stiffened, emitting a strangled little cry. Mortification bled over his face, then he looked away.

"What's wrong?" Carlotta said, then became aware of a sticky wetness on her stomach. She looked down to see a pool of white liquid, and realized what had happened. "Peter…it's okay," she rushed to reassure him.

He rolled over on his back, a stricken expression on his

face. "No, it's not okay. I wanted things to be perfect, not…
premature. I'm so sorry."

Her mind raced, trying to remember if this kind of thing
had ever happened when they were younger, but she didn't
think so. "Peter, it's probably just nerves. I understand.
Don't worry about it."

He was quiet, his arm over his eyes.

She stroked his chest. "We have plenty of time to get
back in sync."

Finally he looked over at her and released an an-
guished sigh. "I suppose you're right." Then a little smile
curved his mouth. "Meanwhile, there's some unfinished
business."

He reached for a box of tissues to mop up her stomach,
then he shifted lower on the bed and kissed her thighs. She
sighed and undulated toward his mouth. He crawled
between her legs and lowered his head to her sex. When his
tongue stroked her core, she remembered in an instant the
way he used to play her body like an instrument. Honeyed
pleasure flowed over her, weakening her limbs. She cried
out and sank her hands into his hair. This was paradise.

Meow.

Her eyes flew open just as Peter's head came up. The
Persian had jumped onto his back and was staring at
Carlotta over his shoulder.

Carlotta frowned and tried to cover herself, even though
she knew her reaction was ridiculous. It wasn't as if the
cat knew what was happening, or what she was looking
at. "How did she get in here?"

Peter made a frustrated noise, then reached around to
grasp the cat while he moved off the bed. "I must've left
the door open."

He carried the squirming feline to the hall and set her down, but she darted back into the bedroom before he could close the door. Carlotta sighed and laid her head back on the pillow while a melee ensued. The cat led Peter on a merry chase around the room while Carlotta's frustration mounted and her libido ebbed. After several minutes, Peter finally nabbed the Persian, deposited her in the hallway and successfully shut her out of the bedroom.

He turned back to the bed with an apologetic smile. "Now…where was I? Oh, I remember," he said, crawling on the bed between her knees. He licked his way back to the nest of wet, dark curls between her thighs.

She closed her eyes in an effort to recapture the earlier passion, concentrating on the delicious trail of his tongue up and down her folds.

Frantic scratching sounded at the bedroom door. *Meow, meow, meow.*

"Ignore her," he murmured against her intimate parts. "She'll go away."

But the cat was persistent, its protests growing louder and louder, the scratching more frenzied. The more Carlotta tried to tune it out, the more distracted she became.

"Enough," Carlotta said, sitting up.

Peter lifted his head. "You don't like?"

She sighed. "I love what you're doing. But fate is conspiring against us. Why don't we take a break and regroup later."

Outside the door, the cat emitted a long mournful howl that sounded as if something large and heavy was sitting on its tail.

"After we drown the cat," Carlotta added wryly.

Peter laughed, then pulled his hand down his face. "So much for best-laid plans. Who knew a cat could be so loud. Do you think she's hungry?"

"Something like that," Carlotta agreed, although she really believed the cat couldn't bear to be away from Peter. "Why don't you feed her? I think I'll take a shower."

"Okay. I'll get out the chops and start dinner." He pulled a pair of boxers and shorts from his bureau. After he dressed, he leaned over to kiss her, then gave her a bittersweet smile. "Promise me we'll try this again."

She smiled. "I promise."

But after he left the room, Carlotta pressed her lips together. That emotion plucking at her, just behind the frustration tightening her chest… It couldn't be relief, could it?

She pushed to her feet, retrieved her wet bikini and smoothed the bedspread. She crossed the hall to her own bedroom, noting the cat had followed Peter downstairs. Carlotta turned on the shower and the stereo. Susan Tedeschi was singing "Alone," and Carlotta knew the words by heart. While she waited for the water to warm, she pulled on a robe and checked her cell phone for messages.

Carlotta frowned—Wesley had called twice and left messages for her to call him.

She punched in his number, wondering if The Charmed Killer had struck again. Wesley answered on the first ring. "Hi, sis."

"Hi. I got your messages to call. What's up?"

"Uh…are you alone?"

"Yes. Why do you ask?"

"Because I've got some news about Coop and I think it might be best if you hear it in private."

Her heart began to thud. "What about Coop?"

Wesley told her about the validated parking receipts from Piedmont Hospital he'd seen in Coop's van, and about seeing Coop yesterday at the hospital.

"What were you doing at the hospital?" she interjected.

"Visiting a friend," he said vaguely. "The point is, Coop didn't see me. I was curious, so I followed him to the office of a neurologist."

She frowned. "Doesn't a neurologist treat spinal cord problems?"

"And brain tumors."

Carlotta reached for the bed and sat down. "Are you saying that Coop has a brain tumor?"

"I don't know what he has, but it makes sense. You were the one who said he was acting strange, not like himself. A tumor would certainly cause a change in personality. And it would explain why he's drinking again."

Trying to process the horrific possibilities, Carlotta massaged her temple. "How do you know that Coop is drinking?"

"Because I smelled it on his breath the other day in the morgue lab. If he's terminal, maybe he figures he might as well drink. Or maybe he's drinking to deal with the pain."

Carlotta grimaced, her eyes filling with tears. Was that the reason Coop had stopped by her house the night Jack had been guarding her? He'd been on the verge of telling her something—that he was dying?

"Sis, are you there?"

She sniffled. "I'm here."

"I knew you'd be upset, but I thought you should know."

"I'm glad you told me," she said, then took a deep

breath. "But we shouldn't jump to conclusions. There might be a perfectly logical reason for Coop to be seeing a neurologist."

But it was evident in the resounding silence that followed that neither of them could think of one.

"Are you going to call him?" Wesley asked.

"I don't believe he'd welcome a call from me right now," she said, thinking of their encounter last night at Moody's.

"Maybe you should go see him."

"I'll think about it," she promised. "And I'll let you know if I talk to him."

"Okay, meanwhile, I won't say anything to him about it."

"I think that's best for now." She sighed. "How's everything else going?"

"Fine. I'm going back to finish installing the security system at the town house later this week."

"Sounds good. How's Meg?" she teased.

"I wouldn't know," he chirped.

Carlotta smiled. Something was afoot, otherwise the mere mention of the girl's name wouldn't push Wesley's buttons. "Have you seen Hannah?"

"Uh…no. What makes you think I would've seen Hannah?"

She frowned at the strange tone in his voice. "Wesley, are you lying? Is Hannah avoiding me?"

"Why would she be avoiding you?" he squeaked. "I gotta go. Call you later."

When dead air sounded, Carlotta disconnected the phone slowly. Something was definitely up with Hannah, but her friend's moodiness paled in comparison to what Coop might be facing.

At the thought of Coop being seriously ill, grief engulfed Carlotta, squeezing the air out of her lungs. The thought of him suffering…of not being in their lives—in her life—was unbearable. She ached to reach out to him, but she knew he wouldn't want her sympathy.

She wrapped her arms around her middle and tucked into herself, rocking. The overwhelming pain was savagely familiar, reminiscent of the helplessness she'd felt when her parents had abandoned her.

A knock on the door sounded. She wiped at her eyes hastily and straightened. "Come in."

Peter stuck his head inside. "How about risotto with our pork chops?" Then he frowned. "Are you okay?"

She touched her forehead. "A sudden migraine. I'm sorry, Peter. Is it okay if I skip dinner?"

He nodded, but from his disappointed expression she knew he realized that skipping dinner also meant skipping sex. "Get some rest," he said. "I won't bother you."

When the door closed, guilt swamped her. Peter didn't deserve her waffling. But she couldn't ignore how the thought of losing Coop had affected her. She needed more time to think.

Miserable and confused, Carlotta pushed to her feet and headed toward the shower for a good cry.

26

Hope you are feeling better. Love, Peter

Carlotta ran her finger over the note he'd left for her on the kitchen counter. Unfortunately, she wasn't feeling better. After a night of tossing and turning over what might be wrong with Coop, she had, as her mother used to say, "worked herself into a state." Add to that the fact that Hannah wasn't returning her calls, Michael Lane was still missing and she was still wrestling with whether or not to let the police know that her father might've had a romantic relationship with one of the victims of The Charmed Killer. She'd come to the conclusion that she might never sleep again.

Still wearing cotton pajamas and house shoes, she stretched, yawning.

Peter's concern only made her feel worse because while he'd offered her nothing but love and support, all the things weighing on her mind were a wedge between her heart and Peter's.

She winced every time she thought about their sabotaged attempt at lovemaking yesterday. The episode had certainly fallen short of the earth-shattering reunion that both of them had hoped for.

The Persian paraded into the room, acting as if she owned the place.

Carlotta frowned down at the cat. "Proud of yourself, aren't you? You've been nothing but trouble since I got here." She sighed. "Did Angela send you to make my life miserable?"

The cat lifted her head and meowed.

Carlotta shrank back, then she stopped and pinched the bridge of her nose. She was officially losing her mind if she thought the blond, green-eyed Persian was channeling blond, green-eyed Angela.

Feeling flushed and overwhelmed she reached across the counter to flip on the switch for the ceiling fan. Patricia Alexander had once offered to share her antianxiety meds, but maybe she should consider getting some of her own.

She poured a glass of orange juice and carried it to the table, along with the notebook in which she was keeping details about The Charmed Killer case. She had a couple of hours before she had to be at work, and she wanted to record the info about the incident in the ladies' room at Moody's before it faded from her memory. The more she thought about it, the more she was sure the unidentified person had been Michael. He'd always made it a point to dress—and smell—as expensive as possible. Even if he couldn't afford to.

Jack had been skeptical, but promised to research recent purchases of the cologne citywide.

Carlotta sipped the orange juice and considered Jack. She hadn't answered his phone call last night because she hadn't decided whether to share Wesley's suspicions about Coop's recent uncharacteristic behavior. Besides, she was half-afraid Jack would be able to tell from her voice that she and Peter had…petered out.

If she kept this up, she was going to have to keep a list of the secrets she was keeping.

The cat sprang up onto the table, walked over to the cloisonné Oriental vase and rubbed against the textured metal surface, her contented purr sounding like the coo of a homing pigeon.

Irrational anger toward the cat seized her. "Get down!" Carlotta said, waving her arms. Startled, the cat hissed at her, jumping back and bumping the vase. Carlotta lunged for the container, but it was top-heavy and it slammed down on the table. The lid flew off and a powdery substance spilled all over the wood surface, then was sucked up in the draft created by the overhead ceiling fan and scattered all over the room…and all over her.

Carlotta pushed to her feet, blinking and sputtering, her arms raised in futility. "Ew, what *is* this stuff?"

As if there was someone to hear her. The cat had high-tailed it out of the room.

She hurried to turn off the ceiling fan, but accidentally increased the speed, creating a sandstorm. Finally, she managed to switch off the fan. When the dust settled, a film of white coated everything in sight like a fine layer of snow.

Peter was obviously more of a smoker than he let on if he kept a container of sand on hand. She didn't see any cigarette butts, but what else could it be?

Then a horrific alternative slid into her mind: Angela had been cremated. Had Peter replaced the silk flower arrangement on the table with an urn containing his wife's ashes?

It made perfect, awful sense.

Carlotta swallowed hard at the revelation, then gagged at the bitter taste of something foreign in the back of her throat. In fact, her mouth was full of grit. *Ew.*

In full-panic mode, she scrambled for her cell phone and called the only person she could count on to help in a situation like this one. "Hannah," she shouted into the phone when her friend's voice mail kicked in, "you have to come help me. I think I accidentally scattered Peter's wife all over the house."

Hannah called back in less than a minute. "I thought Peter's wife was dead."

"She is," Carlotta said. "And I think she was sitting on the kitchen table—'was' being the operative word."

"I'll bring my Shop-Vac."

Carlotta disconnected the call and counted her blessings. When a person offered to come and help you clean up someone's cremated remains, it had to be genuine friendship.

She debated taking a shower in the interim to wash Angela off of her, but reasoned it was better to wait until they got the rest of Angela cleaned up. She stood at the counter, alternately fighting tears and bouts of hysterical laughter as she surveyed the damage she'd unleashed. She hadn't thought she could top totaling Peter's Porsche.

Minus one hundred.

True to her word, a few minutes later, the phone rang and Hannah was at the entrance gate, waiting for Carlotta to buzz her in with Peter's code. On the verge of a nervous breakdown, Carlotta told Hannah to come around to the right side of the house, through the pool area, to the sliding glass door.

"I'm afraid to come to the front door," she said into the phone, looking down at her dusty house shoes. "I don't want to track Angela all over the place."

Soon she heard Hannah's van pull in to the driveway, then the heavy clomping of boots on the walkway leading around to the side of the house. Carlotta deactivated the door and window alarms, then opened the sliding glass door to admit her friend, who was holding a small-canister Shop-Vac.

"Wow," Hannah said, looking her up and down. "This is fucked up, even for you."

"Thanks," Carlotta said, brushing powdery stuff off her shoulder. "It was an accident."

Hannah glanced over the white-coated great room. A hazy film still hung in the air. "What the hell happened?"

"The cat jumped up on the table and knocked over the urn."

"What cat?"

"A stray Persian that just might be Angela Ashford reincarnated."

Hannah squinted. "Are you high?"

Carlotta sighed. "No, but I wish I was. I didn't even know Angela's ashes were sitting on the table. I thought it was just a vase."

"Setting them on the kitchen table is just plain tacky," Hannah said. "And weird, even for the South."

"What am I going to do?"

"Uh…don't sneeze?"

"Helpful," Carlotta said sarcastically. "Seriously, should I call Peter and confess, or do you think we can salvage this…er…*her*…before the housekeeper gets here?"

Hannah reached forward and swiped her finger across

Carlotta's nose, then winced at the pale gritty residue. "How much time do we have?"

"About two hours."

"I'll start vacuuming, you get the broom and dustpan."

Remarkably, within an hour the room started to look familiar again. Carlotta walked to the urn to transfer the contents of the dustpan into it for the umpteenth time. Hannah turned off the Shop-Vac and came to empty the machine's dust bucket into the urn, as well.

"We're probably contaminating her ashes," Carlotta murmured.

"How do you contaminate ashes? It's not like someone's going to eat them."

"Still, you know what I mean." Carlotta studied her friend, then pursed her mouth. "You didn't say anything about Peter's house."

Hannah glanced around and nodded. "Nice place."

"You've been avoiding me."

"No, I haven't," Hannah said, but she didn't make eye contact.

"You're not mad at me over getting fired?"

"It wasn't your fault. Besides, I'll find something else. Thank goodness the one thing Atlantans have in common is eating."

"Have you seen Wesley lately?"

Hannah's back stiffened. "Wesley? What makes you think I've seen Wesley?"

"Maybe because he said the same thing, in the same fake tone, when I asked him if he'd seen you."

Hannah shrugged. "I don't know what you're talking about." She flipped on the Shop-Vac and went back to work.

Carlotta scratched her nose with her knuckle. Something was up with those two.

After two more passes with the broom and the vacuum, Carlotta and Hannah admitted they'd recovered all of Angela they possibly could.

"So this is what's left after they cremate you," Carlotta said, peering into the urn.

"I read somewhere they have to sift out bone chips and teeth."

Carlotta made a face. "It doesn't look like much. What if Peter notices some of the ashes are gone?"

"If you're worried about it, we could add filler."

"We're not going to add filler!" Then Carlotta narrowed her eyes. "What kind of filler?"

"You said something about a cat. Do you have kitty litter?"

Carlotta gasped in horror.

Hannah scoffed. "Spare me the self-righteous outrage. You blew the man's wife onto the chandelier."

She glanced up at the dusty light fixture they hadn't been able to reach. "Okay…maybe just a little filler."

She went into the mudroom and pulled out the bag of kitty litter they'd had to buy for the Persian. When she held a scoop of the sandy gray mixture next to the ashes in the urn, she frowned. "The kitty litter is coarser and darker."

Hannah headed toward the kitchen. "There's gotta be cornstarch here somewhere…or flour."

"Christ, this is turning into a science experiment."

Hannah was opening and closing cabinets. "Where's your blender?"

"It's Peter's blender," Carlotta murmured, then walked to the cabinet where it was stored and pulled it out.

"So," Hannah said casually, emerging with a canister of flour, "have you two had sex yet?"

"No."

"Why not?"

Carlotta sighed. "We tried."

"Don't tell me Richie Rich couldn't get it up."

"He got it up fine. But…he was nervous, and…"

"He shot the pearl jam before he put it in the ma'am?"

Carlotta frowned. "I hadn't heard that particular medical phrase, but yeah."

"You gonna try again?"

"I don't know. I think we're both under too much pressure."

Carlotta plugged in the blender, then tossed in a couple of scoops of kitty litter. Hannah added two scoops of flour, then pulsed the mixture until it was evenly combined. She lifted the lid for a peek. "Looks like a match to me."

Carlotta agreed and they dumped the contents into the urn.

"Do you think it looks like a whole person's worth of ashes?" Hannah asked.

"I think so." Carlotta put the lid back on top and slid it to the middle of the table with a sigh of relief.

"What's this?" Hannah asked, gesturing to the notebook Carlotta had been writing in prior to the incident.

"Just random notes I've been keeping on The Charmed Killer."

Hannah turned the pages, skimming them. "Wow…you got your own little investigation going on here."

"Not really. I promised Peter I would…stay out of it."

Hannah gestured to the sketches of the charms in the margins. "Yeah, I can see that you're not into this at all."

"Randolph's name came up as a potential suspect."

"Wow, I'm sorry."

"I haven't said anything to Wesley."

Hannah set down the notebook. "You and Wesley keep a lot of things from each other."

Carlotta's head came up. "Is Wesley keeping something from me?"

Hannah pressed her black lips together.

"Hannah, do you know something?"

"Just that he seems a little manic to me, and his hands shake a lot. Are you sure he's not on something?"

Carlotta's heart raced, but she tried to keep her voice steady. "He stole two prescriptions I had left on my pain pills. And I found a generic OxyContin tablet on his bathroom floor. But he told me he only took those because of what that animal The Carver did to his arm, but that he'd quit."

"Fair enough."

"Besides, he has to give urine samples when he sees his probation officer. He gets tested for drugs regularly."

"Sweetie, there are additives to mask drugs in urine samples, and people who do drugs know all about them."

Carlotta turned away, feeling like an idiot.

"I don't know anything for sure," Hannah added lamely.

"How could you have noticed it and I didn't? Am I that blind?"

Hannah hesitated, then exhaled. "Okay, I'm shagging Fat Boy."

Carlotta's eyes went wide. "You're sleeping with Chance Hollander?"

"Technically, we're not getting much sleep."

"You give me a hard time about sleeping with Peter, and you're climbing on top of *that* mountain?"

Hannah shrugged. "He's sweet, okay? He fucking worships me. And he's hung like a goddamn mule."

"But...*Chance Hollander?*"

"Forget it, okay? It won't last. It never does."

Carlotta sobered. "Does Chance think Wesley is hooked on something?"

Hannah chewed the side of her mouth. "He...might have intimated something to that effect."

She thought she was going to be ill. "What drug?"

"Oxy."

Carlotta exhaled. "It's rich that Chance is worried about him. He's probably the one who sells it to him."

"He says he's been trying to warn Wesley off."

"From one druggie to another?"

"Chance is a pothead, but that's it as far as I can tell. Most dealers know to stay away from the stuff." Hannah sighed. "For what it's worth, I think Chance really cares about Wesley. I probably shouldn't have said anything, but I thought you should know."

"Thanks," Carlotta said past a tightened throat.

"And maybe it's nothing."

"How am I supposed to know? Wes has already lied to me."

"You might look into one of those over-the-counter drug tests. For some of them, all you need is fingernail clippings, or hair. At least you'd have proof."

Carlotta nodded—one more thing to add to the list. "Thanks for the advice. And for helping me clean up." She glanced at her watch. "I have to get ready for work. Christ, I'm going to be late again."

"Okay, I'm outta here. Call me."

"I will. And Hannah?"

"Yeah?"

"Be careful. There's a guy out there doing horrible things to women."

Hannah face softened. "You, too."

She let Hannah out, and waved goodbye, her chest tight with affection for her friend, and her mind reeling over new revelations about her brother. She kept hoping Wesley would turn a corner, that spending time with Coop had been a positive experience for him. But now it seemed that Coop was also losing his way...

Carrying a heavy heart, she climbed the stairs. When she went into her room, she saw the bed skirt move and her mood took another dive. "Ah, so this is where you're hiding, you bad, bad kitty."

The Persian's fluffy head appeared.

"Do you know how much trouble you caused?"

Meow.

Carlotta thought about her comment to Hannah, that the cat was the reincarnation of Angela. The timing of the stray showing up, the destructive behavior toward Carlotta, the fixation on Peter...it was all so bizarre.

Carlotta wet her lips and looked around the room to make sure she was alone, then crouched toward the cat. "Are you Angela?"

The cat simply looked at her and blinked.

"Are...you...Angela?" she asked, enunciating slowly, in case the cat had trouble understanding her.

The Persian opened its mouth and Carlotta waited, breathless and prepared to levitate if the cat started talking.

Instead, the cat yawned widely, then licked its chops.

Carlotta frowned. "Fine. But I'm putting you on notice—there isn't room in this house for two pussies, do you understand, you little furball?"

She peeled off her pajamas and stuffed them in the garbage can along with her house shoes. Even if she got them clean she wouldn't be able to wear them again without thinking about what had happened.

She shuddered anew and stepped into the shower where she quickly scrubbed her skin and hair. Then she jumped out and dressed in record time, choosing skinny-leg black jeans, a teal-colored swing tunic and long striped scarf. She stuck her feet into the Prada pumps she'd set at the end of the bed, then made a face. Something was in the right one—something squishy…and brown.

She pulled out her foot and from the stench, it was clear what had been deposited in her shoe. "Ewwwwww!"

She glared at the Persian standing next to the door, tail high, almost smiling. Carlotta launched the shoe at the cat, but she darted safely out into the hallway and down the stairs.

And Carlotta could swear the beast was laughing.

27

"Earth to Wesley."

He blinked Meg into focus. "What?"

She sat across a worktable, twirling the end of her blond ponytail. She was chewing gum and blowing little bubbles. Every time the tip of her tongue appeared, his pants got tighter.

"I said I'll be running the job to extract test data from all the databases later this week."

"What's the holdup?"

She blew a bubble and it popped. "What's the hurry?"

"No hurry," he said, then shifted in his seat.

"You're juiced."

Wesley used his sleeve to wipe the sweat from his forehead. "No, I'm not." He hadn't had an Oxy hit since waking up…and he was suffering. "I think I'm coming down with something."

"Too bad. I was going to ask you to go somewhere with me."

He blinked. "Where?"

She studied her blue fingernails. "It's an industry-reception thingy my dad is hosting, and I have to go. I thought if you went with me, it would be less brutal."

He swallowed hard. "Sorry, I can't."

Meg frowned. "I didn't even give you a date."

"Oh. When is it?"

"Tomorrow night."

"Sorry, I can't."

"You can't, or you won't?"

He scratched his temple. "Yeah, see…I'm not good with the whole parent thing."

She nodded. "So you thought you'd just date me and we'd screw and you'd never have to face my dad?"

Wesley squinted. "We're dating? And screwing?"

"Apparently not."

He held up his hands in a T. "Okay, time-out. You've been ignoring me for days."

She shrugged. "My time of the month…I've been moody. Besides, you were an ass about my friend Mark."

"You mean your gay boyfriend Mark with the prissy shorts?"

"See? That's assy."

His mind was chugging to catch up to her passive-aggressive logic, but he gave up. "I'm lost."

"Never mind, you wouldn't have fit in anyway."

Wow, that hurt. He pursed his mouth and nodded, then started loading his backpack to leave. It was true, but… damn.

"I mean, everyone there will be older. You'd be bored to death."

He zipped up his bag and swung it over his shoulder.

"But why don't you come anyway?" she asked.

Wes looked up at her and that was his undoing. Meg was smiling a sexy smile, her cherry-red mouth shiny and plump. He wanted to kiss that mouth. Her eyes challenged him…and she was still twirling her hair. He wondered briefly what she would look like with her hair down and loose around her shoulders.

He considered blurting that her father had hired a P.I. to follow him, and would likely nix the invitation anyway. That if Wesley made it as far as the door of the reception, Dr. Vincent would have him booted out post introductions.

The idea actually cheered him a little. What a gas it would be to meet the great Dr. Vincent, for the man to realize the thug he'd had investigated was smart enough to sneak into his hoity-toity lecture.

"Suit yourself," Meg said with a shrug.

"Okay, I'll go."

Her eyebrows shot up. "You will?"

"Yeah."

She smiled. "Okay."

That mouth—Jesus God. "Okay." He turned and walked toward the exit before he spontaneously combusted. He wiped his sleeve across his forehead and swallowed against a sudden bout of queasiness. He wasn't sure if it was withdrawal from the Oxy, or panic over accepting the date with Meg.

Both conditions left him equally nauseous.

28

As soon as Carlotta walked into Neiman's, Patricia Alexander tracked her down.

"I thought you'd like to know the Bedford Manor Country Club is offering self-defense classes this weekend."

Carlotta gave her a tight smile. "Thanks, but I was told I wasn't welcome at the club."

Patricia frowned. "By Tracey?"

"How did you guess?"

The helmet-haired blonde gave a dismissive wave. "Tracey was just worked up over your friend stealing."

Carlotta glared. "My friend Hannah would never steal."

Patricia looked sympathetic. "There haven't been any purses stolen since your friend was fired."

"That doesn't make her guilty." Carlotta crossed her arms. "And I don't intend to go back to Bedford Manor until Hannah is offered her job back by the caterer."

"Carlotta, don't be silly. Peter's father is on the club's board. If you're going to date Peter, you'll be spending a lot of time there. Pick your battles." The woman turned and walked away.

Carlotta wanted to scream, but Patricia was right. The

club was a big part of Peter's social and professional life. If she and Peter were going to be a couple, she couldn't very well boycott Bedford because they'd fired a member of the waitstaff.

She made her way over to Herb, who was wearing a hole in the carpet next to a rack of bathing suits. He was holding up a tiny bikini comprising of three tiny triangles and a handful of string as if he was trying to figure out the logistics.

"Hi, Herb."

He jumped, then hung the bikini back on the rack, his face red. "Hi, Carlotta."

"I was wondering if there are any new leads on the purse snatcher at the Bedford Manor Country Club."

"Nope. I hate to say it, miss, but it looks as if your friend is the likely culprit. If Ms. Plank hadn't declined to file charges, we would've had to make an arrest. And considering the value of all the purses stolen, plus their contents, your friend would've been looking at time."

"I wish Bebe *had* pressed charges so Hannah could've proved her innocence."

The man nodded politely, but she could tell he, too, believed that Hannah was a thief.

Frustrated, Carlotta returned to her station, tossed back an Excedrin for the headache she was nursing, and tried to concentrate on sales. Her department was busy, but she remained distracted all day. Between tending to customers, her mind jumped from one personal dilemma to another and the helplessness she felt at not being able to resolve any of them. First and foremost, though, her mind kept coming back to Wesley.

Carlotta went back and forth between wishing she'd

trusted her instincts when she'd first learned of the stolen prescriptions of Percocet and found the Oxy tablet on his bathroom floor, and wanting to believe that Hannah and Chance had it all wrong. Wesley knew better than to get hooked on prescription drugs.

Didn't he?

"Hey, sis."

She screamed into her hand, then exhaled in relief when she turned to see Wesley standing there, whip slim and handsomely unkempt. She waved off Herb, who came charging toward her, his hand at his belt holster. "It's okay, he's my brother."

"Wow," Wes said, glancing around. "I guess this means they really think Michael is going to show up?"

"Just a precaution. It's safer for everyone." She put a hand over her still-racing heart. "What brings you here?"

She stared at his pupils as if she knew what to look for, but was diverted by the flush that started at his neck and climbed steadily until even his ears were scarlet.

"Uh…I need a suit."

She raised her eyebrows. "Did someone die?"

He looked sheepish. "Uh, no. There's this…reception thingy."

"For your job?"

"Uh…not exactly."

Realization dawned. "I take it this has something to do with Meg?"

"Uh…yeah."

She schooled her response because she could tell he was already spooked. "Your brown suit isn't so bad."

"The last time I wore it, the pants were a little short. I was thinking of something that might make me look…older?"

She had to bite her cheek to keep from smiling. "Right. Let's go to the men's department and see what we can find."

"Is this a bad time?"

"Actually, I'm just finishing my shift. I can get you my employee discount," she said as they walked, "but I don't have my store credit card anymore."

"I got cash," he said. "As long as it's not crazy expensive."

"We have some good sales going on. So the courier job must be going well, huh?"

"Yeah."

She glanced down at his hands to see if they were shaking, but he had them stuffed in his pockets. "So… Hannah and Chance."

His eyes went wide. "You know?"

"I saw Hannah this morning. How did *that* happen?"

"I try not to think about it. Have you talked to Coop?"

She shook her head. "I'm waiting for the right time. Is he still working at the morgue lab?"

"As far as I know, that's where he spends his days."

And his evenings at Moody's? "Here we are," she said, walking into the men's department. Herb sauntered behind them a few yards, obviously happier to browse ties for a change instead of bathing suits.

"When is this reception?" she asked Wesley.

"Tomorrow night."

"Finding something that doesn't need to be tailored shouldn't be a problem. What kind of event is it?"

"It's for professionals in the medical industry. Meg's dad is a bigwig geneticist."

She ached for how much he obviously wanted to

impress this girl, and her family. She hoped he didn't get his heart broken.

Walking from rack to rack, she offered her opinion on styles she thought would look best on his lean frame. He took a suit and shirt to the fitting room and Carlotta waited outside. Her mind traveled back to the times after her parents left that she'd taken Wesley shopping for back-to-school clothes and waited for him to come out of the dressing room, just like now.

When the curtain opened and he emerged in the dark suit, he was wearing the same expression he'd worn at the age of ten, when he'd come out wearing a Spider-Man T-shirt. "What do you think, sis?"

She bit her lip over how handsome and grown-up he looked in the black pin-striped suit and cream-colored dress shirt. Her brother looked so much like their father, with fine bone structure and great skin. Unlike Randolph, though, Wesley had no idea how good-looking he was.

"I think," she said, walking up to smooth a hand over his lapel, "that Meg is going to fall head over heels for you in this suit."

"Oh, God, you're not going to cry, are you?" But underneath his macho veneer, she could tell he was pleased. When he turned to the mirror, his chest puffed up a little.

"No, I'm not going to cry," she said, peering around his shoulder to his adult reflection. She was worried sick about Hannah's warning that he might be taking drugs, but she didn't want to spoil this moment, not when he'd sought her out to help him on such an important occasion.

Then she noticed that his light brown hair overlapped his collar and she had an idea. "Why don't I give you a quick trim. It'll only take a couple of minutes, and I can do it here."

He craned his neck for a look in the mirror. "You got scissors?"

"I'll get a pair from the tailor. Take off the suit and I'll be back in a sec." She left to gather up what she needed, and came back with tools in hand. Back in his street clothes, Wesley looked like his young, shaggy self again.

"Do you have a comb?"

He removed a comb from his back pocket and handed it to her, then sat on a bench in the dressing room.

When she settled a towel from a janitorial closet around his shoulders and combed his baby-fine hair, she was once again transported back to when he was ten years old, sitting on a chair, grumbling about the fact that she didn't cut his hair right. But a kitchen salon cut saved money, and at the time, they'd barely been scraping by.

Poor thing. As if he hadn't had enough going against him being a skinny kid with big glasses in a new school. The butchered haircut had been a bonus.

Thankfully, over the years she'd gotten better with the shears.

"Be still," she said, her normal reproach.

"Don't take off too much," he returned, his normal comeback.

She held the scissors at an angle and clipped a half inch all around his neckline and ears. "You like this girl, huh?"

He grunted. "Hey, I forgot to tell you that I knocked on the window of that black SUV that was hanging around the town house. The guy had the wrong place. He was looking for an old girlfriend."

She frowned at the change in subject, but nodded.

"That's a relief. All done," she said, pulling away the towel. "Go pick out a tie and I'll meet you at the register."

He stood and ran his hand over his trimmed hair, then grinned. "Thanks, sis." He dropped a rare kiss on her cheek, then strode out of the dressing room.

She watched him go and closed her eyes briefly. She loved him so much sometimes it hurt.

Like right now.

Carlotta pulled a clump of his hair off the towel and dropped it into an envelope. If she took it to Coop tomorrow, maybe he could analyze the hair for her in the lab. She could kill two birds with one stone.

Check up on Wesley…check up on Coop.

By the time his purchases were bagged and Wes walked her out to the Vespa, it was after eight o'clock. He gave his stamp of approval to the scooter, then waved goodbye and headed to MARTA. She removed her cell phone from her purse to call Peter, but the battery was dead. Sighing, she donned her helmet and climbed on the scooter. Dread ballooned in her stomach the closer she got to Martinique Estates.

What if the housekeeper had noticed that the urn had been upended and called Peter? Or what if the scene of destruction was revealed when the sun went down and the lighting changed?

Why, oh, why had she let Hannah talk her into adding kitty litter to the urn, for goodness' sake? In hindsight, it could be perceived as being a little…disrespectful.

When the garage door went up, she swallowed hard. Peter was home already.

She parked the scooter, then went inside, feeling like a little girl who was sure her parents were going to find out just how bad she'd been. She hit the button to lower the garage door, then entered the house through the mudroom.

Just as she feared, Peter was sitting at the kitchen table, looking at the urn, his hands steepled.

"Hi," she said cheerfully. "Sorry I'm late. Wesley stopped by the store, and I helped him pick out a suit."

"I tried to call," Peter said, his tone lifeless.

"My phone battery is dead."

He nodded, then sighed. "Did you think I wouldn't find out?"

Carlotta's heart jumped to her throat. "Peter...I can explain. It was an accident."

He reached under the table and pulled out the notebook in which she'd been recording all the details about The Charmed Killer cases. "Involving yourself in this dangerous case is no accident, Carly."

Her mind raced in confusion before she realized he wasn't talking about the urn—he was talking about the notebook. She almost laughed in relief, but understood that wouldn't be the best response. Walking over to pick up her notebook, she said, "These are just notes, Peter, for my own benefit. I just want to try to keep everything straight in my head in case I'm questioned again."

"That's the point, Carly. If you weren't off moving bodies, you wouldn't be involved in this case."

"That's not true. Michael Lane is the number-one suspect. And don't forget dear old dad."

Peter sighed and nodded. "Have you told the GBI about his connection to Alicia Sills?"

"Not yet. If I do, they'll question you about their relationship."

"I know. And I'll do whatever you want me to do." He

stood, removed the notebook from her hand and set it aside, then pulled her into his arms. "I'm sorry I was angry."

"It's okay. I know you worry."

"More than you can imagine," he murmured, then he kissed her.

She kissed him back, spurred partly by guilt and partly because she wanted him to know that she didn't hold their unconsummated incident against him.

The kiss grew more hungry and intense. Clothes loosened, then fell away as they stoked the fire that had been banked for so many years. Maybe having sex away from the bedroom was the answer, she thought distantly. Less pressure. When they were both naked, Peter stopped long enough to retrieve a condom, then lifted her onto the kitchen counter.

"Where's the cat?" she murmured.

"Closed up in my bedroom."

"Good." She looped her arms around his neck and opened her knees to cradle his hips.

He rolled on the condom with feverish hands, then put his arms around her and latched on to one of her nipples....

And came with a jerking grunt that was half relief, half frustration.

She stilled, wincing inwardly that it had happened again. As his spasms slowed, she searched for something to say. "Peter—"

"Please, don't say anything, Carly," he cut in, his voice thick and his gaze downcast. He pulled away, then gathered his clothes from the floor and walked toward the stairs.

When the door to his bedroom opened and closed, she

put her hands over her face and sighed. Why did things have to be so complicated?

She slid off the counter and put on enough clothes to cover herself, then grabbed her notebook and a carton of yogurt, and headed upstairs to her own room, extinguishing lights as she went. At the top of the stairs she glanced at Peter's closed door and considered knocking. But she was afraid if she forced him to talk, it would only make things worse. At the moment, he must be feeling so humiliated.

Inside her room, she felt strange. For the first time since she arrived, she felt as if she and Peter both wished she wasn't there. Once Wesley got the security system installed in the town house, she would rethink her living situation.

She put her phone on its charger, then turned on the television to CNN Headline News. Since the cable station was located in Atlanta, the city's news was widely reported, and The Charmed Killer dominated every half-hour segment. There had been no more bodies, thank goodness, but everyone seemed to be waiting for the next installment in the horrific saga.

After changing into her pj's, she curled up in one of the upholstered chairs to eat the yogurt. But her body still hummed from being revved up and left running. To get her mind off what she couldn't have, she opened the notebook to review her notes on The Charmed Killer case.

She studied the list of charms—chicken/bird, cigar, car, gun, handcuffs, barrel—again and again, trying to find a common thread. She shuffled the sequence and tried to come up with alternate words where possible—bird, stogie, vehicle, weapon, shackles, keg—but nothing jumped out at her. They didn't seem related to each other, related to Michael, or even relevant in general. If her father was doing these horrible things to communicate with her, she didn't have a clue what he might be saying.

None of it made sense.

When her phone rang, she glanced at the caller ID. Jack.

She connected the call. "Hi, Jack."

"What are you wearing?"

She rolled her eyes, then decided to turn the tables. "I'm completely naked."

He grunted. "And you're by yourself? Are you sure Ashford isn't gay?"

"I'm sure," she said with a sigh. "And how do you know I'm alone?"

"Because you wouldn't have answered the phone if you were with Ashford. Speaking of which, you didn't answer last night when I called."

"That's right, I didn't," she said, allowing him to think what he wanted.

"Come on, admit it. When you close your eyes, you think about me," he murmured.

"Did you call for a reason, Jack, or were you just bored?"

"Both. We got a hit on the cologne."

"With Michael?"

"Yeah. There's a Clive Christian boutique in Roswell. An employee says he remembers a man of Lane's description buying a bottle of cologne three days ago and paying for it with cash."

"What about surveillance cameras?"

"Struck out."

"But still, it sounds like Michael."

"Yeah, but knowing where he's been doesn't help us much. I need to know where he is right now, where he's going to be tomorrow." His voice vibrated with frustration.

"Any developments in The Charmed Killer case?"

"I only know what I read in the papers," he said.

"Since I failed the polygraph, I keep waiting to be pulled back in for questioning again."

He made a noise in his throat. "They might have you under surveillance instead. Which is fine by me," he added. "Especially since Lane could be following you."

"The security guard has been keeping a close eye on me at the store."

"Also good."

"They're not sharing any information with you about the case?"

"Nope. The state guys have been tight with Marquez, but I don't know if that's because of her profiling or because of…everything else."

Carlotta frowned. "Thanks for the update."

"Listen—" he lowered his voice "—I'm stuck at my desk, but since you're naked, I can talk you through it, if you want."

"Good night, Jack."

"Good night."

29

Carlotta got up early, but Peter had already left for work. There was no note on the kitchen counter this time and the house seemed huge and empty and alien. The Persian strutted around, meowing stridently, as if to tell Carlotta that it was time for her to go home.

"Ungrateful puss," she muttered, but checked the cat's food and water before she left the house.

In the garage, she stopped. Now when she looked at the pink scooter, she was sad…and uncomfortable. Maybe she and Peter could talk things through tonight. She understood how embarrassed he might be, but they had to find a way to deal with their sexual impasse.

Or not.

With a start, she wondered if perhaps his condition wasn't a recent development. Could it have been an issue when he was married to Angela? Had it attributed to the couple growing apart, and Angela finding sexual fulfillment elsewhere?

As Carlotta drove out of the garage, she pushed aside thoughts of her and Peter's aborted lovemaking and turned her mind to her more immediate problem: facing Coop. Their last encounter hadn't gone so well. She wondered idly if he was seeing the blonde who'd been wrapped around him that night at Moody's, or if the woman had been a one-night stand. Coop had seemed belligerent toward her, flaunting the other woman and the fact that he was drinking again.

She pulled in to the parking lot of the county morgue and took a deep breath. She didn't like the idea of admitting to Coop that Wesley might be using drugs, but she needed help. And besides, the news just might be jarring enough to make Coop face his own lapse…or open up to her.

After removing her purse from the storage compartment and stowing the helmet, she entered the morgue through the front door and asked for Coop at the front desk. She was given a visitor's pass and directions to the lab. On the way down the hall, she passed Dr. Bruce Abrams, the chief M.E. He had his head down, deep in thought, and seemed startled when she said hello.

"Hi, Carlotta. Did you come to see Cooper?"

"Yes," she said. "To say hello and to ask him about… what you mentioned at the Collins crime scene last week." When Abrams had expressed concern that Coop was turning to destructive behavior.

"Good. I'd talk to him myself, but frankly, I haven't had the time. And something tells me that it would go down easier coming from you."

"You must be incredibly busy assisting with The Charmed Killer case."

The man removed his glasses to rub eyes that were ringed with dark circles. "It's like nothing this city has ever seen."

"I know. Let's hope the GBI makes an arrest soon. Did the murderer leave any DNA at the recent crime scenes?"

The man opened his mouth to answer, then frowned. "I realize that Michael Lane was a coworker of yours, but you know I can't discuss the details of the crime with you."

She played the sympathy card. "My fugitive father's name popped up on a profiler's list, too, so I'm eager for the killer to be found for more than one reason."

His mouth tightened, then he glanced all around before looking back to her. "I can tell you the GBI is expecting results from the state crime lab any day now. I don't know if an arrest will be made, but it's something to go on. We could all use a break. Take care."

She nodded and proceeded down the hall, feeling a little lighter in her soul. Maybe the case would be solved soon. With Michael apprehended, everyone could exhale and life could get back to being just plain crazy.

Carlotta found the laboratory door and knocked before sticking her head inside. "Hello?"

Across the room, Coop was standing in front of a light box studying an X-ray. He turned his head and did a double take. "Uh…hi."

She couldn't help smiling, it was such a relief to see him. "Hi. Is this a bad time?"

He straightened and pushed up his glasses. "No, come on in. Want some coffee? I have to warn you, it's terrible."

"I'll try it."

He walked over to a coffeemaker in the corner sitting between two coolers marked Human Remains and filled a paper cup. He wore a lab coat over gray jeans and running shoes. His brown hair had gotten long enough to pull back into a ponytail. His sideburns were shaggy, his skin pale. It was hard to believe that just a few short weeks ago, they'd been walking hand in hand on Daytona Beach.

Coop had been the picture of male vitality—tanned and lean, with a mischievous smile that made her heart catch. Now his hand shook slightly and when he turned toward her, his eyes were bloodshot. "Here you go."

"Thank you." She took a sip and winced.

"Told you." He laughed awkwardly, then scratched his temple. "I have a fuzzy memory of seeing you at Moody's Saturday night."

"Yes, I was there."

He grimaced. "Was I behaving badly?"

"You were smoking a cigar…and drinking."

"And I seem to recall a woman?"

She gave him a wry smile. "From what I could tell, she was definitely a woman."

"I hope I didn't say anything to offend you. I haven't exactly been myself lately."

"So I've heard. Anything you want to talk about?"

He hesitated, then his expression darkened and he shook his head. "No. I'd rather not involve…anyone. I hope you understand."

Her tongue watered to ask him if he was terminally ill, but after giving him every chance to open up to her, she was forced to respect his wishes to remain silent on the matter.

"So what's up with you?" he asked. "Wesley mentioned you were staying with Peter."

She nodded. "That's right. We thought it would be safer after learning we'd had Michael Lane as a boarder."

"He told me about that, too. Scary stuff."

"Wesley's installing a security system."

"Good."

"Yes, it's…good." She sipped the acidic coffee, and

the silence stretched between them. Grasping for conversation, she looked around the lab. "I understand you're doing more work for the morgue."

"Yeah. I'm working cold cases and generally trying to take the load off Bruce."

"I ran into him. He seems really stressed over The Charmed Killer case."

"Yeah, well, everybody has their own cross to bear."

She blinked at the uncharacteristically cold remark, but chalked it up to ever-present tension between the men.

A knock sounded at the door, then a guy who looked vaguely familiar walked in holding a long file. "Coop, I—" He noticed Carlotta and stopped. "Sorry. I'll come back."

"That's all right, Pennyman," Coop said. "What's up?"

The man held up the file. "I was wondering if you'd take a look at the results of the Nickson autopsy, just to double-check a couple of things."

"That's not necessary," Coop said. "I'm sure everything's in order."

"Still, I'd feel better if you'd look it over," the man said, setting the file on a table. "As a favor."

Coop hesitated, then gave the man a curt nod. Afterward, though, Coop seemed even more preoccupied.

"Unfortunately, I have a favor to ask, too," Carlotta said.

His eyebrows went up. "Shoot."

She set down the coffee and reached for her purse. "I'm worried about Wesley. I think he might be taking prescription painkillers…without a prescription."

Coop averted his gaze.

Her shoulders fell. "You knew?"

"I…suspected he was stoned a couple of times. Do you know what he's taking?"

"I found a generic OxyContin tablet on his bathroom floor. A friend confirmed that's what he might be taking."

Coop shifted foot to foot. "I'm not sure what I can do."

"You can give me proof so I can confront him." She pulled out the envelope that held Wesley's hair clippings. "Can you analyze this hair sample for me?"

He stared at the envelope, but made no movement to take it. "This is a family matter. You and Wes need to work it out."

"I've tried, but he won't be honest with me. I need something he can't refute. Please, Coop."

He closed his eyes briefly, then sighed. "Okay."

Her chest suffused with affection when he took the envelope. "Thank you."

He simply nodded. "I should have something for you in a couple of days."

She smiled. "Thanks for the coffee."

"Anytime," he said, and she thought she detected a wistful light in his tired eyes before he glanced away.

Carlotta left and drove to the mall thinking what might have been. After seeing Coop, she was even more concerned about him. It was apparent he was struggling against some kind of internal demon. But she was so grateful that he'd agreed to help her. If Coop delivered the results in person, maybe she'd have another opportunity to find out what was plaguing him.

Once she arrived at Neiman's, however, she had to shelf her troubling thoughts. The store was having a one-day "private" shopping event, which was anything but private, and meant the biggest savings of the summer. The store was packed. Poor Herb got shuffled around the department like a mannequin. At one point, Carlotta feared for *his* safety.

The hours flew by and the commissions accumulated. She was tired, but pleasantly numb and hungry when she waved goodbye to Herb at the store exit. She knew the man was as tired as she was. And since lots of employees were leaving at once, Carlotta thought she'd give the guy a break. She walked out with Patricia, who chattered about her date with Leo later that evening.

"You and Peter probably have something wonderful planned this evening, don't you?" Patricia asked.

"We'll see," Carlotta said evasively, then waved and veered off to walk to the pink scooter. In truth, she dreaded going home. Things were likely to be even more strained between her and Peter. She wasn't sure how she was supposed to react. If she forced more intimacy and things ended abruptly again, he might retreat altogether. But if she didn't, they would never know.

As she buzzed away from the mall, she could feel her body tensing, and her concentration wandering. She was traveling along a side road heading toward Peachtree Street when she heard a loud thump. Something dark had fallen out of the moving vehicle in front of her. She caught a glimpse of something like a long duffel bag landing in her path before she applied the hand brake with as much strength as she had and swerved to miss it.

She didn't miss it.

And it wasn't a duffel bag, she realized at the last possible second. Exposed bone, charred skin. Horror washed over her, but she was powerless to stop her momentum.

The burned body stopped the scooter cold. Carlotta flew over the handlebars and landed hard on her back, then rolled until she hit something that stopped her. When she opened her eyes, she was staring at the yellow striping of a curb. All around her were the sounds of brakes screeching and horns honking.

She wanted to close her eyes to block out the image in her head, but she knew the longer she lay there, the greater the chances of being mauled by a car. So she pushed herself up gingerly and crawled onto the sidewalk to a fence, as far back from the road as she could go, before turning to look at the scene.

It was chaos. Her beautiful pink scooter was scattered across both sides of the road. Cars were parked at all angles, many with their hazard lights flashing. She couldn't see the body she'd struck, but it didn't matter. She could still see it in her head, the partially burned corpse, with a piece of silver duct tape over its mouth.

To keep the charm in the mouth intact for investigators to find?

30

"Thanks for the ride," Wes said to Chance.

"No problem, dude. Dressed like that, you'd better get laid."

Wes climbed out of the BMW and closed the door, then watched the taillights as the car pulled away, fighting the urge to run after it.

He turned to look up at the "castle on Peachtree," Rhodes Hall, a restored white stone home from the early 1900s, with elaborate arches, a turret and a tower. It was lit up like a medieval torch against the summer night. He'd ridden by it a hundred times, but had never been inside. It was the kind of place rich people flocked to for weddings and private corporate events. Way out of his league. What the hell had he gotten himself into?

He pulled out a handkerchief and mopped his forehead. He'd swallowed an Oxy a little while ago, but with the safety coating intact, it was taking its sweet time getting into his bloodstream.

"Wesley?"

He shoved the handkerchief into his pocket and turned to see Meg walking toward him from the parking lot. Holy crap. Her long hair moved around her bare shoulders, and the red dress fit her like a sausage skin. His dick turned to limestone.

"Wow," she said, smiling wide. "I almost didn't recognize you."

He crossed his hands in front of his crotch. "You look nice, too."

"Thanks."

She tweaked his tie and he caught a whiff of her perfume—Jesus, she was killing him.

"This is going to be so boring," she said. "Don't hate me in the morning."

He swallowed hard. Was that a secret code? Did that mean they were having sex tonight?

"Let's go inside where it's cool," she said. "I'll introduce you to my parents."

He swallowed the bile that backed up in his throat, but followed her up the stone steps—not an easy feat while sporting wood—and inside the historic home. He inhaled and exhaled, trying to lose the erection before he met her father.

When he saw the crowd of suited guests, he was assailed with another bout of nerves. He was sweating again, and thought he might hyperventilate. It seemed as if everyone was looking at him—did he stick out that much?

Meg curled her fingers around his and whispered, "Relax."

When he looked down at her, a strange feeling filtered through his chest, and it wasn't the Oxy kicking in.

"Let's get some punch," she said, nodding to a banquet table.

The event was being held in the hall's reception room,

a fancy-schmancy space with wood floors, a large fireplace and an intricately trayed ceiling. Pretty nice considering no one actually lived in the house.

The punch was pink, and sweet enough to make his teeth hurt, but it was wet and that was all that mattered. He downed one cup, then reached for another.

"Wesley, is that you?"

He looked over to see his probation officer, Eldora Jones, walking toward him. Her boyfriend—make that *fiancé*—Leonard was a few steps behind her.

"Hi, E.," Wesley said with a grin. She looked nice in a yellow swishy dress.

"What are you doing here?" she asked.

"I came with Meg," he said. "Meg Vincent, this is Eldora Jones. E. is…a friend of mine."

Meg extended a warm greeting, but he could tell she was sizing up E., wondering how they knew each other, if they'd ever been involved.

He liked it. "How about you?" he asked E.

"I came with Leonard," E. said, then introduced Meg to her lughead fiancé. "Leonard is a pharmaceutical-sales rep."

Wesley had to fight back a scoff. Wes extended his hand to Leonard and the gym rat ground the bones in Wes's hand. He'd warned Wes more than once to keep his mouth shut to E. about his true vocation.

"And Leonard came at the invitation of his friend Freddy," E. said, indicating another couple who had just walked up.

Wes almost choked on his punch. "Freddy" was Dr. Frederick Lowenstein, the guy who'd sat next to him during the lecture. His wife, Tracey recognized Wesley right away, looking him up and down, eyebrows raised.

"Wesley Wren, you clean up nice," she said in a voice that indicated her surprise that he'd dragged himself up from the gutter to their level.

What a witch.

Freddy Lowenstein stuck his hand out for a shake, then squinted at Wesley. "Have we met before?"

"Maybe at Screen on the Green," Wesley said. "I think you were sharing a blanket with my sister, Carlotta."

"Oh…right," the man said, but he was still squinting, trying to place Wesley. When Freddy was introduced to Meg, he gave her red dress a lecherous look, but his eyes widened when he heard her last name.

"Are you related to Dr. Harold Vincent?"

"He's my father," Meg said drily, then pulled her hand away.

Good girl. She could see right through the old goat.

"Excuse us, please," Meg said, then steered him away from the crowd to the other end of the room. Wesley recognized Dr. Vincent immediately. And since the attractive woman next to the man looked so much like Meg, he assumed she was Mrs. Vincent.

He broke out in a fresh sweat.

They hung back until the couple the Vincents were talking to moved away. Mrs. Vincent saw them and gasped in delight as she pulled Meg into a hug. Wesley was mesmerized. Even though the woman was blond, she reminded him of his mother in the way she carried herself, from the tilt of her head to the way she held her evening bag. Good breeding, his mother would say. There was something fragile about Mrs. Vincent, though, something he couldn't quite put his finger on.

Dr. Vincent also embraced his daughter. It was evident

that Meg was the apple of his eye. Wes hung back to give them a moment, then Meg turned to him.

"Mom, Dad, this is Wesley Wren. Wesley and I work together in the city IT department."

Wesley looked up to Dr. Vincent and saw the man's hand freeze in midair when he heard Wesley's name.

"Nice to meet you, Dr. Vincent," Wesley said, clasping his hand. He almost folded under the man's hostile glare, but stayed strong. And then the man's eyes narrowed. Wesley knew the precise moment Dr. Vincent remembered him from their elevator conversation. The indignant look on the man's face as he drew back slightly gave Wesley the courage to smile. "Nice party, thanks for inviting me."

"You didn't need an invitation," the man said mildly. "You probably could've just walked in and acted as if you belonged here."

"Maybe," Wes agreed.

Dr. Vincent withdrew his hand. "Excuse me, someone just walked in whom I need to talk to. I'll see you later, dear."

Wesley and Meg stayed to talk with her mom, who seemed genuinely nice.

"Are you a student at Tech like our Meg?" Ann Vincent asked, stroking her daughter's hair.

"Um, no…ma'am."

"Do you work full-time with the city?"

He wet his lips. Since he was sure Dr. Vincent had done a background check, considering he'd gone to the trouble of hiring a P.I., it was at least comforting that he hadn't shared the info with Meg's mother. "No, I'm part-time. I also work for the county morgue."

"Really? Doing what?"

He glanced at Meg, who seemed to be enjoying the exchange. "Um…moving bodies…ma'am."

"Oh." The woman looked perplexed, then changed the subject by asking Meg about one of her classes.

Wesley eavesdropped on the easy banter between mother and daughter, envious of their obvious affection and familiarity. As Ann Vincent was being pulled away to meet another guest, she smiled at Wesley. "I hope to see you again, Wesley."

"I'd like that, ma'am."

Once Mrs. Vincent walked away, Meg smiled up at him. "See, that wasn't too bad, was it?"

"I guess not." But his head was killing him, and the sweating was getting worse. He'd brought an Oxy capsule with him, but he didn't want to take it in front of Meg. She'd nail him for sure.

They got a couple of plates of finger food and found a corner to relax, although Wesley almost swallowed a mini quiche whole when Meg sat down and her dress pulled high on her thighs.

"My dad would kill you if he saw you looking at me like that."

Wes glanced up to see she'd caught him staring. "You want me to look or you wouldn't have worn that dress."

"Maybe I wear this dress all the time," she said haughtily.

"Okay, whatever."

Meg leaned in and he got an eyeful of cleavage. "There's only one thing I hate about this dress. It's so tight that if I wore anything underneath, my panty line would show."

He stopped midchew, then swallowed. "Oh, now, that's just cruel."

"Down, boy, I don't put out on the first date anyway. But I do this." She leaned forward and kissed him on the mouth—a good kiss, the kind where you could taste each other. Her lips were as smooth and juicy as he thought they would be. But just as his pants were getting happy, she pulled back and popped another meatball in her mouth.

There she went again, messing with his head. He pulled out the handkerchief and wiped his brow. He wanted to go to the bathroom and take the Oxy, but he didn't want to leave Meg alone wearing that dress...and no underwear. Some guy like that lech Freddy Lowenstein might try to latch on.

Finally, though, he couldn't stand it any longer. Between Meg and her father, his nerves were shot. He excused himself and went to the men's room. He wanted to chew the pill, but resisted the powerful urge. Instead, he ran water into his cupped hand, then tossed back the Oxy pill and chased it with a drink. He closed his eyes when it went down. It would take a while for the painkiller to circulate, but with this one in the pipeline, relief was on the way.

"Got a headache, son?"

Wesley opened his eyes to see Harold Vincent strolling up to a urinal. Anger spiked in his stomach. "Don't call me son. And as a matter of fact, I do have a headache."

"Must be all that hard living," the man said, then faced the wall and unzipped his pants.

"Look, I know about the P.I. you had tailing me. I confronted the guy and he ratted you out. That's why I crashed your lecture. I wanted to see what kind of man would do that to his daughter."

Harold Vincent kept looking at the wall. "I don't care that you know. My daughter's happiness is my only concern."

"Yeah, well, Meg probably wouldn't be too happy if she knew you had me followed like a criminal."

The man zipped his pants, then turned and walked to the sink to slowly wash his hands. "You *are* a criminal. And I got news for you—Meg knows about the P.I. The only reason she invited you is because she knew I wouldn't approve." He pulled out a paper towel and dried his hands. "She doesn't care about you, son, she just wanted to piss me off." He tossed the paper towel in the trash, then stalked to the door.

"Don't call me son," Wesley managed to say before the door closed. He fisted his hands as humiliation crashed over him. He should've known that Meg had an ulterior motive for asking him out. Why would someone like her be interested in someone like him? He caught sight of himself in the mirror, and was disgusted. All that money spent on a suit to impress her, and for what? A few cups of punch and a hard-on. As far as her line about not putting out on the first date, well, she'd never intended for them to have a second date.

He undid the tie and yanked it off, then unbuttoned the collar of his shirt. This charade was over.

Wes walked out of the bathroom and threaded his way through the crowd. He couldn't wait to get out of this place.

Someone touched his jacket sleeve. "Are you leaving?"

He looked up to see E. standing there.

"Uh, yeah…something came up."

"Okay. I'll see you tomorrow?"

He nodded. "Sure. See you tomorrow."

Frederick Lowenstein, obviously eavesdropping, leaned in with an arrogant smile. "No offense, Wren, but I don't think you're Eldora's type."

Wesley set his jaw at the deliberate put-down. "Hey, Freddy, I got one word for you—*dankeshein.*" He stuck around long enough for outraged recognition to dawn on the man's cheesy face, then he split.

He shoved the front door so hard, he practically fell outside. He was eager to escape the party…to escape Meg. She was probably laughing at him.

What an idiot he was.

Inside his jacket pocket his phone rang. He pulled it out and was almost relieved to see it was Kendall Abrams calling. He connected the call. "Yeah, Kendall, what's going on?"

"We got a crispy critter near the Lenox Square Mall. Can you make it?"

"Whoa—slow down. What?"

"A burned body. My uncle wants me to take it. Apparently it's another one of those charm deals."

"Can you pick me up? I'm not too far from there."

"Sure. Oh, I almost forgot. I'm supposed to tell you that your sister ran over the body."

31

"You didn't have to stay home with me, Peter. I'm sore, but I can take care of myself."

Peter's face darkened with the same intensity he'd shown when he'd arrived on the accident scene last night to take her home. "There's no way I'm leaving you at home by yourself today."

It had been a long evening. After the paramedics had checked her over and pronounced her well enough to go home, GBI agents Green and Wick had questioned her for over an hour. Their presence—and persistence—confirmed a charm had been placed in the victim's mouth, but they didn't share any information with her. And she didn't have much information to share with them.

She couldn't identify the vehicle that had dropped the body.

She couldn't identify the driver of the vehicle.

And she didn't know why she'd been the person who just happened to drive over the body. Barring extreme coincidence, she had probably been targeted. But by whom?

Michael Lane? Her father? Someone else?

"Are you comfortable enough?" Peter asked.

"Oh, yes." She stroked the leather of the couch where

she lay in the great room, thinking two days ago Angela had been lying on the couch. And on the table. And the lamp. Carlotta darted a look to the lidded urn just to make sure it was still intact. "I'm so sorry about the Vespa."

He waved off her concern. "I'm just glad you're in one piece. I hope they catch this monster soon. It has to be Michael Lane. Who else could be trying to involve you in the crimes?"

"I don't know," she murmured.

Peter was sitting in an adjacent chair, leaning close. She appreciated his thoughtfulness, but he'd been hovering since they'd arrived home last night. He hovered over her, and the Persian hovered over Peter. She was starting to feel claustrophobic.

"Are you sure you can afford to take the day off?" she asked Peter.

"Absolutely. In fact, I have a lot of vacation time accrued. And I was thinking…maybe we should go ahead and take that trip to Vegas that I bought at the charity auction."

Carlotta swallowed. "Now?"

"As soon as you're feeling better. In light of all that's going on, I can't think of a better time to get away. And maybe a change of venue would be good for both of us."

With a jolt, Carlotta realized she hadn't considered that Peter's sexual glitch might have something to do with making love to another woman in the house he'd shared with Angela.

The doorbell rang, saving her from answering.

"Wonder who that could be," Peter said. He pushed to his feet and walked to the front door. The cat trotted after him.

Carlotta watched from the couch. He glanced through the window, then opened the door. On the threshold stood a teenage girl, who said a few words to Peter, then looked down and threw her arms open to the cat. And the cat actually went to her!

Peter beckoned the girl inside and walked into the great room smiling. "Carlotta, this is Vicki O'Dell. Vicki lives in the neighborhood next to ours and her family owns the cat you found. Isn't that great?"

There weren't words. "Yes, I'm relieved. What's her name?"

"Sheba." At the sound of her name, Sheba meowed loudly.

"She's so…humanlike, we knew she had a home somewhere." Carlotta chastised herself for imagining that the cat was Angela reincarnated. The beast had gotten to her. "I guess you saw the flyers?"

Vicki nodded. "I babysit in this neighborhood occasionally, but this is the first time I've been around in a few days. Thank you for taking care of Sheba for us."

"You're welcome," Carlotta said. And good riddance.

When the girl turned to go, her zebra-print clutch purse tripped a memory in Carlotta's mind. "What a great purse."

The girl looked at it and flushed. "Isn't it? I could never afford Prada on my own, but the lady I babysit for gives me her hand-me-downs."

Carlotta sat up. "Do you mind if I ask who you babysit for?"

"Not at all—Bebe Plank."

"Bebe?" Carlotta's mind raced. "Vicki, I don't mean to pry, but this is very important. When did Bebe give you that particular purse?"

"Let me think. She gave it to me the last time I babysat, so that was…last Thursday."

Carlotta's heart skipped a beat. Thursday was the day after Bebe's zebra-print Prada clutch had been "stolen" from the club. "How long have you been babysitting for Bebe?"

"For about a year now. I think she'd give me a good recommendation if you called her."

"I'm sure she would," Carlotta agreed idly. "In the year that you've been working for Bebe, how many purses has she given you?"

"Gee, I don't know. A lot—maybe twenty or so? But don't worry. It's not something I expect. Bebe is really generous."

With other people's purses…and at least one of her own. To throw everyone off track, maybe? No one would ever suspect a woman whose own purse had been stolen.

"Vicki, you might want to call your parents. I'm afraid the police will want to ask you some questions about those purses Bebe gave you."

Peter called the police and a few minutes later, the girl's parents arrived with shopping bags full of purses. When another doorbell ring admitted Jack, Carlotta was surprised. And Peter looked irritated.

"What are you doing here?" she asked.

"Well, technically, for as many purses and the amount of money that's been stolen, this *is* considered a case for the Major Crime Division." He scowled. "And I'm the only Major Crime detective available at the moment. How are you feeling?"

"I'm fine. Just a few scrapes and bruises."

His gaze swept over her, as if to ascertain for himself

that she was okay. He started to say something, then he turned to Peter and asked if he could borrow a more private room to question the teenager with her parents. As Peter was showing the O'Dells into the office, Jack leaned over closer to Carlotta. "How are you really?"

"I'm okay. Shaken up a little, I guess, when I think about how lucky I was. Have they identified the burned body?"

"They wouldn't tell me if they had, but I know from experience that it'll take a while for the M.E. to make an identification."

"It has to be Michael doing this, doesn't it, Jack? Who else would've dropped a body in front of me? I mean, he did this on purpose, didn't he, Jack?" Tears filled her eyes. "Why would Michael do this?"

Jack's jaw hardened. "We'll get whoever did this... *I'll* get whoever did this."

She sniffed, then nodded. Even if he wasn't officially on the case, she had every confidence that Jack would track down The Charmed Killer. "What about the charm? That's why the body had a piece of tape over the mouth, isn't it?"

"Probably," he admitted. "But I can't tell you about the charm. Sorry, darlin'."

"Jack!"

"Hey, *I'm* not even supposed to know. I'm not going to play fast and loose with the info I do manage to eke out." He pulled his hand down his haggard face. "By the way, have you seen Coop?"

Carlotta frowned. "I saw him in the morgue lab yesterday. Why?"

"He's...missing."

"What do you mean, he's missing?"

"I mean he didn't show up for work today, he's not at home, his van is gone and no one knows where he is."

"Should I be worried about him?"

His mouth twitched downward. "I'm afraid so."

32

Meg was waiting for Wesley the next morning in front of the government building by the bike rack. She was wearing tight white slacks, a buttoned-up blouse and a glare meant to laser holes through him. But he'd eaten an Oxy tablet when he'd rolled out of bed, so he was still feeling good.

Screw her and her rich parents and her plaid-wearing pals.

He braked, then jumped off the bike and locked it up, ignoring her.

"You're not even going to talk to me?" she asked, arms crossed.

"Hi, Meg," he offered.

"That's it? Hi, Meg? Not I'm sorry for ditching you, Meg? I'm sorry for humiliating you in front of your parents, Meg?"

"Oh, cut the crap. I ran into your dad in the john and he set me straight."

"What are you talking about?"

"I'm talking about the fact that you knew your father had me tailed by a private investigator, that the only reason you asked me to go to that party was that you knew it would drive Daddy crazy."

He had to hand it to her—she looked surprised. "A private investigator? I think your drug habit is making you paranoid."

"Whatever," he said, swinging his backpack over his shoulder.

"I saw you talking to that woman."

He turned back. "What woman?"

"That woman in the yellow dress, the one you said was your friend. But it was clear you weren't friends."

"You mean E.?"

"I saw you heading toward the door, but I thought you were just going out for a smoke. Did you make plans to hook up with her?"

Wes studied Meg's face, her body language. Everything in her and about her spoke of money and privilege and success. She could have any kind of life she wanted. But not with someone like him. Never with someone like him.

"Yeah, that's what happened. She and I hooked up, seeing as how you don't put out on the first date. So what?"

Meg's mouth fell open, then her eyes got all hurt looking…like she cared. She turned and stalked away from him.

For a heartbeat, Wesley was sorry he'd lied. Then he decided it was for the best.

33

"Wow, The Great Purse Caper made page two of the *AJC*," Peter said from the table where he was reading the paper and having breakfast.

"It would've been on page one if not for The Charmed Killer," Carlotta murmured, staring at the cloisonné urn.

"It says here that according to the D.A.'s office, Bebe Plank will definitely do jail time."

"She should," Carlotta said. "Stealing from her own friends and neighbors, that's pretty low." But not as low as desecrating the ashes of a person's loved one.

"I guess this means Hannah will get her job back."

"Probably, if she wants it. Did the paper mention anything about evidence in The Charmed Killer case being processed at the state crime lab?"

"No. Are you saying that the killer left DNA at the scenes?"

"I'm not sure what was left, but I was told something was being processed, and it was due back any day."

"Good. Let's hope the GBI gets this guy before anyone else gets hurt. It's unbelievable the things that people do to each other."

"I knocked over Angela's ashes," she blurted, pointing to the urn.

He jerked his head up. "What?"

Her throat convulsed. "It was an accident, I swear. Actually, the cat knocked over the urn, but the ceiling fan sent the ashes everywhere."

He steepled his hands. "Everywhere, huh?"

"Hannah and I gathered them back up as best we could, but I still feel so guilty about it, I had to tell you. Can you forgive me, Peter?"

He stared at her for so long, she was sure he was going to tell her to get her things and get the hell out. "There's nothing to forgive," he said finally. "Angela's ashes aren't here. They're in the cemetery."

She gasped, her shoulders dropping in relief. "Then what's in the urn?"

"Sand from where she and I honeymooned. I've actually been meaning to get rid of it, but the urn is top heavy if it's empty, and I prefer the vase on the table over the silk flower arrangement that was there before."

Carlotta laughed through her fingers. "I've been worried sick you'd find out and hate me."

Peter reached over and covered her hand with his. "I could never hate you, don't you know that by now?"

Her cell phone rang and she glanced at the caller-ID screen. "It's Wes, I should get it."

He nodded and retracted his hand.

She connected the call. "Good morning."

"Hey, sis. How are you feeling?"

"Fine. I'm going back to work today."

"Are you sure that's a good idea?"

"Sure. I feel fine and I'll have a security guard watching me."

"You might want to stay home today after you hear this."

"What's going on?"

"We were called to pick up two more bodies this morning."

"Two bodies? Where?" Peter looked up, his face creased in concern.

He gave her the address and she mentally mapped it. "But that's what? Only two blocks from Moody's Cigar Bar. Are they sure it was The Charmed Killer?"

"Yeah. The charms they pulled out were little books."

"Both of them?"

"That's what I was told."

Carlotta pressed her fist to her mouth. He was killing in pairs now, with less time between the murders. The Charmed Killer's reign of terror was escalating, just as Jack had predicted.

34

Because of the morning body pickups, gratis The Charmed Killer, Wes was late for his community-service work. Not that he was in a big hurry to get there. Since yesterday's little confrontation at the bike rack, Meg had been like an ice maker toward him, to the point that he started questioning whether she'd really known about the P.I. her father had hired. Maybe Harold Vincent had been playing him, betting he'd blow up, walk out, *leave his daughter the hell alone.* Or make her so angry that she'd want nothing to do with Wesley.

Had he played right into the man's hands?

Meg, who could normally be counted on to express her opinion on just about anything, answered questions only when she had to and sat out of group discussions. When it came to talking with Wes one-on-one, it was one-on-none. Which was why he was surprised when a few minutes before he was scheduled to leave at noon, she asked if they could talk privately. He agreed and followed her to a small workroom, secretly relieved and hoping she'd forgive him for behaving like an ass. He'd decided to come clean, to tell her that he hadn't hooked up with E., that she was his probation officer, that he'd allowed Meg's father to goad him into leaving the event.

Meg was wearing a skirt today, so he didn't mind groveling if he had to. Anything to get to that second date. All he could think about was that kiss…

Meg closed the door behind them, then sat down at the worktable and crossed her slender, tanned legs. She was wearing blue crisscrossy shoes that tied at the ankles, and sported pink polish on her toenails. Her hair was shoved up in a messy twist, and she wore her serious glasses—the heavy black ones.

"Look, Meg—"

"You don't get to talk," she cut in, glaring at him. "Not yet, anyway."

She reached into an expandable folder and pulled out a computer printout—the cheap continuous paper used to print programs or large amounts of data. "I ran the Job Control Language you built to pull data from the databases McCormick assigned to you for this encryption project."

Dread began building in his stomach.

"Imagine my surprise when I skimmed the test data and found a defendant named Randolph Wren."

He pressed his lips together. He was sunk.

"I did a little research and found the accounts of your father's alleged embezzling. And it occurred to me that you're trying to access his records, that this whole stunt of breaking into the courthouse database and being sentenced to community service in the very department you hacked into was probably your plan all along."

He'd be fired, and his probation revoked. He'd be thrown in jail before nightfall.

"Now you can say something," she said.

"Are you going to turn me in?"

She studied him with those amazing, quick eyes of hers. "I haven't decided yet. Get out of here."

He looked at the stack of paper on the table, with data printed in neat rows. In there somewhere was information on his dad's case that might or might not help Randolph. He wouldn't know until he was able to analyze it.

Wes pushed to his feet and thought about apologizing for his behavior the other night, but even he could see, at this point, an apology would seem a little disingenuous. He'd blown his chance with Meg, and in doing so, had made an enemy out of the one person who could help him…or take him down.

He went by his workstation to retrieve his backpack, then left the building and jumped on his bike. He'd asked Mouse for the afternoon off so he could finish installing the security system. Chance was supposed to meet him at the town house.

But when he got there, his buddy hadn't arrived yet. He was probably back at the condo doing Hannah or thinking about doing Hannah.

Wes unlocked the garage to retrieve the tools he needed and carried them into the town house. He still had to install contact sensors for all the windows and doors. He began working, conceding that climbing up and down the ladder for tools was no fun, but he actually got more work done because Chance wasn't interrupting every five minutes to talk about porn or his johnson.

The doorbell rang and he sighed. Speak of the devil. He descended the ladder and opened the door.

And blinked.

Mouse and three other guys stood outside, armed with boxes and tools. "I thought maybe you could use a hand," Mouse said. "That's Stuck, Banko and Art. Guys, this is Wesley."

"Hey," they chorused.

"Hey," he said, still confused. "You're going to help me install my security system?"

"We all know how to get around security," Mouse said, "so we know how to make it foolproof."

Wes pulled on his chin, thinking it was insane to have a loan shark's team install a security alarm. Or maybe it was brilliant. "Sure, come on in," he said, stepping aside.

As professed, the men knew what they were doing, making adjustments to components he'd already installed and quickly installing the contact sensors around every door and window in the town house. Mouse supervised.

About an hour later, one of the guys—Banko, he thought—came back into the living room where Wesley was working and motioned for him and Mouse to come into the kitchen. He made a zipping motion across his mouth, so Wesley didn't dare utter a word.

In the kitchen Banko pointed to a hole the size of a silver dollar in the drywall above the window over the sink. Imbedded in the white Sheetrock was a black object. Mouse climbed up on a step stool, then pulled out a switchblade to dig around the edges and study it closer. Finally, Mouse stored the knife, then climbed off the step stool and gestured for Wesley to follow him outside on the deck.

When the door closed behind them Wesley asked, "What's going on? What's that thing in the wall?"

"A listening device," Mouse said. "A good one, professional grade. Installed maybe ten years ago, based on the stamp on the frame. I hope you haven't been talking about anything you're doing for The Carver, little man, or anything else you don't want broadcast. 'Cause someone's been eavesdropping, for a long time now."

Wesley's heart raced. Had their dad planted the device before he'd left, hoping to keep up with him and Carlotta? And could they use it to communicate with him now?

35

Carlotta was looking forward to the end of her shift. She was still stiff and sore from the accident, and standing all day had taken its toll. It was her fault—Peter had tried to get her to stay home another day, especially in light of two more killings. But if she'd stayed home, he would've, too. And frankly, she couldn't bear the thought of spending another day with him hovering.

When her cell phone rang, she assumed it was Peter and was ashamed of the flash of annoyance she felt. But when she checked the caller-ID screen, she was pleased to see Coop's name appear.

She connected the call. "Hello?"

"Carlotta, hi…it's Coop."

She frowned at the unsteadiness of his voice. "Hi, Coop. Is everything okay?"

"Yeah."

"Where have you been? People are worried about you."

"I…took some time off. You don't have to check up on me, Carlotta."

She blinked at his harsh tone. "Well, I'm glad you're okay."

"Anyway, I got the tox screen back on the hair sample."

"And?"

"Are you at work?"

"Yes."

"I'm near there in my van. I can stop by and explain it to you, so you know what to say to Wes."

"Okay."

"See you in a few."

She ended the call and dialed Jack's number. He answered on the second ring. "What's up?"

"I just wanted to let you know that Coop's okay."

"Did you see him?"

"No, I talked to him a couple of minutes ago."

"Did he say where he'd been?"

"No…just that he'd taken some time off."

"Was he drunk?"

"Maybe, but I hope not. He's on his way to the store to drop off something with me for Wes." She was proud of herself for making it sound as if Coop was delivering a sweater instead of the results of a drug test.

Jack made a frustrated noise. "If Coop gets there and he's drunk, do *not* let him get back in his vehicle."

"I wouldn't, Jack. Good grief, I'm sorry I even called. I just thought you might want to know Coop is okay." She disconnected the call, frowning. Everyone was running short of patience these days.

She waited on customers and straightened clothing racks, her head and heart racing over what kind of news Coop was bringing to her. She tried not to read anything into the fact that he wouldn't give her the results over the phone. If the test was negative, wouldn't he just say so?

On the other hand, maybe he wanted an excuse to see her. Cheered by that thought, she kept moving, humming under her breath. A few minutes later she caught sight of him walking toward her…but she smothered a gasp at his appearance.

Coop looked shaggy and tired and inebriated. He gave her a wan smile, and attempted to strike a cocky pose but missed.

"Hi, Coop," she said, trying to hide her concern. He had a couple days' worth of beard growth and his shirt was stained. She hoped he hadn't shown up for work like this, or Abrams would fire him for sure. "How are you?"

"I'm great, but I heard you had an accident. Were you hurt?"

She winced at the stench of alcohol wafting off of him. "No, I'm fine. But how did you hear about that?" The GBI had made it a point to keep her name out of the newspaper.

He pushed up his glasses, seeming not to have heard her. "I did something terrible, Carlotta."

Alarm tickled her stomach—not out of fear of him, but out of fear of his sudden state of confusion and personality shift. "What did you do, Coop?"

His brown eyes looked tortured. He leaned in and whispered, "I killed somebody."

Her breath caught. "You don't mean that."

He studied her for a few seconds, then he smiled. "You're right, I'm just joshing you." From his pocket, he pulled out a folded sheet of paper. "Here are the tox-screen results."

Carlotta took the piece of paper and steeled herself. When she looked back to Coop, though, her eyes went wide.

Behind him, GBI agents Wick and Green were coming

toward her fast, flanked by a small fleet of uniformed officers, most of whom also had weapons drawn. Detective Marquez was with them, her gaze trained on Carlotta.

She shrank back. Surely, they weren't going to arrest her over a failed polygraph?

Coop must have realized something was going on. When he looked over his shoulder, Agent Wick slammed him down on the glass counter.

"Hands behind your back."

Carlotta was horrified. "What's going on?"

Agent Green handcuffed Coop while Agent Wick began reciting his rights. "Cooper Craft, you are under arrest for murder. You have the right to remain silent. Anything you say can and will be used against you in a court of law…"

Disoriented, Carlotta had backed into a clothing rack. When Maria came to pull her out, she slapped at the woman's hands. "Don't touch me. Why is Coop being arrested?"

Maria wet her lips. "Carlotta, Coop is The Charmed Killer."

Carlotta shook her head. "No…that's impossible."

"I'm sorry, I know the two of you are friends. I tried to warn you about the men you let into your life, but I couldn't tell you that Craft was under suspicion."

Carlotta hugged herself to stop the full-body tremors that claimed her. "You're behind this—you and your idiotic profiling. This is a horrible mistake."

"Carlotta."

She looked up to see Jack. "Jack!" She ran to him and put her arms around his chest. "Thank God you're here. Tell them." She gestured frantically to Maria and the GBI agents who were talking between themselves while Coop stood nearby with a uniform on each side, his head down. "Tell them they're making a huge mistake. You *know* Coop. He could *not* have done these things." She was crying now. "Jack, do something."

"It's out of my hands," Jack murmured quietly.

Agent Wick came over. "Thanks for the tip, Jack, letting us know where we could find Craft."

Carlotta pulled away, stricken. "You led them to Coop? How could you do that?"

"It's for his own good," Jack said quietly. "Come on, I'll take you to Ashford's."

She jerked away. "I'm not going anywhere with you."

Jack's face softened—he looked a little dazed himself. "This isn't the time to be stubborn. I'll explain everything in the car." He turned her away from Coop. "Come on, let's get your things and go."

She had to lean on Jack's arm on the way to the parking lot because she couldn't see through the tears. He settled her in the front passenger seat of his sedan, then they headed north on Peachtree. Jack had to take a cell-phone call.

Carlotta looked down and realized that in one hand, she still clutched the paper Coop had given her. She wiped her eyes, unfolded the report and scanned it several times to make sense of the formatting. The chemical that had been screened for was listed in the left column, and the results on the right. She skimmed the results column and stopped on a POSITIVE entry next to "Opiate/oxycodone."

A perfect ending to a perfect day.

She sat back, tears continuing to roll down her cheeks. Jack closed his phone, then reached inside his jacket pocket and withdrew a handkerchief. He handed it to her, his expression drawn. "You going to be okay?"

Carlotta took the hankie and wiped her face. Then she blew her nose and took a deep breath. "I'll be fine. Because this isn't over, Jack. Coop is innocent. You'll see."

* * * * *

Is Coop The Charmed Killer?
Find out in
6 KILLER BODIES,
available from MIRA Books June 2009.
Here's a sneak peek...

When Jack pulled the sedan into the circular driveway in front of Peter's house, Carlotta's stomach clenched. Peter wasn't a big fan of Coop's simply because the man had shown a romantic interest in her. Peter would likely feel vindicated that the good doctor had been so publicly exposed.

She looked over at Jack. "Coop's fall from grace is going to hurt him, isn't it?"

Jack nodded. "He was drunk when he stopped at the scene of an accident and declared a woman dead when she wasn't. She barely survived. Coop lost his job as coroner, and had his license to practice medicine suspended. It doesn't take a psychiatrist to see how something like that could mess with a person's head."

"But he seemed to be dealing with everything," Carlotta said. "I didn't know him when it happened, but Coop seemed at peace with working for his uncle at the funeral home, and moving bodies for the morgue."

Jack shrugged. "Things change."

"But not without a reason," she insisted.

"Everyone has a breaking point," Jack said. "It doesn't have to be a major incident. Maybe being back at the morgue, working in the lab, was too much for him."

She wanted to tell Jack what Wesley had told her about following Coop to a neurologist's office, their concern that Coop was seriously ill. But their suspicions were mere conjecture, and Jack had already betrayed her confidence by calling the GBI when she'd let him know that Coop, who had been missing for a day, was on his way to see her at Neiman's. She wouldn't be so forthcoming with information the next time.

The front door of the house opened. Peter stood on the threshold and waved.

Jack grunted.

Carlotta didn't want to get out of the sedan, but she didn't have a choice. Wesley hadn't finished installing a security system in the town house, and it wasn't as if Jack had offered her a place to stay. She supposed she could get a hotel room, but that seemed silly with Peter offering her the run of his mansion.

She couldn't explain it, but she felt as if she lived in two worlds—in one world was Peter and his lush home in the suburbs that offered her shelter from the other world of Wesley's problems, Jack's issues and Coop's dilemmas. Peter's world was more attractive in every way, but it left her feeling isolated from the people she'd grown closest to.

"Looks like Ashford's waiting for you," Jack said. "I'm sure the GBI will be in touch, will probably want to question you again."

"I refuse to give them ammunition against Coop."

His expression hardened. "Do yourself a favor, Carlotta, and tell the truth. Coop can fend for himself."

Her mouth tightened in anger. "I guess he'll have to fend for himself since his friends have turned on him."

Jack didn't say anything, just pushed his cheek out with his tongue.

Carlotta opened the car door, then turned back. "Jack, aren't you forgetting something?"

"What?"

"My red panties? The ones you stole and said you'd keep until The Charmed Killer was behind bars."

He was quiet for the longest time, studying her. Then the smallest of smiles curved one corner of his mouth. "If it's all the same to you, darlin', I think I'll hold on to them for a while."

She exhaled. "No problem."

Carlotta climbed out of the sedan and walked toward Peter's house, her heart lighter. It was Jack's way of telling her that he didn't believe Coop was The Charmed Killer, either.

Today, that was enough for her.

Tomorrow, she had her work cut out for her. If The Charmed Killer—be it Michael Lane or someone else—had involved her in order to frame Coop for the murders, the criminal had messed with the wrong shopgirl.

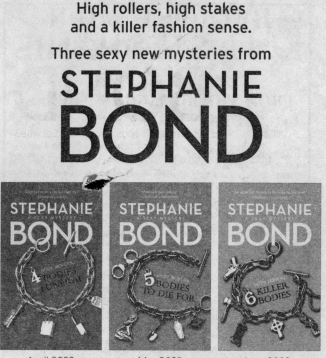

REQUEST YOUR FREE BOOKS!

2 FREE NOVELS
FROM THE ROMANCE/SUSPENSE
COLLECTION PLUS 2 FREE GIFTS!

YES! Please send me 2 FREE novels from the Romance/Suspense Collection and my 2 FREE gifts (gifts are worth about $10). After receiving them, if I don't wish to receive any more books, I can return the shipping statement marked "cancel." If I don't cancel, I will receive 4 brand-new novels every month and be billed just $5.74 per book in the U.S. or $6.24 per book in Canada. That's a savings of at least 28% off the cover price. It's quite a bargain! Shipping and handling is just 50¢ per book.* I understand that accepting the 2 free books and gifts places me under no obligation to buy anything. I can always return a shipment and cancel at any time. Even if I never buy another book from the Reader Service, the two free books and gifts are mine to keep forever.

185 MDN EYNQ 385 MDN EYN2

Name	(PLEASE PRINT)	
Address		Apt. #
City	State/Prov.	Zip/Postal Code

Signature (if under 18, a parent or guardian must sign)

Mail to **The Reader Service:**
IN U.S.A.: P.O. Box 1867, Buffalo, NY 14240-1867
IN CANADA: P.O. Box 609, Fort Erie, Ontario L2A 5X3

Not valid to current subscribers of the Romance Collection,
the Suspense Collection or the Romance/Suspense Collection.

Want to try two free books from another line?
Call 1-800-873-8635 or visit www.morefreebooks.com.

* Terms and prices subject to change without notice. Prices do not include applicable taxes. Sales tax applicable in N.Y. Canadian residents will be charged applicable provincial taxes and GST. Offer not valid in Quebec. This offer is limited to one order per household. All orders subject to approval. Credit or debit balances in a customer's account(s) may be offset by any other outstanding balance owed by or to the customer. Please allow 4 to 6 weeks for delivery. Offer available while quantities last.